The Cat C...
D. B.

One for the Money

After thirty-eight years of marriage, Cat's starting a new life—buying her own apartment house and working for her P.I. license. She'll be using her investigative skills sooner than she thinks . . . when she finds her upstairs apartment comes furnished—with a corpse!

Two Points for Murder

When a high school basketball hero is gunned down, Cat knows there's more to the murder than meets the eye—and she's determined to blow the whistle on the killer. . . .

Three Is a Crowd

Cat missed the protest movement of the '60s . . . she was too busy with a husband, house, and kids. But now she's learning more about those wild years—investigating the death of a protester at a peace rally. . . .

Four Elements of Murder

Cat looks into the death of an environmental activist—and finds herself in a mess of murder and deceit . . .

Five Alarm Fire

For Cat, a pottery class is nothing to get fired up about—until she discovers the cremated remains of a corpse hidden in the ceramic kiln!

SIX
FEET
UNDER

D.B. BORTON

BERKLEY PRIME CRIME, NEW YORK

SIX FEET UNDER

A Berkley Prime Crime Book / published by arrangement with the author

PRINTING HISTORY
Berkley Prime Crime edition / March 1997

The Putnam Berkley World Wide Web site address is
http://www.berkley.com/berkley

ISBN: 0-425-15700-8

Berkley Prime Crime Books are published
by The Berkley Publishing Group,
200 Madison Avenue, New York, NY 10016.
The name BERKLEY PRIME CRIME and the BERKLEY PRIME CRIME design are trademarks belonging to Berkley Publishing Corporation.

PRINTED IN THE UNITED STATES OF AMERICA

10 9 8 7 6 5 4 3 2 1

To Joanne Belknap and Jacqueline Gibson-Navin,
teachers and community workers,
who change lives and manage to survive with their
passion, convictions, and sense of humor intact

Acknowledgments

My thanks go first and foremost to the two women to whom this book is dedicated, Professor Joanne Belknap of the Department of Criminal Justice at the University of Cincinnati, and Jacqueline Gibson-Navin of The Light Center in Columbus, Ohio.

Laura Bordeau and Tracy L. Almanson graciously answered my questions. Frances Bartram, Sue Clark, Laura Anne Gilman, and John Kornbluh served as readers and critics. Officer Scott McManis of the Cincinnati Police Department took me on a high-speed tour of District One.

The autobiographies of Jean Harris have been extremely valuable to me, as has the fiction of Patricia McConnel. But the work that most inspired this novel was a nonfiction work, "The Governor's Task Force on Incarcerated Women, Final Report, June 15, 1992." I recommend it to the current governor of Ohio.

Joanna Cole's and Gloria T. Delamar's collections of jump rope rhymes were useful sources as well.

A special thanks to Ohio Wesleyan University reference librarian Paul Burnam—the voice on the other end of the phone who says, "The sky's the limit!" when I call with reference questions.

Most importantly, however, I owe a debt of gratitude to the incarcerated women who have shared their stories with me.

A tisket, a tasket,
Hitler's in his casket;
Eenie, meenie, Mussolini,
Six feet underground.
—Children's jump rope rhyme

Deep six: A grave. Assoc. with jive and jazz use,
esp. bop and cool use since
c. 1946.
—Harold Wentworth and Stuart Berg
Flexner, *Dictionary of American
Slang*

deep-six Orig. *Navy & USMC.* to kill
—J. E. Lighter, *Random House
Dictionary of American Slang*

One

"Hi, um, I guess you're not home, huh?"

The expulsion of breath scraped our ears like a tinfoil tambourine.

"Well, I guess you know this is Rocky. Ain't likely you'd forget my voice after all these years."

A pause followed. We could hear voices in the background, and an insistent bass in the pounding rhythms of rap music.

"I called you because I didn't know what else to do, and because you always tried to help me out before when I was in trouble, even though I didn't never take your advice."

Pause, then quickly, "I know it was good advice, I just ain't never taken it. But, thing is, I'm in trouble now, big trouble, like the kind of trouble that'll get me killed 'f I don't watch my ass."

The voice faded a little, drowned out by loud laughter in the background.

"—out, now, I been out a week, and I'm clean, but in some heavy shit, like I said, and I don't know what I should do. In the old days, you know I never let nothin' bother me, but now I got kids to worry about."

The rap music came closer, and we heard a syncopated pounding.

"Can't you see I'm usin' this phone, mothafucker? My time ain't up yet!" the voice shouted, making us jump. "Mo'fucker made me forget what I was sayin'," the voice continued petulantly.

"So, they told me you was retired, but I found this number in the phone book and I hope it's the right one. Only you ain't home anyway, 'f it is, so I don't know why I'm sayin' all this, talkin' to a machine."

She paused again.

"Maybe I'll try to call you again. I don't know. You was always good to me. So anyway, maybe if something happens to me, and you hear about it, maybe you'll talk to Arletta."

There was a click, and then a shrill tone, and then just the soft whir of the tape playing out on the answering machine.

"Shit," I said quietly. I looked up at Moses. "Is that it? Did you play back the whole tape?"

"That's it," he said, frowning at it. "I guess her time was up."

Two

Moses Fogg had never wanted an answering machine in the first place. He'd never had one in forty-two years of police work, and he didn't see why he needed one now, when he was retired.

"If I don't answer, I ain't here," he'd say. "Anybody with half a brain knows to call me back."

"Retired is retired," he'd say. "Don't nobody need me to come running no more."

"Any cop knows that good gossip travels faster on the street than through a phone line," he'd say. "For that matter, all I got to do is tell my business to Kevin and it be all over the city tomorrow. Don't nobody need to call up to find out how I'm doing, they can ask Kevin."

This was true. Our neighbor in the old Catatonia Arms Apartments, Kevin O'Neill, is a bartender at Arnold's downtown, and an incorrigible gossip.

But Moses' son Paul is a systems analyst who believes in better living through electronics, and Paul had given his father a combination phone and answering machine for Father's Day.

"I can't figure it out, Cat," he said to me afterward. "It's got more features than an Apollo rocket—intercom this, and two-way memo that, and call-waiting and room monitoring and automatic dialing. You don't even get a dial tone when you pick the thing up to call somebody." He shook his head. "My own son had to show me how to get a dial tone."

"I guess he thinks now that you're retired you'll be jetting off to Cancún at the drop of a hat, and taking golf vacations in Hilton Head," I said.

"Well, if I do, I ain't going to be calling home to check my messages to see if my son needs advice on fixing the toilet again," he grumbled.

But he'd plugged the thing in, even though he rarely listened to his messages. His friends knew enough to call back if they really wanted to tell him something.

Now, after a week of whooping it up at his army reunion, he had actually decided to listen to the tape. His face said that he was sorry he had.

"Who is she?" I asked, setting down a pile of accumulated mail that ran to law enforcement supply catalogs. As a detective-in-training, I had a good excuse for my nosiness, which had been honed over the years through the raising of three children. If you live with kids, nosiness and suspicion constitute survival instincts, take it from me, Cat Caliban. Kevin was a world-class gossip, and I wasn't in his league, but I could hold my own at the beauty shop on those rare occasions when I popped in for a trim.

"Rocky?" He smiled reminiscently. "Just a girl I once knew."

Winnie the beagle was so ecstatic over Moses' homecoming that she was trying to crawl inside his skin. He picked her up and sat down at the kitchen table. I rested my dogs by settling into one of those old-fashioned kitchen chairs, all shiny chrome tubing and slick vinyl.

"Roxanne Zacharias was an accident waiting to happen from the time she was a kid," he said, palming his mustache reflectively. "She says on the tape that she's in trouble, but I don't remember a time when she wasn't. 'Course, I didn't meet her until she first came through Juvie."

He was rubbing Winnie's ears and she flopped over on his lap and heaved a sigh of contentment.

"Her pattern was pretty typical. She'd run away from home, get caught shoplifting, hang out with boys who were doing worse things, do some time at Twenty-Twenty—"

"Twenty-Twenty?"

"Juvenile detention center, 2020 Auburn Avenue." He

grunted. "Vocational school for adult felons. Rocky gradu-
ated and moved on to drugs, prostitution, and theft. She and
her cousin Talia got sent up to WCI—the Women's Correctional Institution—for theft once when they were working together, but I believe this last time Rocky got sent up
for possession. Talia was already back inside for trafficking.
Last I heard, they had three kids between them."

"But you liked her?" I asked.

He nodded. "She was a hard kid to like—mouthy and
tough. But they're all like that. Anyway, she didn't get along
with her stepfather, and I think he was a lot of the problem
in the beginning. It's a long story." He sighed.

"I love a long story," I reminded him, leaning my elbows
on the table. What else did I have to do? I didn't believe in
cleaning the apartment until the fur bunnies started clogging
the heat ducts.

"I used to get an earful about how he beat her up all the
time," Moses said, fingering his mustache. "Some of it was
probably true, but I could never tell how much. I reckon he
was strict, and I've seen him lose his temper with her down
at the station. Mother was an alcoholic, died when Rocky
was nine or ten—somewhere in there. Anyway, she got
moved around from foster home to foster home. She
couldn't adjust, so she just kept running away. She finally
found a foster mother she loved, and the lady had a heart
attack. Lady did everything she could to hold on to Rocky,
but Children's Services said the placement was no longer
practical. I think it finished her off. Things just never got
better for Rocky after that. Had her first kid and her first
felony conviction at sixteen. I don't believe that would've
happened if she'd stayed with Mrs. Weldon."

We let the silence stretch between us, a meditation on
Rocky's fate.

"You want to know something, Cat?" Moses said at last.
"There was one thing Rocky was good at. In fact, she was
so good, the Y was going to send her to these regional youth
Olympics in Ft. Wayne, Indiana. She missed her chance

because she slugged a boy who was hassling her, and ended up down at Twenty-Twenty that weekend." He paused for emphasis. "But Rocky Zacharias was the best damn rope jumper ever to come out of Cincinnati, Ohio. And to this day you can go to any playground in the city where the girls are doing some serious jumping and they'll tell you stories about Rocky Zacharias. Some of the stories are even true.

"You ever seen a good jump rope session, Cat?"

"Not the kind you're talking about," I admitted. "Fifty years ago, I wasn't so bad myself," I added modestly, running a hand through my close-clipped white locks. "But I saw a story on the news once about a national double Dutch competition. That was a whole 'nother sport."

"Was a time I thought maybe jumping would save her, you know?" His bifocals caught the light as he tilted his head back. "She'd never been good at anything before, except getting into trouble. She'd never had anything to make her feel special, and kids need that. She did; she was a needy kid that covered it up with toughness. Being the jump rope queen of Cincinnati got her the kind of attention she never got at home. But I guess it wasn't enough. Much as she wanted to go to Ft. Wayne, she didn't have enough self-control to keep her nose clean. I'll bet that two weeks in Twenty-Twenty was the hardest time she ever did."

"Who's this Arletta she wants you to talk to?"

"No idea," he said.

"So what are you going to do?" I asked. I had been caught by the mixture of feigned toughness, vulnerability, and raw fear in the voice I'd heard.

Moses picked up the sleepy beagle, stood up, and set her gently on his chair. "I'm going to peel me some sweet potatoes for tomorrow."

Tomorrow was Thanksgiving, and all the residents of the Catatonia Arms were going off to their families for dinner. Moses would go to his daughter Chrystal's, I'd go to my daughter Sharon's, Kevin would go to his mother's, and Melanie Carter and Alice Rosenberg would have dinner with Al's parents, who refused to believe that they were a lesbian couple and called Mel "Al's little friend," even though Mel was a five-foot, eight-inch martial arts expert. Moses was the only one who was happy about the situation. On Friday night, we'd all have dinner together at Kevin's, eat leftovers, and dump on our families.

"But what about Rocky?" I persisted, alarmed by the urgency in her recorded voice. "Aren't you going to try and find Rocky?"

"She'll call back," he said, "if she still wants my help after she thinks about it. If not—well, I reckon I'll hear about her, one way or another."

Three

She was showing me where to put her mail while she was away. The room was done in pastel flowered chintz, but her nurse's uniform was starched white and all business. It made a swishing sound loud as a stage whisper when she walked. She wore a little silver name badge pinned over one breast: "Miss Adams."

She was explaining that she never knew how long a case would take, but that I could contact her through the Inspector if I had any questions. I watched her drop a snub-nosed automatic behind a sofa cushion.

She introduced me to her canary, who blinked at me sleepily. Now I was getting instructions on his care and feeding. The bird and I regarded each other doubtfully.

"Why don't you just let him out?" I asked. I never liked the idea of cages anyway, and weather forecasters were predicting a mild winter, so I figured, what the hell? Maybe he would fly home to the Canary Islands, stopping off at Disney World on the way. Cat Caliban, striking a blow for animal liberation.

Nurse Adams stared at me dumbfounded. She didn't have time to discuss it with me, she said, but she strongly believed that the outside world was a cruel and dangerous place for canaries, and he was better off in his cage.

I shrugged in the canary's direction. I'd tried.

Meanwhile, she'd moved on to the fern. And then a funny thing happened: the whole room turned into a lush tropical greenhouse, with the pastel chintz flowers transformed into bold, splashy, exotic blooms like orchids on steroids. The air thickened with heat, and steam rose from my skin. Warm water dripped from serpentine vines overhead and slithered down my face and back. I could barely see the white uniform through the dense mist.

"What is this, Raymond Chandler or Mary Roberts Rinehart? Make up your mind, for crissake," I muttered.

And woke myself up.

I was lying in bed, soaking wet, the sheets clinging to me like long lost relatives to a lottery winner. My usual feline bedmates were nowhere in sight. My eventual—and I do mean eventual—arrival at menopause had been disrupting their sleep as well, and they'd gone in search of less turbulent sleeping quarters.

The bedside lamp was still on, and I found a damp copy of Rinehart's *Miss Pinkerton* crumpled under my left shoulder.

I untwisted the sheets, picked up the book, and started reading where I'd left off. It was four a.m.

So I woke up crabby, and crabby was how I stayed. The less said about the Caliban family Thanksgiving dinner, the better. By all accounts, the recent Reagan-Gorbachev summit had been more successful. More amiable, too.

Maybe you look forward to Thanksgiving dinner with your family. Maybe you see it as quality time with your grandkids. If so, you don't live close enough to your kids to be running a free baby-sitting service. Or your grandkids haven't discovered Game Boys, MTV, punk rock, and other electronic and digital distractions more entertaining to them than you'll ever be. Maybe they live on another planet, or you do.

Maybe in your mind's eye you see yourself surrounded by respectful children and grandchildren, who put a drink in your hand and ask your advice about the stock market or their latest room addition. Maybe you see a glowing fire, a cheerful room with lots of polished wood, and a plate of boiled shrimp and cocktail sauce. If so, you are living in a dreamworld.

In the real world there are Rice Krispies stuck to the soles of your shoes and ground into the carpet, your son is feuding with your daughter, and your daughter-in-law is on her side. Your son-in-law mixes your drinks weak, and he's using tonic left over from last Thanksgiving. Your vegetarian daughter makes gagging noises during the ceremonial carving of the turkey, and her live-in boyfriend has brought wine he made himself after a six-week Continuing Education course in oenology. Your five-year-old grandson is singing Christmas carols because he watched Santa Claus arrive in the Macy's parade on television that morning. One kid is telling another that there is no Santa Claus. The baby is bouncing silver spoons off your kneecaps. And any advice you have to give is drowned out by the sound of other voices telling you how to live your life.

Or maybe you have the kind of kids who always travel at Thanksgiving to exotic places like Hawaii or the Bahamas, or the kind who always go to their in-laws'. If so, want to trade?

When I moved into this apartment after thirty years in a suburban split-level, do you know what my older daughter said to me? She took one look around the place and said, "But where are we going to eat when we all come over for holiday dinners?"

Sharon is bright in her way, but a little slow on the uptake. It's bad enough to have to attend family dinners; to have to cook for them beforehand and clean up afterward was a form of torture I was no longer willing to endure.

Anyway, my head was pounding by the time I returned home from Thanksgiving at Sharon's house, and I was dreading a night of dreams with off-key Christmas carols on the soundtrack. I was lying on the couch with a double gin and tonic perched on my stomach and one arm cocked over my eyes when the doorbell rang.

"Come in," I said. "Only if you're a robber or a rapist, I should warn you that it's a safe bet I'm in a worse mood than you are."

I didn't really think it was anyone with criminal intent, or at least not a stranger. Sophie had nested between my legs and she hadn't moved when the doorbell rang, except to raise her head in a display of mild interest. Of course, her instincts might have been dulled by leftover turkey.

"Was it that bad?" Moses asked. He had already changed from his holiday dinner suit into jeans and a Cincinnati PD sweatshirt.

"I guess you had a good time," I said resentfully.

"Yeah, but I'm wore out," he confessed. I opened one eye to look at him, and realized he was limping. "I'm gettin' too old to play basketball with my kids and grandkids. Took an elbow in my side that knocked me off balance, twisted my ankle when I went down. Come tomorrow, it's gonna hurt to breathe." He felt his ribs gingerly.

"Take a load off," I said, scooting my feet down to give him room on the couch. "Jeremy do that to you?"

Moses grunted. "His mother did it. Girl always did play rough."

"You want something to drink, help yourself."

"Thanks, maybe I will," he said, limping in the direction of the kitchen. "Got to keep up appearances in front of the grandkids. They all into this 'just say no.' Look at me like the creature from the black lagoon if I drink a beer—like they preparing the commitment papers."

I sighed. "I know what you mean." If Nancy Reagan had accomplished nothing else as First Lady, she had succeeded in brainwashing a substantial portion of the nation's kids into regarding all addictive substances as poison. I wasn't necessarily opposed to the idea; if it kept them healthy enough to take care of me in my misspent old age, that was just hunky-dory, as far as I was concerned. But I doubted whether the brainwashing would hold up under a serious assault from the drug culture pimps, who would soon be out in force to offer them instant happiness.

"I came down here to tell you something," Moses said, settling on the couch with a can of beer. "You know Peter

Abrams, Al's friend who works with her at Legal Aid? He was killed by a hit-and-run tonight."

"What?" I sat up quickly, which was a mistake, but I ignored my head. "Oh, no! When?"

"'Bout eight o'clock. Left a family Thanksgiving dinner to go down and pick something up at the office. He was supposed to come back and get them, but he never made it. Got hit crossing Eighth Street."

"Any witnesses?"

"A few. But it was dark, and it happened fast—so fast, it looked intentional. Dark sedan, medium-sized family car like a Chevy Impala or something, maybe with a short in the taillight. That's all anybody can say."

"Intentional?" I echoed, frowning. "You mean he was murdered? But who'd want to kill Peter? He was a nice guy, a really nice guy. I mean, he represented lots of indigent clients, and he worked hard for them, according to Al. Did as much pro bono work as she did, and volunteered in some community programs as well. Oh, hell, Moses, what a shame! He had kids, too, didn't he?"

"They always do, Cat," Moses said sadly. "They always do."

Four

So dinner the next night was more subdued than it usually is when the Catatonia Arms crew gets together. We weren't even in the mood to complain about our families; at least in our families, everybody was still alive, and even if they pissed us off a lot, we loved them and were thankful to have them, I guess.

Kevin was passing around the turnip puree and the chestnut-leek dressing. The cats and dog had all been fed earlier to keep them out from underfoot, and they were sacked out in Kevin's living room, sleeping it off, tummies bulging like tennis balls.

"So Claire shouted into the old lady's hearing aid. 'This is Alice's roommate, Melanie, Aunt Eudora,'" Mel was recounting. I take her descriptions with a grain of salt; to kids their age, an "old lady" could be anybody over fifty-five. "And Aunt Eudora brightened right up and said, 'My sister, Alice's great-aunt Chloe, had a roommate. They lived together for fifty years, and moved together to the nursing home where they died, within six months of each other. Wasn't that romantic?' You should have seen their faces!"

Al laughed. "Mel stuck to Aunt Eudora for the rest of the night. She knows more about my family history than I do."

"That's because the version you got was censored, sweetie." Mel told her.

"Poor Aunt Eudora will probably never get invited back," Al said.

"Or I won't," Mel offered, "which would be fine with me."

"My aunt Peggy is always trying to fix me up with some

'nice girl,'" Kevin said morosely. "This time it was my cousin Trish's college roommate."

"She got a brother?" Moses asked.

I caught myself grinning as I carried plates into the kitchen and stacked them atop Kevin's state-of-the-art dishwasher. Moses and I had both moved into the Catatonia Arms—or the Caledonia Arms, as it was then—a year ago last summer, in 1984. Kevin had come with the property, and Mel and Al were the first tenants I had rented to. Neither Moses nor I had had much personal experience with openly gay people, though we confessed we'd probably known gay people all our lives. Moses is black and I am white, but in some respects we share the experience of an older generation for which homosexuality was a taboo topic. I pretty much take people as they come, and Moses does, too, but he had seemed a little more uncomfortable at first then I was—more easily embarrassed, maybe. He once told me that he had dealt with gay prostitutes and johns as a patrol officer, and later in Juvie, and never felt awkward about it. But at work, Moses had been a professional; here, he was a neighbor and friend.

Yet by last Halloween, Moses had been the belle of the ball at the Stonewall Cincinnati dance, captain of the conga line. By midnight, he hadn't cared who he was dancing with, or if he was dancing with anybody at all. You can go a long way on humility, humor, and *joie de vivre*.

Back in the dining room, the conversation had turned somber: they were talking about Peter Abrams's death.

"The funeral will probably be on Wednesday," Al was saying. "Because of Thanksgiving, a lot of family members were out of town or couldn't have gotten airline reservations on short notice. Margie, Peter's wife, says that there are a few people they haven't even been able to reach yet."

"How's she taking it?" Kevin asked.

"Better than I would," Al said. "She says she wants the kids to remember their father fondly, and she doesn't want to disrupt that memory by creating a lot of noise and confusion about his death. You can tell she's done her share of crying, but in public she's very calm."

"The cops are investigating the possibility that it was a homicide," Mel added. "Right, Al? They're going through his files and appointment books, looking for anybody who could have had a grudge against him."

Moses made a noise in his throat and shifted in his chair. "For a Legal Aid attorney, that could make for a mighty long list."

"Why?" I asked. "I would have thought folks would appreciate Legal Aid. I mean, most of them wouldn't be able to afford legal help otherwise."

"Yeah, Cat, and some of our clients are actually satisfied and grateful," Al said. "But a lot of them aren't. A lot of them think we should have done more for them, or they blame us for every case we lose. They blame us if the whole thing was their fault to begin with, and even if they get what they deserve."

"Did Peter have a lot of dissatisfied customers?" Kevin asked.

"We all do," Al responded ruefully. "Peter was no exception. Don't get me wrong; about half my clients are the salt of the earth—the ones who get me out of bed in the morning and motivate me to keep doing what I'm doing. The other half feed my fantasies about corporate law in a big firm that provides golf club memberships as a company benefit."

"Do you know if he'd been threatened lately?" Moses asked, frowning. "Any logical candidates for a hit-and-run? Somebody angry enough, and crazy enough to kill him, but cowardly enough to take the easy way?"

"I can think of a few," Al admitted. "But let's face it: most of our clients would have to run him down with a bicycle or a skateboard. Most don't own cars. Some of the ones that do have had their licenses revoked, although that doesn't mean they're not driving."

"Car could be borrowed or stolen, too," Moses observed. "Who's working the case?"

"A guy named Bunke," Al replied. "I kid you not, that's his name—Walter Bunke. To tell you the truth, he doesn't look old enough to be out of high school, much less out of the police academy."

"Don't know him," Moses said. "But if he's that young, he could be on a fast track. Could be he's very good at what he does."

Over five kinds of leftover pie, I turned the conversation to Moses' mysterious caller, Rocky Zacharias, the former jump rope queen.

"I don't suppose she called you today?"

He shook his head. "I made a few calls. Talked to her parole officer, who hasn't heard from her but isn't worried. No answer at the stepfather's. I reckon she'll call again when she gets around to it, unless she smokes up all her money."

"Who's this you're talking about?" Kevin doesn't believe in unspilled beans, and he wants them spilled right in his ears.

Moses told them about Rocky and her phone call.

"What did you say her last name was?" Al asked.

"Zacharias," Moses said. "Nope, nobody's seen her, far's I can find out."

"You're wrong, Moses," Al said. "Somebody has. I could swear she came in to see Peter this week, maybe two days before he was killed."

Five

All of a sudden, Moses was very interested in finding Rocky Zacharias. And out of deference to my career plans, he let me tag along. I was pleased to see him back in the saddle, so to speak. If it went well, maybe I could talk him into taking the licensing exam for private investigators, then I could work off his license.

Besides, I wanted to find Rocky myself; whether or not she knew anything about Peter's death, she struck me as a very frightened young woman.

So here they are, folks, reunited in the cause of Truth, Justice, and the American Way: that dynamic duo of crime fighting, those senior Sherlocks who amaze and astonish with their acumen and agility, those geriatric geniuses, Fogg and Caliban, hot on the trail of intrigue, laughing in the face of danger.

Well, actually, nobody's laughing yet.

To tell you the truth, Moses is dragging a game leg, shuffling to the car with that kind of Frankenstein walk that speaks volumes about the stiffness in his basketball muscles and the quantity of food he has put away during the Thanksgiving festivities. Me, I'm hungover, and having a hell of a time getting my jacket zipped up. When I'd gone to brush my teeth this morning, I'd missed the toothbrush altogether on my first pass with the toothpaste. It's that kind of day.

"I still don't see why we have to start so damn early," I grumbled, reiterating a point I had made at midnight last night.

"I thought you wanted to be a detective," Moses said,

folding himself cautiously into the front seat of his Fairlane. He leaned over to unlock my door, and groaned.

"I thought detectives hung out in seedy bars and dark alleys all night, and slept until noon," I said. "That's why I wanted to be one."

Moses started the car, but it died. I leaned my forehead against the dashboard.

Moses tried again. And again.

"It just takes a while," he said.

"You got to stop trying to do those high-speed chases in an eight-year-old Fairlane, Moses," I observed. Moses is a relatively sedate driver, for an ex-cop—but that's a crucial qualification.

Kevin came out of the apartment building carrying his tennis racket and waved at me cheerily. Just wait till you're my age, cookie, I thought, and see how tightly strung you feel at this hour of the morning.

The engine caught, sputtered, and kept going. The whole car shuddered and vibrated like a drunk with DTs.

"I don't see no airsick bags in the seat pocket in front of me," I commented.

"Just needs a tune-up," Moses said.

And then we were off.

"So this guy we're going to see—he's Rocky's parole officer?" I asked.

Moses nodded. "Name's Toby Grisham. Says he doesn't know much, and he's probably right. Rocky's only been out a week, and he saw her right away, so she's not due to check in with him until next month. He lives over in Cheviot."

"And this guy who probably doesn't know much—why are we going to see him?"

"Protocol," Moses said.

"Oh," I said. "That."

"After him, we'll go see some other folks in Rocky's old neighborhood. See, Cat, with somebody like Rocky, you can't track 'em the way you would you or me. Rocky's livin' on the margins in all kind of ways. No telephone, no car, driver's license is probably expired. We can check voter's registration, though."

"Well, excuse me for asking," I said, "but what makes you think she'd rush right out and register to vote? You think she's been brooding about the crime problem the whole time she was inside? Plotting her revenge on society by voting in Ronald McDonald's crowd for four more years?"

He shook his head. "Voter registration's the only kind of ID you can get if you don't have any other ID. For anything else, you got to show a driver's license, Social Security card, something like that. Once you got a voter registration card, you got ID, you can cash checks in the neighborhood. Rocky probably had a Social Security card at some point, but I'm betting she lost it."

"Oh," I said. I tried to think about the implications of that for the state of politics in America today, but I couldn't wrap my mind around it—not without creasing a few neurons that were in no mood to be messed with. So I gave it up.

The day was gray and overcast, and a fine mist had begun to fall by the time we reached Grisham's. It was a brick-and-siding bungalow that looked interchangeable with most of its neighbors, except for the shiny black Harley parked in the carport out front. Moses stopped to run his hand over the leather and chrome. It's that Y chromosome that makes men susceptible.

"Well, it ain't no medium-sized family car with a short in one of the taillights," I observed. "So unless Rocky's parole officer stole a car, he didn't run down Peter Abrams. We're making progress already."

"You better not get fingerprints on that," a voice cautioned. "My dad will go apeshit."

We turned to see a girl, maybe ten or eleven, hard to tell, rounding the house. She was petite with long straight blond hair. Bulging over her ears was a set of headphones connected to a cord that disappeared inside her jacket pocket.

"What does he do when he goes apeshit?" I asked, curious.

"He confiscates my Walkman," she said.

"Sounds kind of petty," I said. Especially for a parole officer, I added to myself.

She shrugged. "Mom gives it back." She headed up the walk toward the front door. "Do I know you, or are you just casing the joint?"

"Fogg and Caliban," Moses said, following her.

"We specialize in cycle thefts," I said.

Moses ignored me. "We're here to see your dad."

She opened the front door, leaned in, and bellowed, "Da-ad!" loudly enough to fetch half the fathers in Cincinnati.

She listened a minute, then said, "I'll be right back," and disappeared inside, closing the door in our faces.

"He's on the phone," she reported shortly afterward. "You can come in and wait, I guess."

She guided us vaguely in the direction of a living room, and departed. There was a television set on, but nobody seemed to be watching it except for a shaggy gray dog that trotted over to sniff our ankles. The room was empty of human inhabitants, but so crowded with human artifacts that it gave the impression of being the tribal gathering place of an extensive clan that had only just left. Open books and magazines lay strewn about, some facedown, some faceup. Some appeared to be using athletic shoes as bookmarks. A disassembled motor from one of those junior science sets graced the coffee table, along with a small plate of gnawed toast corners and a half-empty glass of milk. In one corner stood a music stand, and a saxophone lay on the floor next to it. I got a pin in the back when I sat down on the couch because I had leaned against a skirt somebody was hemming. The ironing board was behind us, and the iron made those popping noises they make when the metal is heating or cooling.

"Weird," I said. "I feel like I've walked into one of those

sci-fi flicks from the fifties, and they've just dropped the bomb."

A kid walked into the room. He wore jeans and a University of Cincinnati sweatshirt and carried a stuffed toy, which, from the size of the ears dragging the floor, was probably a rabbit.

"Hey," he said. "How you doin'? Toby Grisham."

He stuck out his hand, and for a split second I hesitated. Surely this was Toby Grisham, Junior? Then I spotted some fine lines around the corners of his eyes.

This guy is a parole officer? I thought. He could play one of the Beaver's classmates. He had wide blue eyes, a hairless chin and upper lip, a disarming grin, and blond hair combed neatly back from his face. When he turned his head, I saw that he had a ponytail, but it was so small as to be practically invisible.

Luckily, he hadn't noticed my reaction, because he seemed preoccupied by his long-eared companion. He shook hands with us, then seemed to catch a movement in the hall out of the corner of his eye.

"Who's that? Tracy? Get in here!" He bellowed the last part; the Grishams seemed to speak in two volumes: normal and loud.

But the six-year-old waif who appeared seemed unruffled, even though he began to shake the rabbit in her face.

"What was Mrs. Wiggles doing on top of my desk lamp, besides trying to burn the house down?" he shouted. From where I was sitting, I could now see that the rabbit wore a white apron, and that the apron was marred by a large circular scorch mark.

"Well, Daddy, it was like this," the six-year-old explained patiently. "Mrs. Wiggles got caught in the rain last night when she had to go bail her little boy Jerome out of jail. And she wasn't very wet, but just a little wet, and Jerome said, 'Why don't you just let her sleep on top of the lamp, and she'll be dry in the morning?' And I said—"

"I get the picture," he interrupted, and glowered at her. "If

I hadn't smelled the smoke, she would have been one dead rabbit, and she would have taken us all out with her. So don't do it again!"

Like I said before, I love a good story, so I gave her extra points for the explanation. The detail about bailing out Jerome—that was the signature of a natural born storyteller, and a gift like that is nothing to sneeze at.

The storyteller herself, however, unfazed, just nodded and said, "Okay, Daddy, I'll 'splain it to Jerome." She lowered her voice confidentially, "But you know what he's like when he's been drinking."

I put the finishing touches on my hangover by trying to contain my laughter.

"Everybody's a con artist," Grisham said to us. "Listen up, shrimp. Bottom line: you deep-six the bunny and you are looking at a kittenless childhood. If you can't take care of a stuffed rabbit, you can't care of a live kitten." He shook a finger at her. "And don't be thinking you can con Santa Claus because you got the old man in your hip pocket. You can cozy up to Santa all you want, he's still gonna check your file. You read me?"

She gave him her most supercilious six-year-old look, snatched the rabbit, turned on her heel, and retreated at a dignified pace.

Grisham turned to us. "Have a seat, have a seat. Just throw that shit on the floor. Can I get you something?"

I opened my mouth to say, "Alka-Seltzer, if you've got it," but Moses spoke first. "No, thanks, we're fine."

"You want to talk about Rocky Zacharias, right?"

Moses nodded. "What was she in for this time?"

"Possession," Grisham said. "Straight possession. Dumb. She was just under the limit for dealing, as I keep reminding her. Did about a year. Next time, it'll be more."

"Who was she paroled to?"

"Stepfather," Grisham said. "Know him? Big burly guy name of Gordon Nash."

"I've had the pleasure," Moses said.

Grisham snorted. "Ain't that the truth. Well, who else was there? Her aunt's got a record, so she was out. I guess they didn't have too many choices, and Nash was willing."

"I bet he was," Moses said grimly. "He's been trying to run her life for years. Probably enjoys the power he's got now."

"Halfway houses were full," Grisham put in, anticipating an objection. "And they were likely to stay full till after New Year's." He shrugged. "Hey, I'm not crazy about the guy, but at least he cares about her. And living with those two girls would turn any man into Attila the Hun."

"So Rocky had to choose between doing more time and being paroled to her stepfather," Moses said.

"That's it," Grisham conceded. "System stinks, but what can we do? It happens a lot. Woman just wants to go home to her kids and get on with her life, but the parole board isn't about to just cut her loose, and there's good reasons for that. But meanwhile, she's stuck in prison because she hasn't got any place to go when she gets out, and nobody'll take responsibility for her. Worst-case scenario—Children's Services decides to put her kids up for adoption while everybody's screwing around trying to figure out where she can go."

"They can do that?" I asked, aghast.

"Sure," he said. "Happens all the time. And you can't sell halfway houses to the voters because they don't want dangerous criminals living in their neighborhoods, and they'd rather spend money on more police or more jails."

"And are the women dangerous?" I asked. "Is Rocky?"

"Nah, not like people think," Grisham said. "Most of them do time for crimes against property, and most of it's drug-related or alcohol-related."

"More dangerous to themselves than to anybody else, Cat," Moses agreed.

"Now Rocky's got a temper that gets her in trouble," Grisham said.

Moses nodded. "She's a little bitty thing, but if somebody

crosses her when she's in a mood, she thinks she's Muhammad Ali, Bruce Lee, and Superman all rolled into one. The drugs don't help."

"She did AA and NA in prison," Grisham reported, then paused. "Maybe I shouldn't be telling you that, but you put in a lot of time with her in Juvie, right? So I'm probably not telling you anything you don't already know. Hell, most of them do AA and NA if they can. They've all got good intentions, coming out. But life on the street is rough, no doubt about it. A lot of them don't make it."

"NA?" I looked at Moses.

"Narcotics Anonymous," he said. "It's another twelve-step program."

I turned to Grisham. "So you last talked to Rocky when?"

"A week ago Wednesday—the day after she got out. I'm not due to see her again until next month. She's on medium supervision."

"Where's she living?" Moses asked.

"Supposed to be living with her stepfather," Grisham said.

"She have a job?" Moses asked.

Grisham shook his head. "I gave her some names and addresses—we have a few local factories and businesses that regularly hire parolees. I don't know if she made any calls, though. I can check on Monday if you want me to. Normally I don't like to call the employer, in case he doesn't know about the record. But the names I gave Rocky are all employers I've worked with pretty closely, so in that case, I don't mind."

"Her kids with the stepfather?"

"No, they're with her aunt Barbara—you know her? That's where I'd try next.

"So you knew Rocky in the old days?" he said to Moses. "Whyn't you straighten her out?"

Moses just laughed, and I recognized the question as some kind of in-joke, probably an old one for those in the helping professions.

"Why did you say you were interested in Rocky now?" Grisham asked.

"I didn't," Moses said. "But she called me up wanting my help with something, left a message on my answering machine. Then, a couple days later, a Legal Aid attorney we think she went to see got killed by a hit-and-run."

And Moses told him the whole story. Grisham seemed interested, but he couldn't give us any information about what kind of trouble Rocky was in.

"Nothing I knew about," he said. "But the girl runs with a rough crowd, no doubt about it. Say, you ever see her jump rope?"

Moses nodded.

"You did? What was she like?"

Moses paused, stroked his mustache, and gazed at the ceiling. "Like jazz. Like heat lightning. Like the guest preacher at a revival meeting. Like—like the best damn rope jumper you'll ever see."

Grisham walked us to the door, guiding us through an obstacle course of books and shoes and toys. A dryer shrieked somewhere in the bowels of the house.

"Roger!" he shouted. "Dryer!" To us, he said, "My wife wanted the kind with the buzzer. It's convenient, but man, I can't stand the noise!"

Six

"You think Rocky's in there?"

We squinted up at the house through a mist-covered windshield.

"Do I think she's in there?" Moses echoed. "No, Cat. I don't. That would be too easy."

We were still on the West Side—unfamiliar territory to me. Rocky's official address was a pale green two-story frame house that had seen better days. As we headed toward the front door, I noticed that the porch sagged, as if embarrassed to be seen in the company of the two dead evergreen bushes on either side of the front steps and the dead patch of lawn that bordered the crumbling walkway. The weather hadn't been that cold yet this year, so most lawns in Cincinnati still had some green in them; this one appeared to have given up early.

Moses took one look at the doorbell, which was the same vintage as the house, opened a creaky screen door, and knocked.

The teenager who answered the door had dirty brown hair that hung limply to her shoulders. She was probably tall for her age, which might explain her general air of embarrassment. I thought she might be pretty, but as is often the case with teenagers, it was hard to tell. By keeping her head down, she could use her hair to hide her face. She wore an oversized sweatshirt and sweatpants, and orange plastic gloves.

"Hey, Amy," Moses said. "It's Moses Fogg. I'm a friend of Rocky's. You remember me?"

She wrapped a hank of hair around her finger and stuck

the ends in her mouth. She frowned at our shoes and shook her head.

"You were just a little girl last time I was out here to the house," Moses said heartily. "I'm looking for Rocky. She here?"

Amy sucked on her hair and shook her head again.

"She does live here, though?" Moses pursued.

The head changed direction.

"See, she called me the other day, wanted to talk to me, but I wasn't home. You have a phone number? Maybe I can call and catch her in."

The teenager took her hair out of her mouth and studied it, presumably for split ends.

"We don't have no phone," she said at last, eyes crossed in concentration.

"Well, maybe I can leave my number, and you can tell her I came by," Moses said. "Tell her I'd like to talk to her. Can you do that for me, Amy?"

She nodded, almost imperceptibly, at his shoes.

"What are you going to do with your hair?" I asked conversationally.

She looked up at me. "You know what glazing is?" she asked.

"I've heard of it," I said cautiously. I didn't want to misrepresent my familiarity with the cutting edge of beauty technology. My hair stays short, straight, and white, and I resist all of my beautician's campaigns to experiment with it.

"It's goin' to put these red highlights in my hair," she said, with more enthusiasm than she'd shown on the topic of her sister's whereabouts. "I got a friend, Melissa, and she's studying to be a beautician. She's goin' to practice on me. You think it will look okay?"

I felt a quick jab to the heart—a sympathy pang for the pain of adolescence.

"I think it'll look really pretty on you," I assured her. "You've got the right coloring for it."

She flushed and ducked her head. "That's what my boyfriend says," she confided shyly.

Moses handed her a slip of paper.

"That's my number. Tell her she can call anytime," he said. "Your dad around?"

She went back to nonverbal communication, head swinging side to side.

"What about Rocky's kids?" he asked. "They with you?"

She shook her head again.

"You know where they are?" he asked lightly.

"I got to go," she said, panic rising in her voice. She stepped back from the door.

"When's the baby due?" I asked.

She looked up at me again, and started to say something, then stopped.

"I got to go," she said, and closed the door firmly.

We stood there a minute.

"That's what I like about teaming up with an ex-Juvie officer," I observed at last. "Golly, I'm sure picking up a lot of pointers about dealing with juveniles. That's the second one today that's closed the door in our faces. And it's only—what?—ten-thirty?"

"She didn't look pregnant to me," he grumbled.

I shrugged. Some things you can't explain.

"Damn, Cat, she's as young as Rocky was the first time," Moses lamented as we trudged to the car. Only Moses was trudging on one foot, limping on the other. "You sure she's pregnant?"

"You saw the look she gave me," I said. "Anyway, she said she had a boyfriend. Any teenaged girl who has a boyfriend can get pregnant, or didn't they explain that to you at the police academy?"

"Guess I figured Nash would keep a tighter grip on her, but she's gonna end up just like her sister," he said, shaking his head. "Damn, Cat, I wish kids would find a way to rebel that didn't produce more kids."

I frowned. "She was on the verge of answering my

question, but she was too scared to prolong the conversation. What's she scared of, Moses? The same thing Rocky is?"

"Beats me," he conceded. "Maybe she did recognize me, and remembers that I worked Juvenile. That's enough to put the fear of God into any kid. They're all up to something."

"It was more than that, though," I said. "You know how they look when they've done something stupid. This was more than that."

"Yeah, you're right." He sighed. "At her age, Rocky ended up with two kids—twins. Can you imagine having twins at sixteen?"

"I can't imagine having them at any age," I said. "Does Rocky look like her?"

He shook his head. "Different father. Rocky's father was black—she's one of Antoine Dupree's kids. She's light-complected, but you can tell she's got Negro blood. Far's I know, Amy is Nash's daughter."

"Do the sisters get along?" I asked.

"Yeah, Rocky's real fond of her kid sister. Protective, too. But like I said, Rocky's got half brothers and sisters all over the neighborhood, down in District One. She's got a lot of kin."

"Would they look after her, if she was in trouble?"

He gazed through the windshield. "They probably would if they could, those that have their own shit together enough to be able to do anything for her. If nothing else, they'd do what Amy just did—lie for her."

"Which part did you think was a lie?"

"Hard to say," he mused. "Coulda been all lies. Could be she hasn't seen Rocky for days, but she knows she can't say that or Rocky be in trouble with her PO. And I don't reckon I believe that she doesn't know where Rocky's kids are, if they're really with Aunt Barbara. Anyway, I reckon that's where we need to go next—Aunt Barbara's."

"You know where she lives?"

"I know where she *used* to live, but that was a long time ago," he said. "In the life of the neighborhood, centuries."

He made an illegal U-turn in the street, and we headed back downtown. Cops never ticket cops or ex-cops, so even apart from the speed, riding with Moses was always an experience.

"Say, Cat, how'd you know about that hair thing?"

"I could smell it. Not quite like a permanent, and besides, she was wearing gloves, but there was definitely a chemical odor." I grabbed for the dashboard as he swung around the corner. "So I think it's safe that's one thing she didn't lie about."

He gunned the car to run a yellow light and the tires skidded a little on the wet pavement. My hangover had receded, and I was starting to enjoy myself.

Seven

"Don't you never come in here by yourself, Cat, hear?"

We were deep in the heart of Lincoln Court, more familiarly known as the Projects, a twenty-two-acre stretch of brick boxes built as low-income housing and conveniently located just across from the District One police station on Ezzard Charles Drive. The whole place wore an air of neglect, the kind of neglect fostered by the trickle-down economics of an administration that liked to spend money on guns instead of butter. Here we were, five years into the Reagan presidency, and nothing much had trickled down to these folks. Broken glass crunched under our feet, and litter blew against our ankles and stuck to the soles of our shoes. Tattered curtains hung awkwardly in some windows like slips showing, and others were framed by duct tape to keep out the cold. Yet there were signs of vitality, too—music, the smell of cooking, which overpowered a fainter, more acrid odor, and grass that was green if well-trampled in some places and shaggy in others.

Under a covered walkway, several black women had gathered to gossip. Nearby, four little girls were jumping rope. We stopped to watch.

"Fudge, fudge, tell the judge,
Mama's got a newborn baby.
It's a girl full of curl.
Papa's gone crazy.
Wrap it up in tissue paper,
Send it up the elevator.
First floor MISS,
Second floor MISS,

Third floor MISS,
Fourth floor MISS—"

The rope crept up at each floor, until the jumper, a scrawny little thing with brightly colored barrettes on the ends of her braids, missed at last, and collapsed on the ground, giggling.

"Say," Moses said, picking her up and setting her gently on her feet, "you pretty good. You almost as good as another little girl I knew."

"Who?" she asked shyly.

"Little girl name of Rocky," he said. "Rocky Zacharias."

I had to hand it to him: He was smooth. Maybe he had a way with kids after all, little kids, anyway. Maybe it was just the teenagers he had trouble with. Doesn't everyone?

"You know Rocky?" another little girl asked.

"Ain't nobody can jump like Rocky," a third girl insisted.

The first little girl was about to burst with pride. She grinned down at her shoelaces to hide her pleasure at being compared to so eminent a personage as Rocky Zacharias. She was still holding on to Moses' hand, I noticed.

"I seen Rocky jump one time," the fourth—and tallest—girl said to her, "and you ain't no Rocky."

"You lie!" shouted Number Two. "You ain't never seen Rocky jump! Girl, you too young."

Number Four glared at Number Two. "I did so see her! One time, she come over here to see her aunt, and me and Melva Dalby was jumpin', and we axed her would she jump for us, and she did! You can go and ax Melva, too!"

"Actually—" Moses interrupted, an ex-Juvie officer in his conflict resolution mode.

"You lie!"

"Nuh-uh! You the liar! You the one tol' Mr. Edwards you could swim across the pool that time—"

"Actually—" Moses repeated in a slightly louder voice.

"What time you talkin' about?"

"You know! That time me an' you and Henry George was over to the pool last August, and—"

I raised two fingers to my mouth and whistled. All eyes swiveled in my direction.

"I believe that Mr. Fogg has a question he wants to ask you girls," I said. "Isn't that right, Mr. Fogg?"

"Uh, yeah, that's right," he said, after a slight hesitation. "That is, if it's all right with you ladies." He turned to the gossiping women and made a slight bow.

This was a clever diplomatic ploy. Although their conversation had never faltered, the women had kept eyes and ears on us from the time we stopped to talk to the kids. I don't know if the kids were theirs; it wouldn't have mattered. If we'd offered the kids anything, or tried to lure them away, our lives wouldn't have been worth two cents.

They studied us warily now.

"What you want to know, then?" This from a hard-eyed middle-aged woman who was leaning against the wall and smoking a cigarette.

"I'm looking for Mrs. Barbara Hickson, Rocky's aunt," he told her. "I know she used to live over here."

He'd dug an address out of an old book last night. He'd told me it probably wasn't current, but it was a place to start, since there were no B. Hicksons in the Cincinnati phone directory.

"What you want with Miz Hickson?" the same woman asked suspiciously. "You a cop?"

I stifled a grin. People say that if you live around cops, you get to where you can spot one from two blocks away. Moses never credited this principle much where he was concerned, because he was the wrong color to fit the bill for a typical Cincinnati police officer. Apparently, he was wrong.

"Well, I'm trying to find out if Rocky's okay," he said, putting on his most beatific expression. "See, she called and left me a message, wanted my help on something, but she got cut off before she could leave a phone number or address."

That sounded better than just saying that Rocky hadn't

given him any way to contact her, but I wasn't sure they'd buy it.

"I'm just worried about her, is all," he said. "She just got out, and she already in some kind of trouble."

Nobody asked him, got out of what?

An elderly woman wearing hair curlers under a scarf spoke up.

"Miz Hickson don't live here no more. She moved out—must be five years ago now. Packed up all them kids and moved out to Winton Terrace. Ain't that right, Dorice? Ain't that where she went?"

A pregnant woman nodded. "That's where she went, but I don't think she's there anymore."

"Was that the lady used to go to your church, Dorice?" another woman asked. "White lady. Big."

The first speaker answered for Dorice. "Uh-huh, that's her. Used to go with Jimmy DeWitt."

"She live over yonder at Seven Twenty-five," said the woman in curlers. "But then she got Rocky's kids, on top of Talia's two and Richie's, and she say she need a bigger place. Them kids was driving her crazy in that little bitty apartment."

"Seems like I heard she got her Section Eight and moved up on Magnolia." The woman who spoke was thin as my little finger, and she'd been punctuating the conversation with coughs. "Ain't that right, Eva Jane?"

"Somewhere around there," the first speaker admitted grudgingly.

"Federally subsidized housing," Moses answered my frown in response to "Section Eight."

She narrowed her eyes at Moses, sucked on her cigarette, and drew smoke into through her nose. "Who'd you say you were?"

"Moses Fogg," he said. "I used to work in the juvenile section, but I'm retired now. Like I said, I'm just trying to help out an old friend."

His accuser laughed. "Rocky never made friends with a cop in her life."

"I ain't sayin' she was easy to get along with," Moses returned complacently. "I ain't sayin' that. Ain't like we sendin' each other Christmas cards. But over the years, I helped her out a few times, gave her a lot of advice she didn't want to take. Maybe she called me up 'cause she's ready to take it. I don't know."

He smiled down at the little girl who was still holding his hand.

"Thank you for your time, ladies," he said, and made another bow that included the girls, who giggled.

I felt a tug on my arm. It was Girl Number Two.

"How you do that whistle, lady?"

"That wasn't nothin'," Girl Number Four said scornfully. "My brother Junior, he can whistle so loud it break your eardrums."

"You lie, girl!" Number Two took up the challenge. "'F he could whistle like that, he'd already broke his own eardrums. Be deaf on top of dumb."

"You the liar!"

Moses gave up on conflict resolution, and we left, their voices ringing in our ears.

I was getting into the car when I heard an exclamation from Moses.

"Damn, Cat! They got my antenna!"

"Your antenna?" I straightened up and stared at him across the hood, bewildered.

"They cut 'em up, use 'em for crack pipes," he said. "That's a kind of cocaine we seein' more of in Cincinnati these days. Damn, I hate it when that happens! That's the third one this year!"

And to think that the last time I lost an antenna was when my five-year-old son, now thirty-seven, had borrowed it to conduct "Peter and the Wolf" on his record player.

Eight

We had lunch at a little hole-in-the-wall on Fourteenth Street, just off Central Parkway. The tables were rickety, despite the fact that they were partially supported by folded napkins so yellow that they could have been the first paper napkins ever manufactured. I like to think that as soon as paper napkins were invented, some genius perceived their table-leveling properties and put them to use. For all I knew, I could be sitting on a historic site.

A spattered Ezzard Charles presided over our meal, looking belligerently down at us from a wall that had probably seen its last coat of paint before Ezzard got his first pair of boxing gloves. The barbecue was as good as any I'd eaten since I'd left Texas forty years ago, and I was glad I didn't have to fight Ezzard for it.

I didn't have to fight Moses, either, because I polished off my sandwich while he was on the phone to Al, who had spent her morning going through Peter Abrams's office.

"Nothing," he reported, lowering himself into the booth. I noticed he was still favoring his right leg. "She can't find a case file on Rocky, so I asked her to look for one on Barbara Hickson. She found that, but she says everything in it is old. I told her to bring it home anyway, just to look at. She says that if Peter talked to Rocky, he should have kept some notes. I might have to break down and call this Bunke, explain my interest in the case, and ask what he's got."

He chatted up the owners, but they didn't know any Barbara Hickson or Rocky Zacharias. So we moved on.

Our next stop was a small, overstuffed little grocery store, magazine stand, and lottery seller up the street. In one corner of the crowded front window was a hand-printed sign, "Checks Cashed." Moses picked out some candy bars and a gun magazine, and took them to the counter. A tall, bald, stoop-shouldered black man wearing wire rims rang him up. I hung around the front of the store so as not to crowd him.

Moses started in with a comment on the weather, moved on to football in general and the Bengals season in particular, then segued into the past, slid into changes in the neighborhood, and finally arrived at Mrs. Barbara Hickson.

"Yes, I know Mrs. Hickson," the man said. "She comes in here all the time. Kids, too."

"You wouldn't happen to know where she lives?" Moses asked.

"I might," the man said affably. "What you want to know for?" He glanced over at me—a quick, appraising look, as if deciding whether I represented the welfare office or Children's Services.

I turned my back to them and studied the front window. Down low, under the "Checks Cashed" sign, someone had scrawled something in the accumulated grime. I bent down to read it: ELVIS WAS HEER!

"She has a niece name of Rocky," Moses said. "Just got out of prison. Girl called me up 'cause she seems to be in some kind of trouble, but I don't have any way to contact her. I'm worried about her."

"I know the one you mean. Skinny little thing. Got freckles and a lot of attitude."

Moses laughed. "That's Rocky, all right. You seen her?"

The man nodded. "She come in here—let's see—maybe Monday. Had her little boy with her. Kid must look like his daddy, 'cause he sure don't look like her. Cute, though, the way my momma used to say—he so ugly, he cute. Like one of them troll dolls they used to have."

"She say where she's staying?"

"No, I was busy, didn't have time to talk. Just—you know—'How you been doin'? Ain't seen you around.' That kind of thing. Didn't have to ask where she been, though. Got that pasty skin they get from doin' time."

"She look okay otherwise?" Moses asked.

He shrugged. "Not too good. Like she been sick, or somethin'. But her eyes was okay. So if you askin' me is she usin', I say, I don't know. Didn't see no sign of it. She got a cough, but she smoke a lot, too. Bought cigarettes that day."

Moses nodded. "You decided yet whether you're going to tell me where Mrs. Hickson lives?"

The man dipped his head in my direction. "Who's she?"

"Jus' a friend," Moses said, smiling. "Took a notion she want to be a detective when she grow up. Seem to think I can teach her something."

"You workin' for somebody?" the man asked.

"Not me." Moses grinned. "I'm retired."

"Mus' be nice," the man said. "Well, I tell you what. You go on over across the street to that yellow brick building, and ask for Mrs. Hickson there. Somebody be able to tell you which apartment she in."

"Thanks," Moses said. "'Preciate it."

"I wouldn't have told you if you hadn't asked after Rocky—how she looked and all." He walked to the door to point us toward the right building. "But I think you ought to know: you ain't the only one lookin' for her."

"No?" Moses frowned. "What's the other guy look like?"

"White. Medium height. Got more muscles than you got."

"Hair?"

"Don't know. He was wearin' a ball cap, so I didn't notice."

"Age?"

The man paused and thought. "Hard to tell. Got kind of a baby face, but he could be older—forties, even fifties, maybe. Like I said, he was wearin' a ball cap."

We thanked him again, and headed across the street.

"If it was her little boy," Moses observed, "she's got more kids than I thought. The twins were girls."

"And Aunt Barbara sounds like she's running a children's home," I said. "Meanwhile, we got two white guys in this case who look young. But unless the Cincinnati PD allows its detectives to wear ball caps on the job, I'd vote for our friendly neighborhood parole officer Toby Grisham over Walter Bunke."

Moses grunted. And limped.

"That's the same Toby Grisham who claimed not to have made any contact with Rocky since she came to his office last week," I prodded him.

Moses grunted again.

"C'mon, Moses, don't pout," I said, taking his arm. "You still got plenty of muscle."

"All of it sore," he complained, shaking me off. "Let go my arm, Cat. That's the shoulder I landed on when I took Gracie's charge."

On the front steps of the yellow brick building, we found a young man who probably would have sold his grandmother's address to the Big Bad Wolf for fifty cents. So for a dollar, we were escorted to Barbara Hickson's door. He offered to pick the lock for another five dollars, but we declined.

We didn't need his services after all. When nobody answered the door, we tried the handle, found it unlocked, opened the door and walked in. To an empty apartment.

Our footsteps echoed loudly on the scuffed wood floor because there was so little to absorb the sound. A ladder-back chair with a broken leg sat forlornly in the middle of the largest room. A faded rag rug was piled carelessly in one corner. The walls were dingy and heavily marked, as if the previous occupants had run roller derbys in the living room and halls. We found a one-eyed, partially clad, chocolate-colored baby doll lying behind the toilet in the bathroom, and a stained single mattress in the smaller room. We could hear the sound of dripping water coming from the kitchen.

A kitchen towel, gray with dust, was stuffed into a hole in one of the windows.

More alarming was a large crater in the wall where something had struck it with great force, creating a sunburst of radiating cracks and fissures.

"Damn!" Moses said at last, as we gazed despondently at the kitchen. "I got a bad feeling about this, Cat. I don't like to be bringing up the rear if somebody's chasing Barbara Hickson." He absentmindedly shut a cabinet door. "Well, we ain't gonna find nothin', but we might as well look."

"You think somebody else has already searched the place?"

"You know any woman who would go away and leave every drawer and cabinet standing open like that?"

Actually, I knew one—my daughter, Franny. But, as usual, Franny was the exception that proved the rule.

We went over the whole place minutely. We found: three buttons, two safety pins, a book of matches from the Blue Wisp Jazz Club out on Madison Road, a doll's eye, a broken shoelace, three jacks, a box of powdered milk, a can of baked beans, five pens, and a child's jump rope, which had been draped over a hook on the back of a closet door.

Plus one cryptic message, printed in light purple crayon low on the wall in one corner of the smaller room: ELVIS WAS HEER!

Nine

"Cool!" Kevin enthused when we described our discovery. "So maybe the King dropped in from the fifth dimension, or another galaxy, or wherever it is he's hanging out between sightings, and took the family away with him!"

Moses and I exchanged a look over our mugs of beer. Kevin ignored us, leaned over the bar, and stared dreamily into space. Kevin's place of employment, Arnold's, was relatively quiet; the weekday politicoes were out Christmas shopping with their spouses, and the Saturday night crowd hadn't yet arrived.

"He probably has his own press agent in the hereafter," Kevin mused, "only this guy can't spell in English too well."

"I don't know why you want to tell him all our business, Cat," Moses groused. "You know what he's like."

"Well, if Elvis has his own press agent in the hereafter, you'd think he could at least spell 'here' right," I pointed out to Kevin.

"I saw Elvis once." A short white man in a three-piece suit leaned boozily in my direction. "'E was coming out of that hat store—you know that hat store? Whatza name o' that hat store? You know the one I mean." He stared at me accusingly.

A nice-looking young black man in sweatpants and a sweatshirt was sitting next to Moses. "Paragon? Batsakes?" he asked.

"That's it!" the short man said. "Satbakes. I shoulda remembered old Baksatkes. You know why? Because my father bought me my first hat in that store."

"Also because of Elvis," Kevin said.

"Elvis?!" he exclaimed, starting so violently I thought he was going to tumble backward off the bar stool. "Tha's right! Him, too! Why I betcha he went into that store to buy a hat, jus' like me! Good ol' Sabtakes!"

"I don't think Elvis got your taste in hats, Harry," the young black man said. "His wardrobe run to fringe and sequins, man."

"Maybe he was getting his cape cleaned," put in a slender blonde in her twenties. "They clean things, too, there, y'know."

"Elvis was on drugs," the short man pronounced sententiously.

"And you ain't?" the younger man said, nodding at the short man's glass.

The short man narrowed his eyes. "Elvis let drugs control his life. That won't ever happen to me. I'm in control. I'm vinwincible." On this last declaration he brought his hand down on the bar so hard he knocked himself off balance, overcompensated in an attempt to recover, and crashed to the floor.

In the commotion that followed, Moses caught my eye and nodded toward a nearby table, so we extricated ourselves from the melee and snagged it.

"Okay," I began. "So what have we got? Rocky was out of prison less than a week, and she was in trouble. So that means what? She was in trouble before she went inside, but as long as she was inside she was safe? Or that she got in with her old crowd as soon as she came out, and the trouble followed from that?"

"Or she got in with a new crowd she met in prison," Moses observed. "Could be any of those possibilities, Cat."

"But this wasn't the kind of trouble that could get her arrested," I mused. "According to her, this was the kind of trouble that could get her killed. Think she was exaggerating?"

Moses shook his head. "Don't take much to get you killed these days, Cat."

"Yeah, but we're not talking about South Central, Moses. It's not like she could look cross-eyed at the wrong person, or wear the wrong color shirt, and get blown away for that. This is Cincinnati, Ohio."

"Still don't take much," he said, "but I take your point. She wasn't talking about getting killed in the middle of an argument, she meant that somebody might come after her."

I nodded. "So why would somebody come after her? Do you think she knows something that somebody doesn't want her to know?"

The waitress chose that moment to deliver a basket of popcorn, and I reached for it. I know there are party poopers who believe that salt and fat clog your arteries, but I like to think of popcorn as a nutritional whole grain snack. My hand collided with Moses'.

"It could be that," Moses said doubtfully. "But what kind of something? Rocky ain't exactly the type to turn state's evidence."

"Not even if she were implicated, and she were offered a plea bargain?"

"Maybe," he said. "She might if she thought she was going to lose her kids or something. But they're with her aunt, so I don't guess Children's Services is going to bother them. No, Cat, I can't see it."

"What else, then?"

"Usually, that kind of trouble comes from somebody who thinks you owe him something," Moses reflected. "If Rocky was dealing, for example, and she had a stash hidden away that somebody thought belonged to him, or if she owed somebody money for what she'd sold. If he shows up at her door now to demand payment, and she can't pay, she's history. The big boys would say it's nothing personal, just good business sense."

"They won't take an IOU?"

Moses snorted. "Would you? Girl's just out of prison,

got at least three kids and no job skills? No employment history?"

I thought for a minute. "What about that, Moses? Would she have gotten any job training in prison?"

"Sure—laundry, dish washing, home maintenance."

"Don't they have any programs?"

"Well, I think they got some kind of training in clerical work, Cat," he said. "But Rocky didn't finish high school. She'd probably have to start there, 'less maybe they gave her some kind of training to be a beautician. But that don't sound like Rocky."

I didn't think so, either—not from what I'd heard. "Is that it?" I asked. "Clerical training or beauty school? Hell, Moses, this is the eighties! Why don't they train her to be an auto mechanic or work construction?"

"'Cause them Corrections folks don't live in the eighties, Cat," he said. "And the state legislature don't live in the eighties, either. They all live in the fifties when women was supposed to get married and raise children and work for pin money. Too bad, too, 'cause Rocky got a good mind, and she's good with her hands."

"What kind of job training do the men get in prison?" I asked suspiciously.

"Well, now you talkin' 'bout potential breadwinners, Cat. They got all kind of vocational training, and a whole mess of college courses, too. The women got some college, but not like the men."

"What kind?" I sniffed. "Home economics? Jesus, Moses, don't these assholes know that Ward has divorced June and owes her two years' back child support for Wally and the Beave? No wonder she's dealing drugs!"

"Well, Rocky Zacharias ain't no June Cleaver." Moses smiled. "But you right, Cat. Ain't easy supporting kids on AFDC, and once you got a habit, it's impossible."

"But Rocky said she was clean now," I reminded him.

"That's what she said," he agreed. "I hope it's true."

"So what's she supposed to do? Flip Big Macs for a living?"

"She flip Big Macs, she in trouble already," he said. "Old Ronald may build houses for kids in the hospital, but he don't pay baby-sitters' wages."

"Would she have left prison with any money?"

"She probably earned some kind of wages in prison," he said. "It wouldn't be much. Grisham said he'd given her a few leads on job prospects. If he makes those follow-up calls like he offered to, we can find out if she's working any of those places. If not—"

"Okay. So she's broke, unemployed, and running scared," I summarized. "Where would she run to?"

"That's where we goin' next," he said, polishing off his beer and standing up.

"Now?" I asked, surprised.

"Tomorrow," he said. "After church."

I wondered if that meant I had to go to church. Hell, if I thought it would help Rocky, I'd go. Didn't sound like she had too many people in her corner. Elvis, maybe. God would be better.

Ten

"After church" to Moses meant after Sunday dinner at his daughter's house, which let out around two o'clock. That was fine with me. I'd ended up baby-sitting for my grandson, Ben, the night before and I was exhausted. Also, I had a crick in my back from trying to scrub grape Kool-Aid out of the carpet. For his part, Ben had spent half the evening in Time Out for trying to fast-forward my television set, outlining his hand on my kitchen wall with Magic Marker, and throwing Sidney in the bathtub to see if he could swim (he couldn't, but he did a mean dog paddle for a cat). Left to my own devices, I would have spanked the little monster and sent him to bed without a bedtime snack, but my daughter was one of these enlightened modern mothers who considered such treatment child abuse. Personally, I thought Time Out, in which the kid retired to some specified place (not a corner—that would be too punitive) to play with his Game Boy or color or sing songs to himself, was a total washout from the standpoint of either punishment or rehabilitation. Personally, I thought my kids had turned out pretty well, considering their childhood sufferings. They might be dull or bossy or immature or unfit for marriage, but they could be seen in public. These days, that counted for a lot.

"As a former juvenile officer, Moses, do you believe in spanking?" I asked him as we waited for the engine to catch.

"As a former juvenile officer," he replied, turning the key off and letting the engine rest between tries, "I'd have to point out that violence begets violence, and that kids learn from what they see."

"Yeah? And?"

"There's a lot of folks who believe that kids learn from their parents to hit people when they get mad."

"Uh-huh," I said. "So, we got a big problem with kids going around spanking people when they get mad? I mean, that's not our problem, is it? Spanking isn't the same thing as offing somebody with a .357 Magnum, is it? If kids went around spanking the people they were mad at, that would be an improvement, wouldn't it?"

He sighed. "Some folks see violence as one long continuum, Cat. They say kids don't know the difference between being spanked and being slapped or hit."

"Did you know the difference?"

"I reckon I did," he said thoughtfully. "Some folks say it's more humiliating for kids to get hit on their bottoms, because of the sex thing, but I know I would have been shocked if my father ever hit me on the head or slapped me across the face. I always knew there were limits to what he'd do, no matter how mad he got. Hell, I always assumed that the people who loved you always had limits—you know, lines they wouldn't cross." He paused. "And then I started working Juvie. And I learned that not everybody has that kind of self-control, no matter how much they love their kids. Some of 'em are hardest on the kids they love the most."

"So did you spank your kids?"

"Yeah," he said. "But after I started working Juvie, I took to stopping myself every time I raised a hand to one of 'em, and thinking about what I was doing. As a parent, I believe in discipline, and as a juvenile officer, I believe in discipline. Kids needs rules to follow, and they need to know there are consequences for breaking the rules. The consequences don't have to be physical, a lot of times it works better if they aren't. But when kids are little, you can't always expect them to be rational, so the punishment has to be pretty unambiguous and immediate."

"And when do they become rational?" I asked him.

"Mine haven't yet. I only stopped spanking them because they grew bigger than me."

The house where we went in Avondale was an unpretentious frame house, close enough to the zoo so that you could hear the lions roar. Two maples had dropped their leaves in the front yard, decorating it with a riot of golds, greens, reds, and browns. A little boy with a rake taller than he was was attempting to coax the leaves into piles, but an erratic breeze was working against him.

"We're looking for Mrs. Weldon, son," Moses told him.

"I'll go get her," he offered. He seemed glad of the interruption.

A bright red leaf drifted down, and smacked me in the face when the wind abruptly changed direction.

A woman in a pink quilted housecoat filled the doorway. Her head was round as a corsage chrysanthemum, her short gray hair worn in soft, fluffy curls. She was wearing a fashionable pair of glasses with large square lenses and lots of gold trim. One look at Rocky's favorite foster mother and I knew she was just the mother I would have wanted if I'd been a troubled kid.

"Miss Iva," Moses said courteously. "How you been?"

"Uh, uh, uh," she said, shaking her head at him. "Now, ain't that just like a man? Up and disappear into thin air, never call a person up or send you no birthday card, then walk back through your door one day, calm as you please, and ask how you been. What you care how I been, you low-down skunk?"

"Now, Miss Iva, you know you always been my Number One lady." He gave her a kiss on the cheek. "You look just as young and pretty as the first day I saw you."

"Uh-huh. Well, you gettin' ol'." She eyed him appraisingly. "Bet you retired, too. I can always tell by the way a man's stomach hang over his belt."

Moses glanced down self-consciously.

"This your new girlfriend?" She winked at me.

"This here's Cat Caliban. Our relationship is strictly professional."

"Well, I don't b'lieve a word you say, but come on in this house, anyway," she said, stepping back from the door. She wore a pair of old-fashioned felt house slippers on swollen feet, and she swayed from side to side as she led us down a hall into a comfortable living room, talking the whole way.

"I'm sorry y'all caught me in my housecoat, but I usually take a little nap after supper. Course, y'all too young to know about that, but they say them Mexicans takes naps in the afternoon, so my grandson, he calls it my siesta."

Moses said that he hoped we weren't interrupting her siesta, but his apology was waved away. I said a nap sounded good to anybody who'd been up half the night fighting hot flashes. Moses frowned at me like I'd just told an off-color joke, but she laughed and pinched my arm. She offered us lemonade, which I would have declined, but Moses accepted for both of us.

I studied the photographs on the polished walnut table next to my end of the couch as she and Moses went through the preliminaries—her health, his health, their families' health, her daughter's job, her grandchildren's school activities, Moses' retirement, what her various foster children were up to. In the middle of a flotilla of brass, silver, and gold, a picture caught my eye: a skinny, slightly built little girl of twelve or thirteen in shorts, T-shirt, and Keds, wispy red hair sticking out like a Renaissance halo, a smattering of freckles across a broad nose, a gleam of mischief in her eye as she squinted up at the camera, and a jump rope draped around her neck. Her skin was very light, the brown tones in it almost imperceptible.

"That's her," said Iva Weldon, and at first I didn't realize she was talking to me. "That's Rocky."

"You got something more recent?" Moses asked her. "I want Cat to see what she looks like now."

"Honey, I got a whole box of pictures," she replied. "Rocky used to send me her school picture every year she

was in school on picture day." She chuckled. "If you looked
at her school record, you'd probably think that was the only
day you could count on her to turn up regular, 'cept when
she was in detention. But that there's my favorite," she said,
nodding at the photograph in my hand, "because she look so
happy. It's the happiest picture I have." Her voice had
softened.

She heaved herself to her feet and wobbled over to a
built-in cabinet below crowded bookshelves. She returned
with a worn Buster Brown shoe box, soft with age and
rubber banded to hold its split top on.

She slipped the rubber band off and rummaged inside.
"This here's the latest one," she said, handing me a
snapshot. "My son took that the last time she was here
before she went into prison."

The difference between the face in this photograph and
the one on the end table was like night and day. The little
girl had been skinny; this grown woman was thin, almost
emaciated. The little girl's smile had been open, even
triumphant; this grown woman's smile was tentative, artifi-
cial. The little girl's eyes had crinkled with pleasure; these
eyes—these eyes looked haunted, unfocused. In every way
the woman appeared to be a faded version of her former
self—freckles faded, hair faded, eyes faded. And the little
girl's joy had faded as well.

Yet as Miss Iva passed me more photographs and I laid
them side by side on the coffee table in front of me, I
realized just how atypical that first one had been. Year after
year, the school photographs showed a troubled child, then
a troubled teenager, whose eyes were at war with the
photographer's smile.

I returned to the first photo and peered at it closely. Yes,
there was something—something hard to describe—that
proclaimed its kinship with the others. Something hidden
behind the bright smile and shining eyes. Something given
away by the set of the jaw and the wisp of hair that fell
negligently across a barely visible scar at the temple, a

vague sense that the eyes were playing tricks on you, seeming to focus on the camera while one wavered at a glimpse of some inner vision.

"Why was she so unhappy, Miss Iva?" I asked.

Miss Iva frowned down at the photographs. "Well, she lost her mother, you know," she began hesitantly. "And her mother was an alcoholic. So she was unhappy when her mother was alive, but still, your mother is your mother, and she felt miserable when her mother died. And, you know, I believe she blamed herself for her mother's death, the way children will."

She paused, but I felt there was more coming, so I didn't say anything, and neither did Moses.

"Then she didn't get along with her stepfather," Miss Iva continued, and stopped, as if that explained things.

"Was he an alcoholic, too?" I asked.

"No, he was just—strict," she said, and glanced at Moses. "He liked to run the children's lives, and he was hard on them. Well, the boys—that's Rocky's brothers—they run on off not too long after their mother died. That left Rocky and Amy. Amy was just a baby then, so once her mother died, Rocky didn't feel like she could run off the way her brothers did. She felt like she should stay and take care of Amy. Well, she was just a little girl herself, and a baby's a lot of responsibility. And she didn't have good sense. Why, there was a time or two she run off with the baby—you remember, Moses?"

"That was the first time I met her," Moses said. "She'd stuffed a couple of t-shirts, three diapers, a baby bottle, and a jump rope into a bag along with twelve dollars and fifty-three cents she'd stolen from Nash. She thought that was all she needed to get by in the world. We found her at the bus station, trying to buy a ticket to Florida, where Disney World was. That's about all she knew about Florida, except she had a vague notion they had beaches in Florida and it was warm there."

"Well, I didn't never expect her to get boy-crazy, not

Rocky." Miss Iva continued. "But I reckon she run around the way she did to aggravate her father. When she had them first two babies at sixteen, I had me a conniption. 'You can't take care of yo'self, sugar,' I told her. 'What you gon' do with a baby?' I wanted her to go to the midwife, even offered to pay for it. Not that I hold with killin' babies, I don't, but way I saw it, she could either kill it quick or kill it slow, kind of life she was livin'. I would have taken it, Lord knows, if I could have, but I couldn't, and her grandmoma—her mother's mama, that is, the other one never had nothin' to do with her, hard as it was to keep up with all them babies Antoine was makin'—her grandmoma was dead. 'But, Momma Iva, I want this baby,' she told me. 'I can grow up and get a job and take good care of it, you'll see. This baby gonna love me, Momma Iva, and it be the first good thing I ever done in my life.'

"Well, there it was, you see." She looked at me intently. "It like to broke my heart. Still does. All these little girls makin' babies so they can have somebody to love them. What kind of world is this, I want to know, where little girls don't get enough of the right kind of love to satisfy their hunger? And then she went and had twins. Twins! Why, I like to fainted dead when I heard. And them babies not two years old before she got herself arrested again. And then the little boy come along. And I can't do nothin' for 'em—not any of 'em—'cept pray." The last she said almost angrily, though whether her anger was meant for herself, Rocky, or the Almighty, I couldn't tell.

She leaned over and tapped my arm. "You keep your health, honey," she said earnestly. "I'm going to pray for you, too."

Tears started to my eyes. I'm a sentimental old coot, though you can't tell it most of the time, and I was moved by her. I was moved even though the rational part of me pointed out that her prayers hadn't done Rocky a whole hell of a lot of good. But I like to take all the help I can get, and if she could speak to the Lord about my hot flashes, I'd be grateful.

"You got any pictures of the kids in there?" Moses asked.

"Now, wouldn't you know it? I don't have a one!" She looked at him indignantly. "Every time I seen that girl I asked her to send me pictures of them babies. And she always told me she would, but she has never sent me a single one—not a single one!"

"Miss Iva, has Rocky come by to see you since she's been out?" Moses asked her.

Miss Iva nodded. "She come by last Wednesday. She was nervous, I could see that, but she wouldn't tell me what was the matter. Told me not to worry about her, but she always tell me that. Asked me could I keep some things for her."

"What kind of things?" Moses asked.

"A bunch of papers," she said. "Look like letters to me. She say if she don't come back for 'em, I should give 'em to her children."

"Did she tell you where the children were?"

"I b'lieve she said they was stayin' over to her aunt Barbara's, Talia's mother."

"Did she give you an address or a phone number—any way to get in touch with her or her children?"

"No, she say she didn't have nothin' to give me right now. She let me know, she say."

"If she does, will you let me know?"

"If she say it's okay, I will," Miss Iva returned evenly.

"Do you know anybody named Arletta?" Moses asked. "Rocky said in her phone message that she wanted me to talk to Arletta if anything happened to her."

"Oh, yes," Miss Iva said. "That rings a bell. Now, I wonder why. Seem like it was a friend she had in prison. I believe she mentioned an Arletta in some of her letters. Want me to look?"

It took ten minutes of hard negotiation for Moses to get what he wanted. Miss Iva was no pushover. But we left in possession of two things: the packet of letters Rocky had written to Miss Iva from prison, and the other packet.

That was shortly after I had helped her carry our glasses to the kitchen. A refrigerator papered over with photographs and childish letters and drawings had caught my eye, and I had gone closer to inspect it. Somewhere in the house, a door slammed, and the shifting air currents caused the papers to flutter. Down around knee level, I glimpsed some black lettering. I bent over, pushed aside a pencil sketch of a vaguely human figure, and read an inscription done in black marker on the refrigerator itself: ELVIS WAS HEER!

"That Elvis sure gets around," I observed as I fastened my seat belt. "Shorter than I remember, though. Wonder why he's following Rocky around."

In my eagerness, I broke open the mystery packet and unfolded the first piece of paper to see what it was.

"'Dear Momma,'" I read aloud. "'I am fine. How are you? When are you cumming home? If you can pleez Momma I wish you will come home for brother's burthday becuz he is sad and mises you a lot and so do me and Retty. XXXOOO I luv you!!! Patsy.'"

"Oh, hell, Moses!" I said. All my eagerness drained away, and I put my head in my hands.

Eleven

We sat on the floor in my living room, sore backs against the sofa, surrounded by paper. We were thoroughly depressed. The letters were depressing enough, and we'd nursed our depression along with a couple of beers apiece, so now we'd dug ourselves in pretty deep. Winnie was asleep on one pile, no doubt dreaming of a world where all little dogs were loved and well cared for, and all squirrels ran in slow motion. Sidney was perched on the back of the sofa with a gleam in his eye warning us that any minute he might pounce on Winnie and destroy any order we'd managed to create out of the chaos of paper. Sophie had been banished to the kitchen for licking the ink off of Rocky's letters, several of which were draped over the back of the sofa to dry. She'd sent her emissary Sadie to remind us that it was dinnertime, and Sadie was stepping delicately around the pages. Sadie was better at this sort of thing, not only because she wasn't in the cathouse, so to speak, but because she had a flair for tragedy. She stopped a few feet away, looked at us plaintively, and yowled.

"I know what you mean, Sades," I said. "I feel the same way."

To summarize what we'd just read: prison, or at least the Women's Correctional Institution, is crowded, noisy, hot, oppressive, demeaning, unhealthy, sometimes brutal, and always fundamentally chaotic. The rules change daily, or hourly, depending upon who's enforcing them. The guards seem to fall into three categories. The first comprises ordinary people whose presence in the prison defies explanation, although there is a handful of visionaries and do-gooders among them. The second encompasses a large number of people, relatively uneducated and unskilled, who probably couldn't get a job anywhere else. In the third and largest category, which overlaps to some extent with the second, are people who enjoy the power their jobs permit them to exercise, and who are drawn to prison work because it encourages not only the use but the abuse of that power.

The women prisoners themselves range from submissive to rebellious, but most are held in check by the promise of parole and the threat to their children represented by further incarceration. Most are trying to survive a day at a time despite multiple addictions, poor health, and abysmal health care, not to mention loneliness, hopelessness, and constant anxiety about their children. Most left domineering if not brutal fathers, husbands, and boyfriends on the outside, so their relationship to the guards is a familiar one. Many learn to hustle on the inside just as tirelessly as they ever did on the outside—everything, from phone privileges to toilet paper and tampons, has a price. Most of the women are on antidepressants.

Not that Rocky ever came right out and said any of this in her letters. In fact, Rocky's prose implied an education that barely exceeded junior high. But she had a gift for storytelling, and after forty-eight letters, you didn't have to be a cryptographer to translate the specifics into generalizations. Rocky's tone was sometimes angry, sometimes bitter, sometimes sad, and sometimes determinedly cheerful and optimistic, especially after one of her weekly AA or NA meetings. But most often it was neutral, matter-of-fact, as if strip searches, shakedowns, missed medication, petty insults, confiscated packages, violations of privacy, and squabbles over shifting interpretations of changing rules were the most common occurrences in the world, and I guess in her world, they were. Like I said, the stories spoke for themselves.

The other set of letters, from Rocky's kids to their mother, told their own story of heartbreak. The letters in their packet appeared to cover several of Rocky's trips inside, but their content and themes didn't vary much. When are you coming home? they asked, over and over again. Why can't you come for Christmas, for my birthday, for the school festival? Why don't you call us more often? I wanted to tell you about my spelling test, my bike accident, the kitten that followed me home from school, the bad boys that hang out on the corner, my dream about us, but Aunt Barbara said I couldn't call you. Why can't we come and see you? Aunt Barbara says she doesn't have money for the bus tickets to Marysburg, so will you send us some money? We were coming to see you in Dion's car, but then it broke down and we couldn't come, even though I was going to wear my new dress and bring you the ashtray I made for you in school and Patsy wanted to show you her arithmetic test that she got an A+ on. Brother is sick again and Retty is in trouble at school for beating up a boy who teased her about you. Why can't we come there and live with you? Aunt Barbara says she has too many kids to keep track of, and so she fusses at us all the time and won't let us turn the radio up. She is always mad at the welfare, and she says if we aren't good, they will come and take us away. My teacher says that anybody who wants to can be good and stay out of trouble if they try, so why can't you? Don't you want to live with us all the time like a real family? I am sending you a million kisses, a jillion hugs. I am praying for you every night. I hope you will be good so you can come home soon. I LOVE YOU!!!

These letters, in pencil, pen, and brightly colored crayons, lay scattered about us like so many knives.

The pile that Winnie was sleeping on consisted of all the letters that made any reference to Arletta. Arletta's name only appeared in letters from the most recent incarceration. She seemed to be a good friend of Rocky's—so good, in fact, that Rocky was apparently planning to live with her after they both got out, or so she told Miss Iva. Arletta had four children and what Rocky referred to as "some health problems," which didn't make her a good risk to be Rocky's housemate to my mind. But nobody had asked me, and Rocky seemed confident that, prior experience to the contrary, she and Arletta would get good jobs and a nice apartment for their children, and they would make something of themselves so that their children could be proud of them. And she would be the mother she always intended to be.

Off to the side were two items that didn't seem to belong to anything else. They had been buried in the middle of the children's letters. I picked them up now, and scrutinized them again for the umpteenth time. Both were photocopies of some kind of log pages, one dated 6/8/85 and the other 6/21/85. On each page was a handwritten list of names, followed by a time and the name of a medication. At least, I was assuming that they were all medications, because the ones I recognized were insulin, Librium, Valium, Haldol, hydrocortisone, Nembutal, Vivactil, and most prominently, Elavil. None of the names in the left-hand column on the earlier page was one I recognized. But on the second page, six names down the list was an "Arletta D. Sandifer," along with a notation indicating that on June 21 at 10:13 in the morning, she had received a dose of insulin.

"Shit, Moses, what's the good of sending these women to AA and NA, and then pumping them full of prescription drugs?" I asked. "This stuff they're giving out like candy is probably more addictive than some of the drugs they were arrested for."

"They don't give out candy, Cat," Moses said. "Just drugs."

"Well, maybe they should give out candy instead," I pointed out. "It can't be any worse for them than this shit."

"You got no argument from me," he said. "Add to that any contraband drugs they might get hold of, and you got the risk of drug interactions. Lot of these women ain't that careful about what they're putting in their bodies."

"So what does it mean?" I asked, passing the page to him to look over. "Is this illegal? Is somebody writing prescriptions or passing out drugs illegally? If so, why keep a log of any kind? And what did Peter Abrams have to do with any of it? You think somebody wanted to sue the prison for medical malpractice?"

"Beats the hell out of me, Cat." He sighed. "I don't even know if you can sue the prison. You have to ask Al about that. As far as anything else somebody might do with the information—you and me might get worked up over something like the overmedication of women prisoners, but I doubt anybody else gives a damn. 'Less, of course, they think taxpayers' dollars is subsidizing wholesale drug use. But I'd be willing to bet that if the warden came back and said that drugs helped keep inmates under control for less money than a prison guard's salary, everybody would be slapping him on the back for coming up with such a good idea and saving the state all that money."

"Yeah," I agreed. "But what do you make of Arletta's name on that second list?"

"Way I figure it," he said, "Arletta has diabetes."

"Gee, Moses, thanks for sharing your razor-sharp mind with me," I said. "Almost makes me despair of rising to your level of investigative insight."

"Well, you asked me, Cat," he grumbled. "That's all I see in it. When I see more, I'll let you know. Meanwhile, why don't you call up to WCI tomorrow, and see what you can find out about Sandifer?"

Afterward, I suspected that he'd set me up. I decided he knew exactly what would happen when I called the next day. First, I got put on hold a jillion times, as Rocky's kids would say. Then, I was told that the lady I needed to speak to, Mrs. Rush, was out to lunch. I refrained from pointing out that she wouldn't be out to lunch if I hadn't been put on hold for an hour, nor did I intimate that everybody there seemed permanently out to lunch. When I called back an hour later, I was told that she was back from lunch, but nobody knew where she was. I was told to call back. After another twenty minutes on hold when I called back, I finally spoke to someone who claimed to be Mrs. Rush, but as soon as I started explaining what I wanted, she interrupted to tell me that I needed to call back and ask for Mrs. Goforth. I did, and was informed that Mrs. Goforth was—guess where? Next time around, I snagged Mrs. Goforth.

I told Mrs. Goforth that I wanted to speak to Arletta Sandifer. Mrs. Goforth explained that I couldn't speak to an inmate unless my name appeared on her approved telephone list. I told her that I was investigating a homicide, in case she thought I was trying to get Arletta to switch her long-distance service. She didn't budge. When I asked how I could get my name on the approved list, she said that I would have to speak to Arletta Sandifer.

When my daughter Franny was a classics major during a brief sojourn at San Jose State, she had told me the story of this guy who spent his life rolling a boulder up a hill, only to have it fall back to the bottom every time he reached the top. Need I say more?

I asked Mrs. Goforth if I could come and see Arletta Sandifer in person. She said that I could only do so if my name appeared on Sandier's approved visiting list. How could I get my name on that list? I would have to speak to Sandifer.

Then, just for spite, she admonished me that I would have to follow all the prison regulations regarding approved visiting attire, and that anything I brought with me would be searched for contraband and subject to confiscation.

I couldn't help it. My curiosity got the better of me.

"Really?" I asked. "Like what?"

"Drugs, both legal and illegal. Personal items, such as toothpaste, deodorant, and tampons. Makeup. Hair color. Nonregulation clothing," she said sternly. "Just for a start."

Was she serious? Did she really think I was going to all this trouble to smuggle in a bottle of Secret and some Supp-hose?

I hung up, stymied, and considered my options.

I dialed again and asked for the prison chaplain. He was not in, I was told. Did that mean he was not in his office, or not on the premises? That question netted me another five minutes on hold. Then someone new came on the line, and we went over the whole thing again. She cut me off in the middle and put me on hold again. Or rather, she dropped me on a hard surface and left me there, rubbing my ear and listening in on a gossip session going on in the background. The first voice picked me up again, and told me that the chaplain was on a hospital run. He wasn't expected back this afternoon, the voice added, to my undying gratitude.

When I reported all this to Moses, he sat placidly, threading a needle while I gave him this blow-by-blow account. He was sitting at his kitchen table, patching a pair of jeans.

"How can they run a prison that way?" I fumed. "They must have—what?—a couple hundred inmates at least?"

"More than that, Cat. More than a thousand."

"If they're that inefficient, it's a wonder anybody gets fed!"

"Don't matter anyway, Cat," he told me. "Arletta Sandifer is deceased."

"What!" Shock battled anger in my chest. Shock won. I didn't even bother asking him how he'd found out. "When? What did she die of?"

"That," he said, biting off the thread and looking at me over his bifocals, "is what we going to find out."

Twelve

So we had two dead people and one missing. The problem was, one of the dead, Arletta Sandifer, had died inside, and the other, Peter Abrams, had died outside. Moses reminded me that the two deaths might not be related, either to each other or to Rocky's disappearance. Abrams's death might have been an accident, and Arletta Sandifer, whom we knew to have been in poor health, might have died of natural causes. But when pressed, he admitted that he had a "bad feeling" about the whole business.

"So we might be looking for someone who was inside when Sandifer died, and outside when Abrams died?" I asked. "Shit, Moses, what if this is one of those gang things—you know, somebody inside with connections outside?"

He shook his head. "Girls don't run in the kind of gangs you're talking about, Cat. Least, not in Ohio, they don't. Not even in Cleveland. Only kind of connections they got outside is their dealer, their pimp, and their boyfriend or husband, assuming those aren't the same person."

"So we could narrow our investigation if we found out when Sandifer died, and who was paroled between that day and the day Abrams died."

"Maybe," he said gloomily. "But what I'm trying to tell you, Cat, is that you can only narrow down one line of investigation, on account of you don't know for a fact that those two deaths are related. For all we know, you could have been right the first time, when you said that Rocky was probably in trouble before she was arrested, and stayed safe only as long as she was in prison. So even though I think we need a cause of death on Sandifer, our first priority is to find Rocky, not to do the police detectives' job for them."

Moses was right, especially given what we knew about Arletta's health. Rocky had said she was in poor health, and we knew from the medication log that she was diabetic. So her death would probably turn out to be attributable to "natural causes," if you considered a lifetime on the streets to be natural. But that didn't explain the medication log itself, or why Rocky had hidden parts of it in a packet she'd given to a friend for safekeeping.

So I spent the rest of the evening going through Rocky's letters to Miss Iva and taking detailed notes. This time, I wasn't just looking for Arletta; I was scrutinizing everything that Rocky said about her life inside for some clue to the trouble she was in. After a while, I had assembled quite a cast of characters.

Most frequently mentioned were Arletta and Talia. Arletta was clearly Rocky's best friend inside, often referred to in the course of a story and sometimes quoted. I got the impression that one of the things she was serving time for was parole violation, because Rocky vowed that when they moved in together she would make sure that Arletta followed all the rules. Coming from Rocky, that was hardly reassuring. But Arletta and Rocky apparently spent a lot of time living in this fantasy future together, and knowing that Arletta hadn't even made it to parole caused an ache in my chest. I found myself wondering what would become of her four children. They had been placed in foster care when Arletta had been arrested, and their mother had worried about them constantly. Was there anyone to worry about them now?

Talia, I gathered from an occasional yoking of her name with Aunt Barbara's, was Rocky's cousin, and I thought I remembered Moses saying that Rocky had been arrested with her cousin on at least one occasion. Talia was portrayed as a crazy woman, always willing to take a risk, always trying to calculate how to turn a situation to her best advantage, always leading with her mouth. She spent a lot of time in "the hole," as Rocky called it, which I took to mean solitary confinement. Talia had been in the hole for cutting a heart in the crotch of her underpants, for arguing over the length of her shorts, for putting a braid in her hair and dying it purple, for not telling where the purple dye had come from, for fighting in the medication line—you name a rule, Talia had broken it.

Talia, Arletta, and Rocky had all been sent to the hole over the great jump rope incident. Someone appropriately named Charity found a length of rope in the storeroom she was cleaning and smuggled it out for Rocky. Rocky used Talia's contraband scissors to cut the rope to an appropriate length, and then the three sneaked down to the kitchen pantry while they were supposed to be working and jumped rope. They paid for half an hour of pleasure with three days apiece in the hole. But for Arletta, the punishment had been even more severe: the next time she requested a medical pass, she was turned down, and had nearly slipped into a diabetic coma by the time she'd been loaded into an ambulance.

I didn't like the sound of that.

On another occasion, Talia had persuaded Rocky to go looking for the Tombs, a legendary dungeon said to be located under the main building. Rumor had it that this place was the original "hole," and that women were tortured and died there before it was sealed off. The closest they came was an underground storeroom before they were intercepted by a CO and written up. But Talia still swore that the place existed, and that she would find it someday.

Some of the other women mentioned in the letters belonged, according to Rocky, to her "family"—a group that modeled itself on families of blood and marriage. Although Arletta Sandifer was apparently the oldest in this group, the woman whom Rocky called "Mommy" was a woman named Precious McKinney. Rocky called Precious "the sweetest person you'd ever want to meet." There was a "Grandmomma," who was an older woman named Clara, as well as siblings in addition to Talia—women named Opal, Ronnie, and T.J. In the family, Arletta was "Aunt Letty," and Rocky was "Daddy." No surprise there.

Rounding out the cast of characters were the guards, who weren't called guards but "Corrections Officers," or COs. Some of these rated several mentions because they were unusually bad, unusually good, or just unusually stupid. Among them was a woman Rocky called "Leech," who was a slow-witted, small-minded woman who clung to the rules for stability, but who was always two rule changes behind. "Wiseass," a male CO, figured prominently in stories of mean-spirited assertions of power and authority, and he was often backed by Becker, apparently a female CO. "Romeo," also sometimes called "Roaming Romeo," was as proud of his nickname as he was of his sexual exploits with the prisoners, not recognizing the scorn with which his name had been bestowed. "Saint Rheba" pressed religious tracts on the prisoners and offered to pray for them if they'd accept Jesus Christ as their personal savior. "EZ" and "Smoky," a male and female CO, respectively, were well-liked for their easygoing personalities, and because they didn't patronize the women and treat them like recalcitrant children.

The only other names notable for the frequency of their recurrence were Mrs. Tunney and Mrs. Connors, who apparently came in from the outside to run educational programs and support groups for the women. That these women retained their own names spoke volumes about Rocky's attitude toward them: she considered them saints. I noted them down on my growing list of prospective contacts.

Nowhere in the letters did Rocky mention Peter Abrams. Nowhere did she explain why she might seek legal counsel when she left prison.

There was plenty of drama here, though. Rocky reported four deaths—one heart attack, one AIDS-related, two of unspecified causes—and three suicide attempts, one successful. In one case, a woman had grown despondent after she miscarried. In another case, a woman had gone into labor while being transported to a hospital in Columbus; her baby had been born with severe brain damage and died, and the distraught mother was blaming the waist shackles that the women had to wear during the transport. Several women beat up other women, apparently either girlfriends or rivals. In fact, although Rocky's letters skirted rather than confronted sexual matters, perhaps out of deference to Miss Iva's real or perceived prudishness, you couldn't read between the lines without coming to the conclusion that the whole damn place was a hotbed of passions that made *Days of Our Lives* pale by comparison.

I also scrutinized the letters for allusions to events taking place in life outside the prison. In one letter from August of this year, Rocky noted that Talia's boyfriend Orlando had gotten out of prison, and that Talia had said that it was the first time she'd been glad she was inside and not outside. Rocky herself confirmed that Orlando was "crazy," and hoped that he'd be back inside before she and Talia got out. In another letter she mentioned that Orlando had begun writing to Talia, trying to sweet-talk his way back into her good graces. In another she reported that Orlando had come to visit Talia, even though he was not included on her list of authorized visitors, and she had refused to request the authorization; now she lived in fear that he would hurt her children. I put Orlando at the top of my list of potential suspects.

Rocky worried about her sister Amy as well. She wanted to get Amy away from her stepfather, whom she described as "mean." But her own experience with foster care discouraged her from expressing any hope in that direction. Rather, she seemed to acknowledge that if Amy could just "stick it out" for another year or two, she'd be old enough to make it on her own. On the other hand, she didn't have much faith in Amy's judgment of men, a blindness that she conceded might run in the family. She didn't approve of Amy's boyfriend, and didn't want to see Amy "under his thumb." At one point, she proposed that Amy could come and live with Arletta and her. "But Daddy Gordon better not mess with us then," she'd added. I moved Gordon Nash up on the list.

The rest struck me as idle chitchat—Aunt Barbara's emergency surgery for kidney stones, how Brother broke his arm falling out of a tree, how Retty baked her first cake and didn't know to grease the pans, how Amy fell off the back of a motorcycle and broke her wrist, how Patsy won a prize for collecting the most pennies for UNICEF.

But where, in all this accumulated drama and comedy and despair, was the clue to Rocky's present trouble? What scrap of information pointed to something that somebody could get killed for? Was the real tragedy inside or outside? I was damned if I knew.

Thirteen

On Monday morning, Moses worked the neighborhoods on his own. He thought he might have more success without a white woman in tow, and I'd conceded the point. After all, if somebody else was looking for Rocky and Barbara Hickson, we didn't have any time to waste.

Rocky and Talia were both half white, Moses had told me, since Rocky's mother and aunt were both white, but all of these women lived in a more fluid racial universe than the average American. Both Rocky and Talia had grown up in predominantly black neighborhoods and had black lovers, and at least some of their children had resulted from these unions. I asked Moses how Barbara Hickson managed to fit in, in the Projects and other black neighborhoods.

He shrugged. "It ain't something I can explain to you, Cat," he said. "She fits in 'cause she looks like she belongs. Plus she always be traveling in a gang of brown and black kids. Now, you—you look like the Welcome Wagon lady from Mariemont."

"I don't!" I was appalled.

"Well, your hair's cut a little on the butch side, maybe, but you know what I mean."

I didn't argue with him; instead, I went out for a little reconnoitering of my own. I walked downtown alleys your average Welcome Wagon lady would never set foot in, and which would have gotten her soles stuck with gum wrappers and tobacco and studded with broken glass if she had. Behind the IGA store across from Findlay Market, I found a couple of pals of mine sorting through the Dumpster for recyclables.

Checking a nearby wall for stains, I leaned one shoulder against it and explained my problem.

"Ain't too likely we see the lady with the kids," Curtis said. He emptied a bottle into a rainbow pool at his feet, and tossed it to Steel, who dropped it into a plastic grocery bag with a clink.

"She ain't gonna put those kids on the street if she can help it, Cat," Steel said. His restless eyes scanned the area as if he were still in country.

What I saw was a dirty alley and the backs of run-down tenements, brick walls stained with unmentionable substances and decorated, here and there, with the graffiti of people who could print better than they could spell. The air had a boozy, funky smell, overlaid with the acrid stench of burned coffee and old fry grease. What they saw was their living room.

"But if we see the other chick, Rocky what's-her-name," Steel continued, "we'll let you know."

"Man, you mean to tell me you ain't never heard of Rocky Zacharias?" Curtis asked, pausing, hands on hips, to look at him reproachfully. "My sister's girls, they was full of Rocky when they was little. Rocky this and Rocky that. Rocky gone and jumped over the moon with that cow they always talkin' 'bout. Way I hear it, y'all coulda used Rocky over there in them minefields in Vietnam. If we find Rocky, I'm gonna get her autograph first. Then I'll call Cat."

We chatted for a few minutes about mutual friends, then I said I had to go.

"Say, Curtis," I said, turning back. "Do I look like a Welcome Wagon lady to you?"

"I wouldn't know, Cat," he said. "Ain't no Welcome Wagon lady never showed up to welcome me nowhere."

Telling Curtis anything was the street equivalent of telling it to Kevin, so there was nothing to do then but go home.

I was sitting at the desk in my office, snoozing over the goddamn computer manual, when Moses called in the afternoon. After my teenage cousin had transformed my office into an IBM showroom last summer, I had reluctantly promised to sit down some rainy day and try to figure out how to run the damn equipment. Today it was raining, and I'd run out of things to amuse myself with while waiting to hear from Moses. I could either wash the kitchen floor, do laundry, or read the computer manual. I quickly discovered that I had made the wrong choice.

"Oh, good," I said to him. "I been reading the same sentence for the last ten minutes."

"That interesting, huh?"

"It's not that," I said. "That was the last sentence I could understand, and it was the one about where to find the on-off switch, and how to turn the thing on."

"Cat, you supposed to start with the tutorial," he admonished me.

"This *is* the fucking tutorial, Moses! There's even this cartoon owl in the margin, pointing this wing at a statement in bold print about hard and soft drives, and floppy disks. *Floppy disks!* I ask you! Does that sound to you like something you'd pay IBM a couple thousand bucks for?"

"Well, I wouldn't, but then I didn't want no phone answering machine."

"Shit, Moses, I think this is Delbert's idea of a joke," I said. "I bet he stashed the real manual behind the bookcase or something."

"Well, you ain't got time to look for it now, Cat," he said. "We going to see Barbara Hickson."

I met him in front of an overgrown vacant lot on McMicken Street. Broken glass crunched under our feet as we walked. The rain, which had turned into a fine mist, had washed most of the dirt and litter into the gutters, but the sidewalk had buckled, heaved, and sunk over the years like a roller coaster, and the water had collected in slick, iridescent puddles.

In front of a yellow brick apartment building, three little girls—two black, one Asian—were jumping rope. Two young teenaged boys—one black, one Asian—were sitting on the steps talking. The Asian kid was holding a basketball. Moses nodded at the boys, and we entered the building.

We studied the mailboxes in the hallway. Most weren't labeled, but the boxes didn't look all that secure.

"Watch for the cops, Cat," Moses said. "I'm about to commit a federal offense."

I didn't ask why he hadn't asked the kids which apartment was Mrs. Hickson's. I figured that if any of them were her kids, and if the family was on the run for some reason, we wouldn't get a straight answer anyway.

Moses grinned at me over an American Family Sweepstakes envelope.

"How the hell does Ed McMahon know where she's living?" I asked.

We climbed two flights of battered stairs and walked down a dim hallway to the accompaniment of soap opera organ music and laugh tracks. The fetid air smelled of mold, sweat, coffee, and something unfamiliar—an unfamiliar cooking smell, I guessed.

The American Family—or at least part of it—was at home. Trained detectives that we were, we knew because the door was open, and because someone inside was raising her voice.

"I told y'all if you was goin' to fight over that television, we'd get rid of the damn thing!" it said. "Now, turn it off! Retty, did you pick up your clothes like I asked you to? Lizzie, did you wash out your gym blouse? Where's Brother? I told you girls to keep an eye on him! Do I have to do everything myself around here? 'Cause I got news for you all: if everything ain't done like I told you when I get back from fetchin' Gabriel, there's goin' to be hell to pay! I mean it!"

Moses rapped lightly on the doorjamb, and she turned her fury on him. She was a big, raw-boned woman with long black hair, neither thick nor thin but falling in limp waves down her back. Her face looked weathered, and it had aged more than her hair had. She had startling blue eyes, and she might have been pretty if she weren't so angry.

"What the hell do you want?" she snapped at Moses. "Whatever it is, we don't want to buy it, and we ain't gonna contribute to it, so you can just take your ass on out of here!"

Moses laughed. "Good to see you again, too, Mrs. Hickson."

Her eyes darted to me, and then back to Moses, narrowed now, suspicious.

"Who the hell are you?"

She made some kind of gesture to the kids behind her back, and they slipped out of the room.

"Moses Fogg," he said placidly. "I'm a friend of Rocky's. Used to be in Juvenile Division. Don't you remember me?"

"Juvenile?" she echoed, glancing at me again. She picked up a cigarette out of a nearby ashtray and took a puff, studying him. "Yeah, I reckon I do remember you. Used to give Rocky hell."

"I was just trying to tell her like it is, Mrs. Hickson," Moses said. "Talia, too. I just wanted to keep 'em out of trouble, if I could. Knew too much about what might happen to 'em if I didn't."

She choked on her cigarette and coughed.

"Yeah, well." She turned away from us, took a few steps, and sank onto the couch vacated by the girls. It had the look of a government-issue waiting room couch, but she had thrown a colorful spread over it. When she spoke again, her voice had dropped. "Thanks for reminding me."

"Can we come in and talk to you? Just for a minute."

We were still standing in the hall.

"Look," she said, turning wet, angry eyes on us, "if you come to offer condolences, fine. Just say you're sorry, and leave. If you come to say 'I told you so,' then you can go fuck yourself. If you brought *her* 'cause you got some notion you're gonna get my kids away from me, think again."

I was taken aback. After Moses' crack about the Welcome Wagon lady, I'd deliberately dressed down. I was wearing jeans, a turtleneck, and a denim jacket. I didn't think I looked like a goon for Children's Protective Services.

But Moses had snagged on something else she said.

" 'Condolences'?"

This heightened her rage. "Well, I know cops don't send flowers to the funeral of every kid they've ever arrested," she spat. "But seein' as how you was such a good friend and all, I thought maybe you come to pay your respects."

"Who died, Mrs. Hickson?" he asked.

"What?"

"I'm sorry," he said. "I didn't know. Who died?"

She studied him for a minute, then took a swipe at her tear-streaked cheeks and looked away again.

"Never mind," she said. "It don't matter. What did you come here for?"

"I want to know who died," Moses persisted softly, passing through the doorway and into the room. He took a chair near the couch.

I hung back. I turned my head away from her pain and tried to pretend I wasn't listening. Just above the baseboard, in blue ballpoint on a dull mustard wall, I saw it: ELVIS WAS HEER!

"My daughter, that's who died," she was saying. "My daughter Talia. She hadn't been out a month. She got herself cleaned up, got herself a job, went to those meetings regular—you know the ones I mean. All she wanted was to make herself a good life for her and her kids. And she was beaten like a goddamned dog, and left to die in the street!" She took a drag on her cigarette. "Well, I reckon they've closed her file down at Juvenile. So what are you doing here?"

"I'm looking for Rocky," he said, and told her about the phone call. "Were they in some kind of trouble together, Mrs. Hickson? Do you know who killed Talia?"

She blew out a breath. "They was always in trouble

together, them two. As for who killed Talia, I reckon it was Orlando Walker, but I don't know nothin' for sure. They damn for sure ain't gonna pull no overtime in Homicide over no ex-con. Not when they got one with a record for drugs and prostitution."

She thought for a minute, then continued. "Them two shared everything, the bad and the good. The bad—that included Orlando Walker. So if he killed Talia, I reckon he might go after Rocky next. He's crazy enough, that's for damn sure."

"I need to find Rocky, Mrs. Hickson," Moses said. "I need to make sure she's okay, and find out what she wanted from me."

"Well, I can't help you there," she said, stubbing out her cigarette. "I don't know where she's got to. Ain't been by to see the kids in more'n a week. I reckon I'll hear from her one of these days, if she keeps her ass out of jail."

"Aren't you worried about her?" Moses asked.

"Hell, I'm worried about all of us, mister," she said in a tired voice. "I'm worried about all of us." She leaned back against the couch and put a hand to her forehead.

"Is there anything I can do for you? Anything you need?" Moses asked awkwardly.

A faint smile appeared. "Yeah. I need me a new life. You got one of those?"

She opened her eyes as Moses stood up, and followed him to the door.

"I left my name and number there on the table." he said. "Will you tell Rocky I came by next time you talk to her? Will you ask her to call me again?"

She didn't say yes or no.

"There is something you can do for me," she said, leaning against the door. "You can keep your mouth shut. I don't know how you found us, but I'm prayin' you're smarter than Orlando Walker, in case he takes a notion to visit us."

"Is that likely?" Moses frowned.

"How would I know?" she said. "The man's crazy, and

two of these kids are his. But don't ask me how a crazy man thinks."

I felt her tired eyes on my back all the way down the hall, as she calculated where to move next.

Out on the sidewalk, the girls were still jumping rope. Two more had joined the original crew, while the boys were nowhere in sight. Sneakers thudding the pavement, the jumper sang in a clear voice:

"Room for rent,
Inquire within.
When I move out,
Let Felicia move in."

Fourteen

"So—you know this Orlando?" I asked Moses as we sat in the car.

Moses nodded. "Orlando 'Walkman' Walker. I know him as much as I want to know him. He's crazy, all right. Had more attitude than brains to start with. Now that the drugs have stolen what there was, he's pretty much all attitude."

"Could he have killed Talia, do you think?"

"Oh, sure. Coulda killed her, and not remembered it two hours later," Moses said grimly. "Wouldn't even have to have a reason."

"But he didn't kill Peter Abrams," I said.

"No," Moses agreed. "That required more presence of mind than Orlando is capable of."

"And he didn't kill Arletta at WCI," I added glumly. "Shit, Moses, is there any kind of pattern here at all?"

"Hell if I know, Cat," he responded, turning the key. "But the only way we going to find out is to find Rocky."

"You think Mrs. Hickson was telling the truth about not knowing where Rocky is?"

"I doubt it," he said. "Woman's keeping Rocky's kids. I expect she knows how to get in touch with Rocky if she needs to."

"She's going to move again," I observed.

He nodded.

"She ought to move anyway," I said. "This isn't much of a neighborhood to raise kids in."

"You think the Projects are better?" he asked, looking at me.

"At least the Projects have laundry rooms," I pointed out.

"And there's stores you can walk to. You can even walk to the Farmer's Market. Same thing in the heart of Over-the-Rhine. But around here, there's not much of anything, except more run-down houses and apartment buildings. Say, Moses, were those Asian kids Vietnamese?"

He shook his head. "Cambodian, probably. Lot of Cambodians live right around here."

He'd been cruising slowly, and now he pulled up next to a little corner grocery, about five blocks from Mrs. Hickson's apartment. It seemed to specialize in beer and lottery tickets.

He left me in the car while he went in to ask about Rocky.

I was making some notes in a small notebook I carry around when he burst through the door of the shop and sprinted for the car.

"Damn! Damn!" he shouted, wrenching the key in the ignition and flooring the gas pedal as we pulled out of a U-turn. "Bastard's one step ahead of us, or one stop behind us! Should've kept my damn eyes open!"

There were no little girls jumping rope in front of Barbara Hickson's building when we pulled up.

I reached the front of the building before Moses, who had paused to get something out of the glove compartment. A small crowd of frightened kids had gathered in the vestibule by the mailboxes.

Moses pushed past me and bolted up the stairs. By the second-floor landing we could hear shouts above us.

In the third-floor hallway, we passed a black woman standing at the door of her apartment.

"My husband is in there!" she hissed at me. "He got two little kids of his own to look after! Sweet Jesus, what he have to go and be a hero for? If he comes out of there alive, I swear I'm gonna kill him!" Her voice shook with anger, but tears glinted in her eyes.

Just outside the open door to the Hickson apartment, Moses stopped to listen. I heard Barbara Hickson's voice first.

"I told you, I don't have what you want. I never had it, and Talia didn't have it, neither." Her raw voice trembled. "And Rocky don't have it."

"Bullshit!" a high-pitched man's voice shouted. "That's bullshit! You been jerkin' me around, you been fuckin' wit' me!" The last was accompanied by a crash, as if a chair had been turned over. I heard the sounds of children crying, those syncopated gasps of breath caught in the chest.

"Come on, man!" This was another man's voice, a gentle drawl. "You scarin' these kids, brother. What you want to be scarin' these kids for? Mrs. Hickson done told you she don't have what you come for. Now, if you still got a problem with that, why don't you and me go on outside the building and talk about it? You don't need to be botherin' nobody else."

Moses was easing into the doorway. I was two steps behind him, not wanting to be in his way.

"Bullshit! That's bullshit, too!" the first man exploded. "Who are you, motherfucker, to tell me what I can do with these kids? These *my* kids, motherfucker! These *my* motherfuckin' kids, and I do what I want with 'em!"

Inside the apartment, glass shattered and a woman screamed.

"Hell, I do what I want with 'em! If I can't have my money, bitch, you can't have my kids!"

I saw Moses' jaw tighten just before he moved. I heard a scramble inside, screams and shouts, and then a gunshot.

When I reached the door, they were frozen in a tableau, Moses partially blocking my view of the only moving object: a man sinking slowly against a shattered window. The man was holding a very small boy, whose limp body hung from bony shoulders, and whose feet were bare. Two other children, a teenage boy and a girl of eight or nine, sat clutching each other on the couch. Between Moses and the man were two other people: Barbara Hickson, who still held a carving knife clenched in her fist and pointed in the man's direction, and another man, apparently the father from down the hall, a man wearing some kind of khaki uniform with the name of a local dry cleaner stitched across the back.

He was the first to move. He crossed to the window and gently pried the little boy from the dead man's grip. He stroked the boy's hair and murmured soothingly to him. I moved to Barbara Hickson, took the knife out of her hand, slipped an arm around her to support her, and walked her over to a couch. The man handed the little boy to her, and she buried her face in his hair. The other children—the two on the couch and two others who had been watching from the hall—gathered around her.

"Cat," Moses said quietly, "go call the cops."

But when I picked up the phone to dial, I heard sirens approaching, so I hung up. I wondered why the cops hadn't arrived sooner. Everything had happened quickly, and no doubt my own sense of time was distorted. But it also occurred to me that Cambodian refugees, like poor black people, had good reason to mistrust the police.

The next two hours passed in a blur. A female officer took the younger kids into the bedroom, and after a while, to my surprise, I heard giggles and cries of excitement, accompanied by the click of dice and the clatter of markers on a game board. Someone made coffee, and Barbara Hickson sat at the kitchen table gripping her mug and cursing Orlando "Walkman" Walker as her fear gave way to rage. Out in the hall I could hear the man in the khaki uniform making soothing noises, while his wife's voice rose in tearful anger. In the living room I could hear the soft pop of the photographer's flash as he commemorated the scene of Orlando Walker's demise. I was in the kitchen, perched on a counter and waiting my turn to make a statement. I wasn't sure where Moses was, but I caught the low rumble of his voice now and then.

A crowd of local reporters and a television newscaster or two was gathered in front of the building when Moses and I emerged. An eager-looking young man with salon-styled hair stuck a microphone in Moses' face.

"I understand, Mr. Fogg, that you're something of a hero," he said. "Everyone is praising your courage in saving that little boy's life. Can you tell us your feelings right now?"

Moses gave him, his microphone, and the video camera behind him a look that should have short-circuited all their wiring.

"I feel the way anybody would who just took another human life," Moses said slowly. "It doesn't take courage to shoot down an unarmed man. So if you want a hero, son, you go find the man who walked into that room to go up against a crazy man with nothing *but* his courage."

Fifteen

"He would've thrown the kid out the window, Moses," I said quietly, as Moses sat behind the wheel staring into space. "He was flying high, you couldn't have reasoned with him. He was moving fast. You did what you had to do."

"Don't you think I know that, Cat?" he responded dully. "That don't mean I have to like it." He gazed out the window and focused on something in the distance. "Maybe in a day or two, I'll be glad I was in the right place at the right time, and I'll be glad I was armed. If I think about it long enough, maybe I'll even get around to thinking the Lord put that gun in my hand. Right now, though—" He paused, sighed. "I feel like shit." He fitted the key into the ignition. "I feel like shit."

I respected his feelings, and kept my mouth closed all the way home.

The story of Orlando Walker's death, when I got it out of Moses later that night, went pretty much the way he'd predicted. Orlando and Talia had been in business together before they'd been busted. Although he'd been in charge of the operation, the drugs had been found in her apartment, so she'd drawn a longer sentence than he had. Moses figured she'd also done extra time as punishment for keeping drugs on the premises when she had small children around—an extra penalty for being a bad mother. According to Moses, nobody ever thought to punish Orlando for being a bad father, even though he had brought the drugs into the apartment in the first place, and talked Talia into holding them for him. After their arrest, Orlando became convinced, against all reason and experience, that Talia had kept a stash hidden from the cops, and he had plotted to retrieve it ever since. As soon as she'd been released, he started looking for her. Both she and her mother went into hiding, but separately; like Rocky, Talia had tried to protect her children by staying away from them.

But what had happened next? Had Walker found Talia, argued with her, and beaten her to death? Barbara Hickson told the police that she didn't know. When she had accused Orlando of her daughter's murder, he had denied responsibility.

"Bitch musta fucked wit' some other motherfucker," he'd claimed, "got to her 'fore I could lay my hands on her. You think I want the bitch dead when she got all my money?"

With Talia dead, he'd come after her mother, unshakable in his conviction that he had a fortune waiting for him somewhere, and Barbara Hickson knew where it was. Infuriated by her denials, he tried to demonstrate his power by confiscating the nearest thing that belonged to him—his son. The rest we knew.

"So did he kill Talia, or not?" I asked Moses later that night as he soaked his right ankle. He had ignored his basketball injury at the moment of crisis, and now he was paying for it.

"I'd give it about fifty-fifty," Moses declared. "You can't rely on anything a junkie says, Cat. Whether he's lying to you, lying to himself, or just don't remember, it all comes to the same thing. You don't go to a crackhead for truth."

Moses raised his foot, scrutinized his ankle, and poked it gently.

"You don't think it's over, do you, Moses?" I asked.

"No, I don't," he said. "It's possible that Rocky was running from Orlando—that she figured he'd come after her next if he thought Talia had hidden something from him. And she had good reason to be scared for her kids. The little boy was hers."

It took a minute for this to sink in.

"Wait a minute," I said. "The kid he tried to kill was

Rocky's? And Orlando was the kid's father? You mean both Rocky and her cousin—?"

"Like Mrs. Hickson said, those two shared a lot of things, Cat," Moses told me. "Not that they were both sleeping with Orlando at the same time—at least, not that I know. I suppose they could've been. But I seem to recollect that Rocky passed him on to Talia a few years back. Or he moved on himself, who knows? If you talked to all three of them, you'd probably get three different versions."

"Only we can't talk to any of them," I pointed out morosely.

"Anyhow, Walkman don't match the description of the other guy who was looking for Barbara Hickson," he said, settling his foot back in the water. "You know—the young-looking muscular white guy that the store owner told us about."

"Yeah," I agreed. "Plus, he doesn't explain Peter Abrams. If Rocky was running from Orlando Walker, what would she need to see an attorney about? A restraining order wouldn't be worth the paper it was written on. She'd know that."

"You right about that," Moses conceded. "Rocky ain't the type to go to the cops for protection."

"Well, she went to one cop," I reminded him gently. "And that one saved her little boy's life."

I bent down and put my fingers in the water.

"Don't you want some more hot water in there?" I asked him. "It's lukewarm."

I ran the tap until the water heated up, filled a pitcher, and poured it. He shifted in his chair and winced.

"I stopped by the IB this morning and met Walter Bunke," he said. "Seemed like an okay guy, Cat. They found Peter's red spiral notebook in the pocket of one of his sports jackets, but there wasn't anything about Rocky in it."

"Say, Moses," I said. "You don't think maybe Talia really did have a stash, and Rocky knew where it was and wanted to turn state's evidence to get Orlando off her back. I mean, she wouldn't do it when Talia was alive, but after Talia died? She might have gone to Peter to find out how to do that."

"It's a thought," he said slowly. "If the old Rocky knew about a stash, she wouldn't be looking to give it away when she could sell it on the street herself. She says she's gone straight, but they all say that when they're just out. I don't see the Rocky I knew having any more to do with the law than she had to, but if she was desperate to protect her children, she might've been willing to cooperate with the narcs. If that's the way it happened, there's only one person who can tell us, and that's Rocky."

"So we're back to hunting Rocky." I sighed.

He picked up a deck of cards and shuffled them.

"Come on, Cat. Help me take my mind off my misery."

Our plan was to return to Barbara Hickson's the next day and have another chat with her about Rocky. That was our plan. But nobody came to the door, and our knocks had a hollow sound I didn't like much.

All the kids were presumably in school or day care, which cut down on our prospective sources of information. We knocked on doors until we raised a petite Asian woman, who gazed at Moses with awe. The loud sound of a game show in progress explained her reaction. In case she had missed the significance of Moses' heroics on the scene yesterday, they had been depicted by our local newspapers with more than a touch of drama. The man in the khaki uniform whom Moses had tapped as man of the hour hadn't offered the prime-time appeal of Moses' James Bond imitation. The woman stared at Moses openmouthed, as if Superman had stopped by to use her bathroom.

"We're looking for Mrs. Hickson," Moses explained. "We—"

"Gone," the woman interrupted in her eagerness to be helpful. "All gone."

"You mean, they've moved out?" I asked.

She nodded, and stepped out into the hall as if to

demonstrate what "gone" meant. She flapped a hand in the direction of the Hickson apartment.

"Gone-gone," she reiterated, nodding, then pointed to the door to the stairs at the end of the hall. "All gone."

"When?" Moses asked.

She looked surprised. "Night," she said.

The television announcer's voice rose with enthusiasm. "Your new car!" he shouted gleefully. Somewhere, on the sunny side of the country, where money grew on palm trees as tall as a freeway overpass, a crowd roared.

"Last night?" Moses echoed.

"Yes, yes, night—yesterday. Yesterday night." She studied our faces to see if we were following.

"Do you know where?" I asked.

She frowned at me and shook her head. I didn't know whether this meant she didn't know or didn't understand.

"Where they were going," I continued. "Where is their new house?"

She raised her eyebrows at us and shook her head. At last she said, "No-body know." She stared hard at the door of the Hicksons' former apartment. "Crazy man dead," she said with some satisfaction. "You." She pointed up at Moses. "Good." She nodded. "Now—all gone. Kids. Mother?" She looked at us questioningly, then corrected herself. "No, mother—not mother. Mother dead."

Cheesy organ music was attempting to drown out the rhythmic clapping of the studio audience.

The woman shifted her finger from Moses to the door across the hall from her. Her finger moved down the row of doors, and stopped again at Barbara Hickson's.

"Door Number One, Door Number Two, Door Number Three," she said, and gave us a meaningful look when she reached the third one. "No prize," she said softly. "No luck."

She might not know English very well, but she had a pretty good handle on the American Dream, I thought.

Sixteen

Sometimes we professional investigators reach what we call a dead end, and this felt a hell of a lot like one of those. It would have been one, too, if the light on Moses' answering machine hadn't been blinking when we got home.

The first message was from Toby Grisham. None of the prospective employers on the list he'd given Rocky had heard from her. Officially, he didn't have any reason to go looking for her yet, but he asked us to keep him informed. In the background we could hear a television set, someone playing scales on the piano, and an odd whistle.

The second message was from Gordon Nash. It had a trace of a Southern accent.

"Mr. Fogg, this is Gordon Nash. I understand you came by the house the other day looking for my stepdaughter, Roxanne."

I had to stop and think who he meant.

"I don't know if you remember me," Nash's voice went on, "but I believe we met at Jeannie's funeral." He paused. "As you probably know, Roxanne was paroled to me, but it seems she's run off again. So, seeing as how we have a mutual interest in finding her, I figured maybe you and me could join forces. I know you always tried to straighten that girl out, and I appreciate your efforts. Why don't you give me a call sometime, or come by the store?" He left two numbers and the address of a discount carpet store across the river in northern Kentucky.

The third call was from Rocky.

"Hey, it's, um, me, Rocky." She laughed nervously. "I

feel like a fool talkin' to this damn machine all the time. Anyway, I want to thank you for what you done for my baby. I just—well, you know what I want to say." The voice choked, then recovered. "I'm glad you was there. I reckon maybe my higher power was lookin' out for me, after all."

She was drowned out by the sound of a siren.

". . . you not to worry about me no more. I'll be all right, but I ain't goin' back to Daddy Gordon." She coughed a few times—a smoker's throat-scraping hack. "So, the thing is, I don't want you to come lookin' for me no more. I know I said I was in trouble, but I reckon I can handle it." She seemed to take a deep breath. "I gotta go now. Maybe I'll see you around sometime."

And that was it.

We replayed it a few times, in case we missed something crucial under the sound of the siren, but we couldn't make out the words, and they didn't seem all that important compared to the words we'd heard. Rocky didn't want to be hunted, and she definitely didn't want to be found. The trouble, whatever it was, was not over.

"You know what, Cat?" Moses said. "I bet you could buy some new carpet tonight, have it installed by Christmas, and not pay a penny until June."

"You could be right, Moses," I said.

He was still brooding over Orlando Walker, I knew, though he wasn't talking about it. I wanted to keep his mind on other things.

The next call came through on my line. The phone rang while I was sacked out on the couch, taking a nap. It interrupted a dream in which Sharon McCone, Nurse Adams, Kinky Friedman, and me were all sitting around in Kinky's loft, shooting the breeze, while Kinky's cat sat on top of the canary cage, trying to get at the bird inside. Me and Kinky were maintaining that if we were the canary, we'd rather be on the outside of the cage, where the cat was, than on the inside with no options.

"Start talkin'," I said into the phone, half asleep.

There was a shocked silence on the other end.

"Hello?" a voice ventured at last.

"Yes?" I said irritably, the way you do when somebody interrupts a really good dream.

"I'm trying to reach a Mrs. Catherine Caliban," the voice said doubtfully.

"You've got her," I said, squinting at the clock. We were definitely in the danger zone for telephone harassment. "But she doesn't want aluminum siding or cemetery plots, and her charity of choice is the Foundation for Cockroach Preservation."

Silence.

"I believe, Mrs. Caliban, that you were trying to reach me," the voice said, a bit frostily. "This is Herman Graebel, chaplain at the Women's Correctional Institution."

"Oh, yes," I said, "Mr.—uh, Reverend—Graebel. Thanks for getting back to me." Sidney had come running when he heard the phone. I crossed my eyes at him, and mimed putting a gun to my head and pulling the trigger. He tumbled backward off the couch and rolled over with glee. That's what makes him such a gratifying audience: the old routines are his favorites.

"What can I do for you, Mrs. Caliban?" The voice had thawed slightly.

I told him that I was trying to track down Rocky Zacharias. I told him that a mutual friend had heard she was in trouble, and that every time we went looking for her, we turned up a dead person.

If this information worried him, he concealed it well.

"I'm afraid many of our inmates live in a violent world, Mrs. Caliban," he said.

"You mean, they live in a violent world when they are inmates?" I asked.

"Oh, well, no, I didn't meant that," he said. "Although we do get our share of incidents. I meant that the world they live in on the outside is violent."

"Suppose I were to tell you that one of the dead people is an attorney for Legal Aid?" I said.

"I wouldn't ordinarily expect violence in that direction, no," he said after a brief pause. "What is it you want from me, Mrs. Caliban?"

"I'm looking for Rocky, Reverend Graebel. Can you give me any help?"

"I'm sorry," he said. "I didn't know Rocky that well. I don't get to know all the inmates, I'm afraid."

"But I thought she was in a couple of twelve-step programs," I said, "working on turning her life over to a higher power."

"Oh," he said, "that's quite possible. But I'm not involved in the twelve-step programs. And even if I were—you do know that the twelve-step programs guarantee absolute confidentiality and anonymity, Mrs. Caliban?"

"I'm not asking you what she said at the meetings, Reverend," I reassured him. I would have, only I hadn't thought of it. "I'm just trying to find someone who knows her, who might know where she is."

"Again, I'd caution you that neither AA nor NA will confirm the identity of any of their members. But, if you're looking for someone who might know Rocky, you want to talk to Mrs. Tunney," he said. "She runs an organization out of Columbus called CAMAWAC."

"CAMAWAC?" I echoed.

"The Capital Area something-or-other. Hold on, I've got it here somewhere. Here it is. Capital Area Multiracial Alliance for Women and Children. They run several support programs here—you know, personal development programs. I don't know what their policy is on anonymity, but Mrs. Tunney should be able to tell you whether she knows Rocky or not."

I recognized the name from Rocky's letters, and remembered how highly Rocky had thought of her. Graebel gave me a phone number, with an air of having solved my problem and mentally moved on to the next one on his list.

"Speaking of incidents, Reverend," I said. "While Rocky was there at WCI, one of her best friends was a woman named Arletta Sandifer."

"Yes?" he said cautiously.

"I understand that Arletta Sandifer is dead. What can you tell me about her death? I assume, as chaplain, you would have to know something about that."

I heard him draw a long breath. "I feel very badly about Arletta's death. We all do. The truth was that she was a diabetic in poor health. Perhaps if she'd had more extensive medical care—who knows? But she wouldn't have had better care on the outside than she received here."

"Are you saying she died in a diabetic coma?" I asked.

"Yes, that is what happened," he affirmed. "I don't know how much you know about diabetes, Mrs. Caliban. Fluctuations in the body chemistry require a constant monitoring to get the insulin dosage right. She received regular medical care here, of course. But sometimes, it's just not enough, is it?"

"By regular medical care, you mean—"

"Just that," he said sternly. "Regular medical attention, from a doctor or nurse."

"I see." I thought about the medication logs Rocky had photocopied, and considered how to frame my next question without giving too much away.

"I wonder if you can tell me," I said, "how prescription medication is dispensed. Do the women get their prescriptions filled at the prison pharmacy, and then take the medication on their own until the prescription runs out?"

"Oh, no, certainly not," he said. "That wouldn't work at all. You have to realize, Mrs. Caliban, that prescription drugs are controlled substances for a reason, and our women are, quite frankly, not very responsible when it comes to drugs. If we gave the women a week's supply of medication at one time, do you know what would happen?"

Sidney had clambered back up onto the couch and was gnawing on the telephone cord.

"No. What?"

"All the pills would disappear overnight," he assured me. "Every woman would swear she'd lost her pills. Meanwhile, the nurses would be swamped with drug overdose and drug interaction cases. We'd probably get a few suicide attempts by women who'd sold or traded their antidepressants. And the methadone market would destabilize the entire population. Not to mention the various problems that would develop when the women simply forgot to take necessary medications."

"I see," I repeated, feeling my way. "So where prescription drugs are concerned, the women are given one dose at a time?"

"Where any kind of drugs are concerned," he said. "Even Tylenol is given out by request only. Nonprescription drugs can be abused, too, after all."

"That makes sense," I conceded. Always concede something when you can, I say; it keeps the conversation going. "But what about conditions like diabetes and epilepsy, or even heart conditions—anything that might cause a sudden crisis? What if someone needs emergency medication?"

"There's always a nurse on duty," he said, then cleared his throat. "Help is always available."

How far away? I wanted to ask, but didn't. I let the silence stretch between us.

"I see," I said.

Seventeen

"This here's a good color for you, Cat," Moses said, patting a reddish-orange square of carpet. "Matches that dye they put in the kitty tuna."

I nodded. "Is it stain repellent?"

"Now, that carpet there is Scotchgarded," a voice said behind us. I turned to see a burly man with light blond hair and a plaid sports coat. He reached out a meaty hand embellished with a thick diamond ring, and ran it over the carpet. I don't know what this was supposed to demonstrate. The pile was short as a military haircut. "That's a nice piece of carpet, for the price. But if it's stain resistance you want, why, I can show you a carpet that will practically clean itself."

We allowed ourselves to be led to another display.

"Now, I sell a lot of fine carpet here," he continued. "There's not a piece here that isn't quality. But this carpet"—he patted it confidently—"this carpet cannot be beat for stain resistance. I want you to see something."

Before I could stop him, he'd snatched up a coffeepot and poured a stream of brown liquid on a light beige carpet sample lying on a counter next to the display. He tilted the carpet square up, and we watched as the coffee ran down and pooled on the counter.

He looked up at us expectantly.

"Gee," I said. "Just like linoleum."

He chuckled appreciatively. "You have said it, ma'am. That is just exactly right. Now, did you ever think you'd see a piece of carpet that could do that?"

I hadn't really thought about it much, to tell you the truth.

I mean, this is not the kind of thing that keeps me awake nights. What does keep me awake nights, ever since a case I'd worked last summer, is the way we are poisoning the earth with environmental toxins, many of them developed at chemical plants where people lie awake nights thinking up ways to make carpet repel stains. Somehow, visiting a neighborhood that featured both a high concentration of chemical plants and a high cancer rate had permanently changed my outlook, and I was beginning to think maybe I should look for a nice rag rug.

Moses, meanwhile, was asking how much the wonder carpet cost. It turned out he was right about how I wouldn't have to pay anything until June. Plus I could get free padding if I placed my order before midnight tomorrow night. Our salesman implied that he had fought the good fight with those stingy bastards at the carpet factory, who must be in the same class with the sales managers at all the car dealerships, and he had won.

"Actually," I said, stepping on Moses' rising enthusiasm, "we came looking for Mr. Nash."

"I'm Mr. Nash," he said, obviously gratified that I hadn't yet said anything that would cancel the sale.

"I'm Moses Fogg, Mr. Nash," Moses said. "And this is Catherine Caliban. Is there someplace we can talk, if you're not too busy?"

"Mr. Fogg," he said, light dawning. He shook Moses' hand, then clapped Moses on the shoulder. "I'm sorry, I didn't recognize you. I guess it's been a while. Why don't y'all come on back to my office? We can talk there, and Mrs. Caliban can think about that carpet." He smiled at me.

As we followed him, I asked myself whether he might be described as youthful in appearance. I decided that he could, because he still had a full head of hair, and it was that light blond that never showed gray. He had the flush of alcohol or high blood pressure or both in his cheeks, but his skin was smooth for a man his age. Was he muscular? His shoulders strained at the seams of his jacket, so yes, I supposed he could be described that way. We stopped at the door of a stuffy office that smelled of new carpet and old cigar smoke, but another salesman was sitting behind the desk, talking to a middle-aged couple.

"Let's go on back to the warehouse," he said.

We passed through a door and into a large warehouse, where the air was cooler and the carpet odor stronger. Rolls upon rolls of carpet were stacked in neat piles. I remembered Nash's neglected front yard and decided he'd been spending too much time around synthetic fibers.

"I'll tell you the truth, Mr. Fogg," he began. "That gal is going to run me into an early grave, if she don't settle down. Now her mother—God rest her soul—had some influence over her. But she won't listen to me."

Given Rocky's record, I wondered just how much influence her mother had had, and whether it had been all the wrong kind.

We leaned against rolls of carpet. I picked a nice deep pile shag of a color my daughter Franny would have called baby poop brown, except during the brief phase when she'd been an art major at Antioch, when she'd have called it burnt sienna. Nash fired up a cigar, doing that fishlike thing with his mouth that cigar smokers do when they're trying to get the thing going.

"When was the last time you saw Rocky, Mr. Nash?" Moses asked.

"Call me Gordon, Moses," Nash said through his teeth. He puffed a few more times, then seemed satisfied. "Hell, you're practically one of the family."

This hardly seemed like much of an honor to me; given how dysfunctional the Nash-Zacharias family was, you'd think they'd want to keep it to themselves, not go spreading it around. Maybe Nash figured they needed a cop in the family. Me, I would've recruited a shrink.

"The last time I saw Rocky was maybe a week after she got out," Nash said. "She got out on a Monday—that'd be the week before Thanksgiving, week before last. So I reckon it was last Tuesday she took off."

"How did she seem to you?" Moses asked. "Did she seem nervous? Happy? Excited?"

"Hell, she seemed like she always did—sulky and bitchy. Girl's got an attitude problem—always did." He studied the end of his cigar the way cigar smokers do, as if the *Bhagavad Gita* were inscribed in its ash.

"But we understood that Rocky was off drugs and determined to go straight," I said. "We heard that she'd gotten into Alcoholics Anonymous and Narcotics Anonymous while she was inside. That would suggest a change in attitude, wouldn't it?" I couldn't bring myself to say that Rocky had turned her life over to her higher power; somehow, it didn't seem to go with the acrid smell of cigar smoke and the cloying odor of new carpet.

"Hell, Catherine," he said, promoting me into the family as well, "she's been in and out of AA and NA and God knows what all. Shit, I can't keep 'em all straight. But it all adds up to one thing, and that's BS. She knows how to say what the parole boards want to hear, she's been working the system long enough."

"So you think she was still on drugs?" Moses pursued.

Nash raised a cautionary hand. "Now, I didn't say that. All I'm sayin' is that straight and bitchy or stoned and bitchy, it don't make a whole hell of a lot of difference to me. The girl's got an attitude problem that won't quit." He paused and grimaced in what I took to be a frown as he studied a crack in the cement floor. "No, I think maybe she was clean. But I reckon she'd about reached a point where she couldn't take it any longer. Girl never could keep a promise, to herself or anybody else. I reckon that's why she ran off like she did. Because I made it perfectly clear I would not have drugs in my house."

I turned away so he wouldn't see me wince. I was thinking about a young woman who'd been moved from house to house, and finally from prison back to her stepfather's house—a young woman whose fondest dream was to have a home she could call her own.

"So you don't have any liquor in the house?" Moses was asking with a straight face.

"Oh, well, yes, of course, I have that," Nash said. "But I keep a sharp eye on it, you'd better believe."

Judging from the flush in his cheeks, I didn't have any trouble believing that Nash checked his liquor supply daily.

"So you think Rocky ran away because she didn't want to follow your rules?" Moses asked. "Is that what Amy thinks?"

"Hell, who knows what she thinks," he said, looking uncomfortable. He looked around him vaguely and I could swear he was hoping he'd set a drink down someplace nearby. "How I wound up raising two girls by myself, the Lord knows." He sighed. "But if that's the way He wanted it, so be it."

I hoped the Lord was keeping track of his job performance. Because if he was expecting to go to glory on the basis of his record as a father, he was in for a shock, or I am the Archangel Michael.

"Have you asked Amy if she knows where her sister is?" I asked.

"Sure, I've asked her. But if I get two consecutive words out of her in a day, I'm doing good. She's at that awkward stage, you know."

Yeah, I thought, teenage pregnancy, you jerk. And then, I wondered if he knew about it. And I wondered if I could figure out a way to find out without telling him.

"Girl don't seem to think about anything except that idiot boyfriend of hers. Well, hell," he said, unexpectedly grinning at us, "maybe it's hormonal. I reckon we all went through that stage. She might know where Rocky is," he mused. "Then again, she might not. But I reckon I could have her watched—you know, put a tail on her. What do you think, Moses?"

Where would we get someone who could blend in at the

high school? I thought. Someone who knew about glazing, New Kids on the Block, and Air Jordans.

"I don't think we're there yet, Gordon," Moses said seriously, putting a hand on Nash's shoulder. "That's a pretty drastic step, and a long shot. I don't think we've exhausted our other possibilities."

This was news to me. What possibilities did he have in mind?

"Have you talked to Barbara Hickson lately?" Moses continued.

"No, I have not," Nash said. He took his cigar out and pointed it at us. "And that's another thing. Those kids should be with me. They do not belong with an ex-con who's raising them on welfare and food stamps. Hell, she's moved them all over the city! And she's got them all mixed in with the kids of two other junkie ex-cons! Now, what kind of a person do you think that is to be raising kids?"

This really pushed my buttons. I opened my mouth to point out that he had no room to talk, seeing as how he'd done a piss-poor job of raising two kids himself, but Moses headed me off at the pass. Moses claims I narrow my eyes and tighten my jaw when I'm about to torpedo somebody, but I think he's exaggerating.

"Are you hoping to get custody of Rocky's kids, then?" he asked.

"Well, I'm going to do my damnedest, Moses," Nash said. "But my hands are tied." He held out two meaty paws that kind of undercut his claims of helplessness. "I don't know where the kids are, and I don't know where their mother is. But when I find 'em, I'm going to do everything in my power to get the courts to let me give 'em a good, stable home."

I almost conducted by own little stain resistance demonstration on the carpet closest to hand, but I settled for rolling my eyes at Moses, who frowned at me.

"You don't happen to know where they are, do you, Moses?" Nash asked.

Moses shook his head. "I've got a list of former addresses, that's all."

"You see?" Nash persisted. "That's just what I'm talking about. Now, how are those kids going to get by in school if they're changing schools every month or so? That's not right. No, sir, it's not right."

"I suppose you know that Mrs. Hickson lost her daughter recently," Moses said.

Nash looked unconcerned. "No, I hadn't heard anything about it. Is that Talia you're talking about?"

"That's right. She was found beaten to death in the street."

"Well, it doesn't surprise me, kind of life she led," Nash said philosophically. "And that's just how Rocky will end up, if she's not careful. That's just what I've told her, too, a million times, but that gal won't listen. Talia was a bad influence on her, ever since they were kids." He delivered this last sentence as if it were a eulogy.

"Did Rocky ever mention a friend of hers named Arletta Sandifer?" I asked.

"Name doesn't ring a bell," he said.

"Let me ask you this," Moses said. "Do you know any reason why Rocky would want to visit a Legal Aid attorney the week after her release?"

"A lawyer?" He looked around again, spotted something on the floor a few yards away, and went over to pick it up. It was a soft drink can, and he tipped his cigar ash into it. "No, not really. These cons and ex-cons are always talking to lawyers, though, aren't they?"

"I don't know. Are they?" Moses asked. "Did Rocky go to see lawyers a lot?"

"Hell, I don't know, Moses," Nash said. "Like I said, she didn't confide in me. I'm talking about my general impression, now. Convicts always have some beef about the system, don't they? Always whining about their rights being violated. Hell, if they hadn't violated somebody else's rights, they wouldn't be in prison in the first place, would they? I say, once you're busted, you don't have any rights."

"You mean convicted?" I said.

"Come again?"

"Convicted, not busted. Once you're convicted, you don't have any rights."

"Well, yeah, sure. Convicted."

"Just checking."

I couldn't wish him a period without a tampon or a Midol, or a difficult labor with a shackle around his waist. But I confess that I wanted him strip-searched in the worst way.

Eighteen

We replayed Rocky's last message on the answering machine that night.

"She says she won't go back to Daddy Gordon," I pointed out. "But then she talks about being able to handle whatever trouble she was in. I don't know, Moses. It doesn't sound to me like Nash was the trouble she meant."

He sighed. "It doesn't sound that way to me either, Cat. But it could mean that."

"You're a trained cop," I said. "How did he seem to you?"

"Well, Cat, if you askin' me did I catch a glimmer of guilt in his eyes when I mentioned Talia's death, then no, I didn't see it. And I didn't catch no violent start when we mentioned Rocky's visit to Legal Aid either."

"Me neither," I agreed. "But he did get up and walk away at that point. He turned away from us. Maybe he was hiding something."

"Or maybe he was just putting out his cigar, which for my money, he should've put out of its misery before he ever lit it."

"That guy's been sniffing too much carpet glue, Moses," I said. "He probably can't even smell the damn thing."

"Well," Moses said, "he wouldn't get my vote for Father of the Year, but he's right about the kids needing stability. From his perspective, he's probably been a good father. Jean was an alcoholic, so she was a washout as a mother. Rocky had more stability after Jean married Nash than she'd ever had before, when they were living on welfare. You can't blame Nash for all of Rocky's problems."

"But she started running away after he came on the scene, not before, right?"

"Yes," Moses admitted. "But just because she didn't get along with him, or didn't respect his authority, doesn't mean he was a bad father."

I gave him a look. "Would you want him for a father?"

He sighed again. "Look, all I'm sayin' is there's a lot of different kinds of fathers in the world. Ain't none of them perfect."

"And all I'm saying," I drawled, "is that between perfection and making your kids want to run away from home there's a gap you could drive a tour bus through."

A moment of silence followed. Then he asked, "Didn't your kids ever try to run away from home?"

"Sure," I conceded. "But they never got far enough or left long enough to be picked up by the cops. Did yours?"

"No," he said.

"That's what I'm talking about, then, Moses," I said. "And you know the difference after working Juvie all those years."

"Yeah," he said at last. "Kids like Rocky don't run away from home. They run away from the place where they live because they're looking for a home."

The next morning was Peter Abrams's funeral, and we all went. I scanned faces for anybody who looked either guilty or smug, but to tell you the truth, my own eyes quickly became too bleary to make any fine visual distinctions. As far as I could tell, though, there was nobody in attendance who wasn't genuinely stricken by Peter's death. Moses pointed out Walter Bunke to me—a good-looking young man with wavy dark blond hair and a mustache. Even his eyes looked a little pink.

Afterward, I went Christmas shopping. When I'd gone home to change after the funeral, I'd called the number for CAMAWAC in hopes of speaking to Mrs. Tunney about Rocky, but I'd ended up talking to an answering machine.

So I'd started my day depressed and moved on to frustrated, and Christmas shopping did nothing to improve my mood. Two menopausal incidents, one involving sneeze-related leakage and one involving hyperventilation in the toy department of Lazarus, contributed to my foul temper. By the time my daughter Franny served me stir-fried tofu and homemade wine for dinner, I was already expecting the worst. When Franny announced that she was going to study psychology at U.C., I got a sharp pain right between my eyes.

I'm not against education, believe me. My younger daughter's college career of more than ten years had taken her from coast to coast, and I'd dutifully tried to keep up with her schools and her majors. But I'd lost track somewhere in California. And now she'd come home to study psychology. I wasn't surprised by the field. I'd been expecting it for years. To tell you the truth, I couldn't figure out why it had taken her so long to get around to it. But I'd always hoped that when she did, she'd be in some kind of study abroad program in Zaire or Australia, as far away from her family as possible. I did not look forward to becoming the object of my daughter's scrutiny, and I certainly had no intention of letting her practice psychoanalysis on me. Garf, her live-in boyfriend, offered to use acupressure on my headache. I declined and went home.

There was nobody at home to complain to, and maybe it was just as well. Kevin was at work, and Moses was baby-sitting. I didn't know where Mel and Al were. For that matter, I didn't know where the cats where. The way my day was going, they were probably out torturing the neighbor's pet gerbils. Sidney would probably come home in a patrol car.

I fixed myself a gin and tonic and turned on the television. But I wasn't in the mood for family comedy, so I switched it off and picked up Mary Roberts Rinehart.

I can't tell you when I first became aware of the noise in the basement. I had probably heard it for quite some time before it registered. I paused, glass suspended, and listened.

When you live with three cats and a dog, not to mention all the human housemates and their attendant friends and relatives, you don't take strange noises too seriously. You listen long enough to ascertain whether the sound you're hearing calls for any action on your part—typically, animal rescue or some kind of cleanup. If it doesn't, you ignore it.

I couldn't figure this one out, so I set my glass down and went out the door and into the foyer. Now I could hear it more distinctly. And it definitely sounded human—like whispered conversation.

I went back into my apartment, dragged a chair into the bedroom closet, clambered up and felt around on the shelf until I found my Diane, wrapped in an old Notre Dame sweatshirt of Kevin's. Maybe you think I should've called the cops. The truth was, any creature with the brain of a walrus and opposable thumbs could break into our building through the basement windows, and some of my friends had chosen to enter that way in the past. At the time, they were hiding out from the police. So I didn't want to jump to any conclusions. Besides, I'd been hoping someone would break in and steal all my computer equipment, so I could collect the insurance money, pay off my Visa bill, and go back to living in the fifties when advanced technology gave us Melmac, and all you had to know about electronics was how to adjust the rabbit ears on your television. If there was a burglar in any basement now, I was willing to strike a deal.

Everything was quiet as I approached the basement door from the foyer. I switched on the light. Nothing moved. Nothing made a sound.

I surveyed what I could see of the room from where I stood on the steps. There were plenty of dark nooks and crannies—back behind the luggage on the utility shelves, on the other side of the furnace, under the shrouds that draped Mel's exercise equipment, behind the freezer.

Sophie stood in the middle of the floor and blinked at me sleepily. I narrowed my eyes at her. It was no good asking her whose side she was on; her loyalty could be bought for a scratch behind the ears.

My head throbbed as I considered all the places I would have to search.

As it turned out, I didn't have to.

A series of dull, staccato thunks issued from the clothes dryer.

I descended the stairs and approached it warily.

Before I could open the door, I heard a voice behind me.

"Oh, Lord, Patsy, she's got a gun!" it wailed. "Don't shoot, lady! We didn't hurt nothin'!"

A skinny black girl stepped out from behind the furnace. A second one, about the same size, popped up from behind the freezer. They both had their hands up, like we were playing cops and robbers. Or rather, they had three hands up. The fourth held Sadie, whose ears were back and whose hind legs were scrambling for purchase on the little girl's hip. Since she didn't have one, Sadie was having a hard time.

"I'm not going to shoot," I said. "My warranty doesn't cover it."

I bent down and opened the dryer door. Out tumbled Sidney and a little black elf. The elf had a tiny body and a comical face, with ears mounted to the side of his head like satellite dishes. His face was screwed up in distress, his lip protruded, quivering, his crumpled eyes were leaking and his nose was running. His jacket was torn, his blue jeans were muddy, and his shoes were untied. He was a natural disaster—the perfect ending to a thoroughly rotten day.

"I told you we shouldn't never have brung him!" the second little girl, presumably Patsy, said to the first. She set Sadie down on all fours, strode over to the elf, and whacked him upside the head.

His yowl sent a pain right up my spine and into my skull.

I put the gun down, so I wouldn't be tempted to end it all right there by shooting myself.

"It dark in there, Patsy!" the elf managed between sobs. "I was scared!"

"You gonna be scareder than that, time I get done with you!" she threatened him.

I had sunk down on the basement floor with my back against the dryer, drawn my knees up, and laid my head down on my knees.

Somebody noticed that I wasn't following the script.

"You okay, lady?" the first girl asked. "'Cause we didn't mean to scare you none. We was jus' waitin' for Mr. Fogg. We ain't s'posed to talk to nobody we don't know, and we didn't know this was your house, too. We got cold outside."

"That's right, lady," Patsy added. "We was jus' waitin'. Only Brother start in on he have to go to the bathroom, like we didn't tell him to go 'fore we left home." She took this opportunity to box his ears again. They made a big target.

He howled, and I bit down on my arm to keep from screaming.

"Quit that, Patsy!" the first girl said with authority. "You makin' him worse! Don't aggravate him!" She turned to Brother. "Hush up, now!"

"But Patsy keep hittin' on me!" he wailed. "And that l-l-lady gonna shoot us!"

Over my arm, I gave him a look that could shatter glass.

"That lady ain't gonna shoot us," the first girl said soothingly. "She's a friend of Mr. Fogg, don't you 'member? She gonna help him find Momma for us."

The elf turned his face toward mine, and I was nearly blinded by the transformation. A radioactive smile now stretched from ear to ear and lit up his eyes.

"You gonna find my momma?" he asked.

Fifteen minutes later, Rocky's kids were lined up on the couch in the living room, two pairs of tennis shoes propped against the coffee table, a third pair—too short to reach—bobbed up and down in the middle. They had canned caffeine, I had the hard stuff.

"I'm Retty," the first one said. "That's short for Loretta.

And my sister named Patsy. We're twins, even though we don't look nothin' alike. Momma a big fan of country music, so we named for Loretta Lynn and Patsy Cline. You know who I mean? We call him Brother," she said, bouncing her knuckles on her brother's head, "but his real name—"

"Don't tell me, let me guess," I said. "It's Elvis."

The elf's eyes popped open, and his eyebrows sprang to his hairline. "How you know that?" he said.

"I get around," I said.

"You so dumb," Patsy told him. "This lady was at the apartment yesterday when—" She saw him frown, and evidently thought better of whatever insult she was planning to deliver. "You know," she finished.

"My daddy dead," Brother informed me gravely. "Mr. Moses, he shot him."

"Didn't I just tell you she was there?" Patsy threw a look that apologized for her brother's stupidity while asking sympathy for having to put up with him. "She know all about that."

"My daddy was sick," Brother explained defensively. "That why he acted so crazy. Aunt Barbara says he sick from some medicine he took."

Patsy rolled her eyes at me, but Retty put an arm around his shoulders.

"Speaking of Aunt Barbara," I said, "does she know where you are?"

"Nuh-uh, 'cause we runnin' away," Retty said.

"I see."

"You ain't gonna tell on us, are you?" Retty asked anxiously.

"Well, that depends," I said. "How come you're running away?"

"'Cause we don't want to live with Aunt Barbara no more," Patsy said.

"We want to live with Momma," Brother said wistfully.

It was hard to decide where to take this conversation. I

was walking into treacherous terrain, and there were dangers wherever I stepped.

"Why don't you want to live with Aunt Barbara?" I asked.

"'Cause she say she got too many kids, make her mad all the time," Retty said.

"Yeah," Patsy agreed. "She all the time fussin' at us."

"She makes me eat these nasty old greens," Brother chimed in, "and she don't let me watch *Miami Vice* on TV."

Score two for Aunt Barbara, I thought.

"We movin' all the time now," Patsy said. "We s'posed to be in hiding. Every time we make friends, we got to go someplace else and start over again."

"Are you *still* in hiding?" I asked. "Is that what Aunt Barbara says?"

"Uh-huh." Patsy nodded.

"I don't like that place we in now," Brother contributed. "Them stairs is dark and they smells nasty."

"We want to stay with Mr. Fogg," Patsy says, "until y'all find Momma."

I opened my mouth to say something, but Retty beat me to it.

"We wouldn't be no trouble," she said softly. "We could live in y'all's basement."

I looked at her. Sadie, having recovered from, and apparently forgiven, her moment of peril, had curled up on Retty's lap and fallen asleep. What had gone so wrong in this child's life that she would rather live in a basement than go back to where she came from?

And where the hell was my resident juvenile officer when I needed him?

So far I hadn't heard anything that approximated child abuse or endangerment, just your typical little league grousing. The woman had raised her own kids, evidently on a shoestring. They had not turned out well, by all accounts, and to be fair to Gordon Nash, I had to consider the possibility that she was at least partially to blame for that.

Then, just when she thought she could retire from motherhood, her kids and her sister's kid had started dumping their kids on her. As if that weren't enough, these kids were the ropes in a whole series of tug-of-wars between their mothers and a collection of possessive, irrational, violent types which included at least one father and one grandfather, some of them, if not all of them, on drugs of one kind or another. And the kids' complaint was that she was crabby? Who wouldn't be?

But did that explain why I was less sympathetic to Gordon Nash, who just wanted to give these children a good home, than to Barbara Hickson, who would probably have been eager to give them up to anybody with a home to offer them?

No, I thought to myself as I studied their tired, cranky little faces. It's because Barbara Hickson could be you. You, Cat Caliban, whose heart sinks every time your youngest daughter shows up on your doorstep with a backpack, a guitar case, and a duffel bag full of dirty laundry. You, who refuse to baby-sit any grandchild still in diapers. You, whose five-year-old grandson once spent three hours in Time Out because you forgot you put him there. You, who take the older grandkids to the mall because that way you don't have to supervise them. Barbara Hickson could be you.

For a fleeting moment there, I caught myself thinking that the basement wouldn't be a bad place to put them if we got stuck with them for a while.

I shook off the thought, cleared my throat, and asked, "Has Aunt Barbara ever hit you?"

But that didn't come off right. What I meant was, has she ever hit you really hard and in inappropriate places such as to cause serious damage or permanent emotional scarring? I was prepared to take whatever they told me with a grain of salt.

"Uh-huh, she hit us all the time." This from Brother in an injured voice. "This one time, she hit me for spilling some pop on the rug, and it wasn't even my fault!"

Obviously, Aunt Barbara hadn't paid a visit to Grandpa Nash's carpet store, or he hadn't made her a deal she couldn't refuse.

"Sometime, she get so mad, she hit everybody," Patsy said.

I framed my next question carefully. "Did anybody ever have to go to the doctor because she hurt you?"

"No, it ain't like that," Retty, the mature one, explained. "It ain't like child abuse or nothin' like that."

I had forgotten how sophisticated kids were these days.

"Nuh-uh!" Brother was bouncing up and down excitedly. "Member that time with my wrist, Retty? What about that?"

"That was 'cause you was pullin' away, fool," Patsy said in disgust. "You did that your own self. That ain't what she's talkin' about."

Me, I was beginning to suspect that Brother came in for more abuse from his sister than from anybody else.

"She hit us when she gets mad," Retty confirmed, "mostly on the butt. Sometime she hit whatever she can reach. But she don't hit that hard. It's just—I don't know. It's so many of us, and we always crowded. And she worry all the time."

"We rather live with Momma," Patsy summarized.

"Do you have any idea where I can look for your mother? Where she might be?" I asked.

They shook their heads.

"She used to be in prison," Brother confided in a whisper. "But she ain't there no more."

"She know that, fool." Patsy corrected him without much spirit.

"When was the last time you saw her?"

"Saturday," Retty answered. "She come to see us on Saturday, say she don't know when she come again."

It crossed my mind that Barbara Hickson had lied to us about when she had last seen Rocky, and I wondered what else she had lied about.

"And she didn't say anything about where she was going?" Retty shook her head sadly.

"Does Aunt Barbara have a phone where she is now?"

"No."

"Do you know where she is? I mean, could you find it?"

"You gonna take us back home?" Patsy asked.

"I didn't say that," I responded cautiously. "But we need to let her know you're safe so she won't worry about you, right? It will be up to Mr. Fogg to decide what to do, since he's the one you came to see."

I heard a car door slam out back.

"And if I'm not mistaken, that's him now."

The door from the living room into the foyer stood open. I wasn't taking any chances on missing Moses when he returned. The front door opened and closed, and then Moses appeared in the doorway. I noticed that he was favoring his right leg only slightly now, but he'd developed a full-blown limp in his left. Three pairs of eyes swiveled to the door and locked on his face.

"Grandpa Moses," I said. "I have a surprise for you. The sleep-over is at your house tonight."

Nineteen

That was Wednesday. By Friday, our house bore an unsettling resemblance to Toby Grisham's living room. I don't know where all the toys came from, but I suspected some were transferred during Moses' negotiations with Barbara Hickson on Thursday. Some seemed to have spontaneously generated in our basement, though calmer reflection told me that some of my housemates must have had them in storage there. Why anyone would save a fortune-telling eight ball from the fifties was past my understanding, but Kevin insisted that it would be valuable someday. I pointed out that it would only be valuable if I didn't throw it down the basement stairs the next time I tripped over it in the foyer.

Barbie's wardrobe, which was more extensive than my own and ran to dry-clean only space-age synthetics, was strewn all over the building. I found one of Barbie's bright red stiletto heels in the sugar bowl, and Mel found its mate in her medicine chest.

"Even Al doesn't wear them this high," she said when she brought it down to me.

"Barbie doesn't dress for success," I pointed out, downing my fifth and sixth aspirins of the day.

"Not that kind of success, anyway," Mel observed. She lifted her foot, studied the bottom of her boot, and peeled off a red hot.

Aspirins stuck in my throat, I was searching for a clean glass. Every glass I owned had some kind of bright red liquid coating the bottom.

Mel didn't notice. She was backing a Tonka tow truck up

to a red caboose and making mechanical noises. She was leaving tire tracks in the spilled powdered sugar.

I gave up, chose a glass at random, added water, and swallowed. It tasted vaguely like cherry cough drops.

Sidney appeared, with a doll-sized Western bonnet hanging rakishly over one ear, and one of its ties dangling from his mouth like a mouse tail. I bent down to liberate him, and my fingers brushed something sticky in his fur.

"So Moses reached an agreement with the kids' aunt?" Mel asked. She retrieved some Leggos from the floor and started fitting them together.

"They're here for a visit," I said. "That's the understanding. To give their aunt a rest."

"Don't they have to go to school?"

"They'll start again on Monday. They hadn't started going yet in their new neighborhood, so that's where they'll go on Monday. Moses is going to take them."

"It must be hard, changing schools all the time." She had built a small pyramid. On top she placed two plastic cows and a Revolutionary War soldier. "They seem like smart kids, though."

Sadie strolled in and examined the mess in her food dish— soggy Cheerios and milk. She lapped tentatively at the milk, then thought better of it, and remained crouched, staring at her dish as if willing it to fill with tuna fish.

"I don't even know why we have all these toys," I said to Mel. "They'd just as soon sit in my office and play Minesweeper on my computer. I didn't even know I had Minesweeper on my computer."

"Where are they now?"

"Cooking lessons at Uncle Kevin's."

"Good," Mel said, sniffing the air. "I hope they're making something fattening. So, in exchange for this little vacation, did Moses get anything out of Barbara Hickson? Such as why Rocky went to see Peter Abrams?"

"She says she doesn't know why. She says she knows Rocky's running away from somebody, but she doesn't know who or why. She thinks Talia knew, but Talia didn't tell her either."

"Is Gordon Nash included among the 'somebodies' Rocky could be running away from?"

"He's one of them," I confirmed. "And he's the one Barbara Hickson claims to be running from, so he won't get the children. Well, and Orlando Walker—she was running from him, too. But where Rocky's concerned, there's somebody else, too. At least, Barbara thinks there is, and she thinks it's connected to the prison somehow. But whether it has to do with something that happened in prison, or something she learned in prison, Barbara doesn't know."

"Did Moses show her the medical logs?"

"Yeah, but she didn't know anything about them. He also asked whether Rocky had given her anything to keep, but she said no."

"Do you believe her?"

"Yes," I said slowly, "about that, I do. After all, Barbara has been moving around a lot. That doesn't make her a very good candidate for holding on to something for somebody. Besides, if she had anything, it would endanger Rocky's kids."

"So does that mean you also don't think Barbara is holding on to a major drug shipment, which she moves from apartment to apartment under a pile of dirty clothes in a laundry basket?"

"I think that's a safe assumption, yes," I said. "If she had convertible assets like that, she'd be living in better places than the ones she's living in, and in neighborhoods where she'd be less likely to be recognized."

"Do you think Orlando Walker's mythical stash exists?"

"I don't know," I admitted. "But I hope nobody else thinks it does."

"Has Moses found out anything about the police investigation into Peter Abrams's death?"

"He says there's nothing to find out, really. The investigators have done a lot of interviews and read a lot of files, but they don't have anything definite—just a handful of disgruntled clients with violent tendencies."

"Maybe it's one of them," Mel said. "Maybe Peter's death doesn't have anything to do with Rocky. I mean, I believe Al when she says Rocky came to see him, even though they haven't found a file or any notes on her. You don't forget a name like Rocky Zacharias. But that doesn't mean she had anything to do with his death."

"No," I agreed. "But an awful lot of people who met up with Rocky have turned up dead."

"So what's your next move?"

"The woman from that Columbus group called back," I said. "You know—the group that conducts programs at the women's prisons. She knew Rocky pretty well, I gather. She wouldn't say anything on the phone, but she agreed to meet with us. Moses and I will drive up some day next week, when the kids are in school."

When the kids are in school. It had been years since I'd uttered those words, or planned my life around school schedules. Just hearing them again on my lips sent a chill up my spine.

"I don't know, Cat," Mel said. She'd reached under the table and come up with a multicolored blob of something with the unmistakable sweet doughy scent of Play-Doh. She flung it at the refrigerator and it stuck there. "I think it's kind of fun having the kids around. Don't you?"

Twenty

No woman should have to cope with menopause and kids at the same time. It isn't natural. Whether God in Her infinite wisdom saw fit to delay the Change until the kids were grown and out of the way, or whether the schedule had been arrived at through survival of the fittest, I wasn't prepared to say. What I could say was that all those grandmothers out there who were raising their kids' kids without killing them deserved a medal.

By Sunday, I could no longer distinguish the panic attacks caused by hormonal imbalance from the ones brought on by logical causes, such as Brother tossing a Frisbee off the roof. Every time I had a hot flash, I looked around to see what was burning.

Not that I had the kids all to myself, you understand. But they moved so fast, it seemed like I did. And once Kevin and Al put them on roller skates, they moved even faster.

That was an idea I had vetoed, incidentally, but no one had listened to me. That was why Moses was now confined to his recliner with an Ace bandage wrapped around his left wrist, an ice pack against his hip, and a bottle of prescription Tylenol at his elbow.

"Cat," he said faintly, eyes closed, "could you get me a beer out the icebox?"

"No," I said. "I could not. Not while you're on drugs. And if you expect me to wait on you hand and foot while you take a vacation from your child care duties, you got another think coming. I'll bring you a pitcher of orange juice and a glass, and you can pour some whenever you're thirsty."

"You cold, Cat," he said without opening his eyes. "Don't

be that way to a dying man. You be sorry when they read my will."

I snorted, and left his orange juice next to the Tylenol.

His pitiful voice reached me at the door. "Where my faithful dog at? I like to see her face jus' one more time before I go."

"She's parked in front of the VCR down in Kevin's apartment, watching *101 Dalmations* with Brother for the forty-second time."

I blessed Retty for that suggestion. Nineteen-ninety-five had been a small price to pay for some peace and quiet.

I paused on the stairs and listened, and then felt the panic rising in my throat. It was too damn peaceful and quiet. Something was bound to be wrong.

I could still hear barking coming from Kevin's apartment, and when I looked through the door, I saw two little bodies side by side on the carpet, two heads propped on forelimbs, two sets of ears tuned in to the TV, one tail wagging. So that wasn't the problem.

I stepped out of the building onto the front stoop and froze. Retty and Patsy were speaking to a man dressed in a brown suit, a navy parka, and very dark sunglasses.

The sun was out, although it was cold, but trust me when I say that a person could have only two reasons for wearing shades this dark. Since we didn't have any aboveground nuclear tests scheduled for Northside that I knew about, I presumed he didn't want to be recognized.

But as I approached, he whipped out a small black cardholder and flipped it open to show me a badge and ID.

"I'm Officer Wyszanski," he said. "Criminal Investigation. And you are—?"

"I'm somebody who would like to see you do that more slowly, and without the shades," I said.

His businesslike expression didn't change. He removed his glasses and showed me his ID again.

"Thanks," I said. It looked like him, all right.

"Always good to be cautious, ma'am," he said.

"Was there something you wanted to ask the girls?" I asked.

He showed mild surprise. "Are these your kids, ma'am?"

"Second cousins," I said smoothly, watching Retty's mouth drop. "They're visiting me while their mother recovers from surgery."

"Is that so?"

"Oral surgery," I affirmed, one hand on Patsy's shoulder. "Very painful. You ever had a root canal, Officer?"

He ran his tongue around his gums and looked uncomfortable. "May I ask your name, ma'am?"

"Catherine Caliban," I told him, watching his face. As far as I could tell from his absence of reaction, he hadn't heard of me from either my friends or my enemies in the Cincinnati PD. "To what do we owe the pleasure of your visit?"

"I believe you knew Peter Abrams, Mrs. Caliban? I'm making some inquiries about his death."

"Really?" I raised my eyebrows. "I understood that someone else was working on that—Officer Bunke, was it?"

"That's right, ma'am," he agreed easily. "Officer Bunke is in charge of the investigation. I'm just following up a few things for him. I wonder if we could go inside?"

I realized that this was a polite way of indicating that he was freezing his ass off, and possibly that he was bribable if I had a cup of coffee and a cookie or two lying about.

We left the girls drawing in chalk on the sidewalk. I hoped they weren't writing profanity.

I handed him a cup of coffee and set down a plate of cookies on top of a Strawberry Shortcake coloring book. The cookies looked as if they'd been decorated by someone on a bad acid trip. Maybe he should've left his sunglasses on after all.

"I'm following up this lead on a connection between Peter Abrams and a Roxanne Zacharias." He tapped a small spiral notebook with a ballpoint pen. "Alice Rosenberg—I believe she's your tenant?"

"That's right."

"Alice Rosenberg remembers that this Roxanne Zacharias had an appointment with Mr. Abrams the week he was killed." He looked up at me. "We're trying to reconstruct his calendar, you understand. We have his Legal Aid appointment book, and his personal notebook, but we haven't yet found anything that mentions Miss Zacharias, so we're checking anything that anybody remembers about that week."

"Uh-huh."

"Do you know Roxanne Zacharias, Mrs. Caliban?"

"No," I said. "I've never met her."

"Oh," he said, and seemed to consult something in his notebook. "But I understood you were looking for her."

"My friend, Mr. Fogg is looking for her," I corrected. "I'm just going along for the ride."

"That would be Moses Fogg." He nodded. "I believe he lives upstairs?"

He'd been living the last time I'd laid eyes on him, so I said, "Yes."

"And why is he looking for Roxanne, Mrs. Caliban?" he asked. "Do you know that?"

I shrugged. "She's a friend of his. As to why he's looking for her now, I think you'd better ask him."

"Mmm." He tapped his teeth with the pen. "Have you had any luck in tracing her, Mrs. Caliban? You see, if she did talk to Abrams that week, we need to talk to her. Not because we suspect her of anything, you understand, but just—"

"To eliminate her from your inquiries," I finished for him.

"Excuse me?" He glanced at me in confusion. "Oh. Oh, right. They say that on TV. Well, that's as good an explanation as anything. See, we don't really have a lot to go on in this case, Mrs. Caliban. A hit-and-run, well—" He spread his hands to suggest the futility of the situation. "To tell you the truth, we may never solve it. But we have to give it our best shot. So, have you had any luck in tracing Roxanne Zacharias, Mrs. Caliban?"

"Nope, sorry," I said truthfully. "Moses can probably give you a better account of where we've looked than I can, but we haven't turned up anything."

He studied my face with the kind of frown that could either be directed at me or at the state of the universe.

"She's violated her parole, of course," he said at last, "which means she probably won't come forward voluntarily. But if you find her before we do, and she has some information for us, would you tell her we might be able to work something out?"

"If she had information, couldn't she just call in from a phone booth and give you an anonymous tip?" I asked.

"She might," he conceded. "But then again, she might be a witness, and we might need her for identification purposes, or even to testify in court." He handed me a card. "This is all highly unlikely, of course. She probably doesn't know anything about the Abrams case. Maybe she went to see him about the condition of her parole, didn't like his answers, and walked. That's much more likely. But just in case."

I fingered the card. "This isn't your card," I pointed out.

"My partner's," he responded evenly. "I may have to be out of town some time over the next week or so. Officer Ross will be able to make the same kind of arrangements I could as far as the parole violation goes."

"Couldn't she call Officer Bunke as officer in charge?"

"Sure, if she'd rather," he said. "He's got more on his plate, though, so he might not get back to her as fast as we would. But sure, she can call any of us."

I squinted at the card as he headed upstairs to interrupt Moses' death throes. Something funny had just happened here, and I wished I knew why.

Twenty-one

I didn't have a chance to talk to Moses until after the kids were in bed—something else I thought I'd never say again—and by then we were both functionally brain-dead. Make that all; Mel, Al, and Kevin were also lying prone on the floor cushions in Mel and Al's apartment, or sprawled on the futon. They were passing around bottles of wine and aspirin.

Even the dog and cats had had it. Sidney and Winnie were curled up together, Sophie was lying on Kevin's stomach, and Sadie, who had snagged a cushion all to herself, was lying on her back, four paws up, like roadkill with rigor mortis.

Brother had pitched a fit at dinner because Kevin's beef stew had tasted funny. When Kevin explained what was in it, Patsy dropped her fork in horror, and Retty announced that they were all underage, and primly requested a peanut butter and jelly sandwich.

"How long did you say they were staying?" Mel asked Moses.

"I don't want to take them back until we know they're safe from whatever kind of trouble Rocky is in," he answered. "Besides, we only got the three, and five adults to supervise 'em. Think about Barbara Hickson, raising our three and three more like 'em by herself."

"She must have a system," Al theorized.

"She must have a prescription for Valium," Kevin said.

"I wish you wouldn't call them 'our' three, Moses," Mel said.

"Maybe we could send 'em to boarding school," I proposed. "I'd be willing to take up a collection for that."

"Yeah," Kevin agreed. "A nice, strict military academy in South Dakota."

"They're not bad kids," Moses admonished us. He shifted on the futon to resettle his bruised hip, and winced. "They're just kids."

"Remind me not to have any, sweetie," Al said to Mel.

"I'd divorce you," Mel threatened darkly.

Before Moses could say anything, Kevin put in, "We know they're not bad kids, Moses. They're kind of cute, in their way."

"Yeah," Mel agreed. "They look real cute when they're asleep."

"We don't want to see 'em hurt, Moses," Al assured him. "You know we'll protect them."

"Yeah, when I saw that guy talking to Retty and Patsy today, I just about lost it," I said. "He's damn lucky I didn't take him out."

"You mean you were packing, Mrs. C?" Kevin asked.

"No," I said. "I would have sat on him and hollered for Mel."

"What about that guy, Moses?" Mel asked. "Was he legit?"

"Seemed to be," Moses said. "Had the ID, asked the right questions. I give 'em credit for following up on Al's information that Rocky went to see Peter before he was killed. Means they're being thorough."

"But how did he know that we were looking for Rocky?" I asked.

"Said he heard it from Gordon Nash," Moses responded. "Don't have any reason to doubt that, do you?"

"I guess not," I conceded. Moses and I had hardly been discreet. By now, half of Cincinnati, including everybody in the Projects, must have known we were looking for Rocky. "But why did he give me his partner's card?"

Moses shrugged, then winced again. "Said he might be

called out of town in the next few days. Doesn't sound that suspicious to me. If he was trying to hide what he was doing, why encourage us to call someone else?"

"Unless the someone else was in on it," Kevin said. "You know, a confederate." Conspiracy theories were always Kevin's theories of choice.

"Course, he doesn't really have a partner, Cat," Moses added. "Not in the Investigations Bureau. But maybe he explained it that way because he thought it would make more sense to you."

"Still sounds pretty fishy to me," I said.

"But the guy was a police officer, Cat," Al pointed out. "Moses says his credentials were legitimate. So how do you think the cops might be involved in whatever trouble Rocky's gotten herself into?"

"That's a very good question," I acknowledged. "Are they looking for Orlando Walker's mythical stash? Do we know for sure that he's attached to homicide, Moses, and not narcotics?"

"It would be easy enough to find out," Moses replied. "And he'd know that. He knows I'm an ex-cop."

"But he knew you weren't going to find out today when he showed up on your doorstep," Kevin said. "So maybe he wanted to surprise you into revealing something."

"Surprise me?" Moses said irritably. "Look, I'm an ex-cop. If I knew about a drug stash, I'd be the first one to report it. They know I ain't about to set up in the drug trade. Ain't no drugs ever disappeared from the station house on my watch. My record is clean."

"Yeah, yeah, we know all that, Moses," I said. "But what if you found out that one of your former juvenile offenders was holding—someone you'd formed an attachment to over the years, someone you'd still like to help if you could?"

"Then I'd advise her to turn herself in and plea-bargain," he said.

"But you'd have to find her first," Al said. "And maybe this cop today—what was his name?"

"Wyszanski."

"Right, Wyszanski. Maybe that's what he was trying to figure out—how close you were to finding her."

"Did he ask you about the kids?" I asked. "Who they were, I mean?"

"No."

I sighed. "That means either he bought my story, or he knew who they were all along. Shit, I wish people would at least wear team jerseys so we could tell how many teams are in the fucking game!"

"Suppose it wasn't about drugs, or at least not about Orlando's stash, which we don't really believe exists anyway," Kevin continued. "Why else would the cops be interested in Rocky? Apart from Peter's death."

He passed the bottle around while we thought about it.

"Rocky knows something," I said at last. "We're back to that."

"But what about?" Kevin asked. "It has to be something that the cops know about, too."

"Talia's murder?" Al offered.

Moses shook his head. "Rocky was still inside when that happened."

"Arletta Sandifer's death?" I suggested.

Moses shook his head again. "Rocky was already out when that happened. Anyway, it wouldn't involve the Cincinnati cops. Even if that was a homicide, it would be out of their jurisdiction."

"Hell, Moses, this doesn't make any sense!" I rubbed my eyes. "People are dying all around Rocky, except that she's never in the right place at the right time. It's like, she's never anywhere you think she ought to be! The only reason we think she's anywhere at all is because she leaves messages on your answering machine. Are you sure it's her voice?"

"It's her, all right," he said. "Anyway, the kids saw her a week ago yesterday."

"Well, I'm tired of running around in circles!" I complained. "Why don't you leave a message on your answering machine telling Rocky to get her ass over here so we can straighten out this shit and send her kids home?"

"You the one wanted to make a career out of investigation, Cat," Moses said. "Not me."

Kevin intervened with a change of topic. "Personally, I'm glad the little monsters have taken the Nancy Reagan pledge," he said, eyeing the nearly empty win bottle. "More for us."

I was halfway down the stairs when Moses called me back to listen to his answering machine.

"She must've called when we were eating dinner," he said.

I'd been out of patience since about seven the night before, when Brother had dumped a whole bottle of salon formula shampoo in the bathwater. Getting him out of there had been like rescuing him from a burning building; I'd had to feel my way through a wall of bubbles.

"And it took you this long to notice?" I groused. "Wasn't the light blinking?"

"The light's always blinking," he said shortly.

"Hi, um, it's me again. How come you don't never answer this phone?" I could hear her breath in the silences. "Um, anyhow, I heard you got my kids. I really appreciate what you're doing for me, and I'm real glad they're with you right now. I know they're a handful, but they're good kids, really, and I know you'll make 'em mind." Her voice softened. "You tell 'em I love 'em, and I'm coming to get 'em real soon—soon's I can straighten things out." There was a long, drawn-out sniff. "Well, I got to go now. Thanks for everything"

And then she disappeared again.

Twenty-two

My plan for Monday, the kids' first day back at school, was to spend it flat on my back in the company of Miss Pinkerton and her canary. Moses had a similar plan, but somehow we ended up on the road to Columbus to interview Mrs. Tunney of the Capital Area Multiracial Alliance for Women and Children. Maybe it was the wistfulness in Rocky's voice when she talked about her children that heightened our sense of urgency. Or maybe it was the tantrum Brother threw when we sent him off to kindergarten with a brown paper bag instead of his Smurfs lunchbox.

"I didn't know kindergarten only lasted half a day," Moses was saying as we watched the farmland fly by on I-71. "Did you know that, Cat?"

"I knew it," I said, "but I'd repressed it."

"What do mothers do?" he said. "I mean, I got lucky because some kid in the after-school care program had the flu, but I can't count on that happening every day. And do you know how much it costs?" He turned to look at me. "When I complained, they handed me some kind of financial aid forms. Cat, it was more paperwork than I signed when I bought my house!"

"I think you get better at filling out forms if you rely on any kind of government assistance," I mused.

"At least I can read," he said. "A lot of folks can't even read the forms."

A few minutes later, he glanced at his watch.

"Girls get out of school at three-thirty," he said. "Three-thirty! What kind of time is that? You know any jobs that end at three-thirty? I guess they're old enough to get home by themselves, but what if they weren't?"

"If they weren't, you'd stay home and go on welfare because you couldn't earn enough to pay for after-school care for three kids," I said.

"Damn, Cat!" he exclaimed. "What they want to send 'em home at three-thirty for, anyway? No wonder the Japanese are eating us alive. Why don't they keep 'em in school and teach 'em something?"

"Manners, for instance," I said. "Respect for their elders."

"I be happy if they just teach Brother how to double-tie his shoes so he wouldn't be tripping over his shoelaces all the time," Moses observed. "Another two days, and I'm going to break down and buy him some of those shoes with the velcro tabs."

"They'd better have Smurfs on them, or he won't wear them."

The CAMAWAC offices were located in a vintage yellow brick office building right next to the freeway in downtown Columbus. The neighborhood, like the building, had that slightly run-down look you see wherever nonprofits and social service agencies congregate. The beige carpet inside ranged from shabby to threadbare, the walls did not appear to have been painted since the last glacier receded, and all the office furniture and equipment looked outdated.

The reception we received was warm enough, though.

Natalie Tunney was a tall, medium-brown woman, broad-shouldered, with wavy black hair cut very short. She wore a loose-fitting cotton tunic over pants, and an armful of brass bracelets. She waved us back to her office.

"The receptionist's desk is just for show," she said. "The only one we have is a part-time volunteer, and she's usually too busy answering the phone to do much receiving."

She glanced at her watch, and waved us toward a comfortable old couch with an afghan thrown over its worn upholstery.

I like to see what people have hanging on their walls. It

tells me a lot about them. Natalie Tunney's poster collection was quite a colorful and eclectic mix, featuring slogans from "Stop the Violence" to "End Apartheid" to "Every Mother Is a Working Mother." I recognized a poster of Alice Walker from a book jacket I'd seen. There was also a poster in Spanish from WIC—the government food supplement program for women, infants, and children.

"Just what is it that CAMAWAC does, Mrs. Tunney?" I asked.

"Oh, a little bit of everything," she said. "Mostly we organize support groups focused on women's and children's concerns. Some of them are kind of general—sort of an eighties version of consciousness-raising groups. Others are more focused, like groups for women with serious or chronic illnesses, or survivors of domestic violence or incest. We have a few groups for kids, like kids who are recovering from a loss. We also provide some educational programming—like workshops on caring for the elderly, or self-help workshops on maintaining your mental and physical well-being."

"That sounds like something I should sign up for," I said.

"Don't I know it!" She smiled at me. "We all need that one."

"You're not the teacher, then?"

"Teaching people how they're supposed to do it, and doing it yourself are two different things," she said. "Haven't you ever heard that old saying about how those who can't do, teach? Anyway, we're an all-volunteer organization; I'm the executive director and the only paid employee, and sometimes I wonder about me. We get most of our funding through grants and contracts."

"Contracts?" Moses asked.

"Sometimes somebody calls us because they want a specific workshop, or they need us to organize a support group at a particular site—a nursing home, for example, or even a large company. They don't always have somebody on staff who can provide the services we can."

"Is that how you got involved with the women's prison?" I asked.

The phone rang. She excused herself and picked it up. After a brief chat, she referred the caller to Children's Services.

"Sorry," she said. "It's just that we've turned in this major grant proposal, and I feel like I need to answer the phone in case they have any questions. Now, where were we?" she asked.

The front door banged shut and we heard a woman's voice. It preceded into the room a short, chubby woman in a powder blue polyester pantsuit and a crocheted poncho. She had straight yellow-blond hair that fell in her eyes like a horse's mane and pink-framed glasses to match her pink nose. She jingled when she walked. She was wearing little gold bells in her ears, a large jingle bell around her neck, and little jingle bells on her shoelaces. She seemed to be in the middle of a conversation, apparently with us.

"—know I don't like to be late, but as Natalie can tell you, it's always something."

She sat several large shopping bags on a chair, turned her back on us, and began rummaging through them.

"Now, where did I put—? Here it is. Whoops, no, that's Josie's kitty treats. Here," she said to Moses, who was standing as if in suspended animation, "would you hold this a minute?" She handed him a cookie tin. "I could've sworn—no, here it is! I put it under Pete's bear to keep it warm. I wanted you to have them fresh out of the oven."

She produced another cookie tin, opened it, and handed it to Moses.

"Peanut butter cookies. Have one," she said, and beamed at him. "I'm Hazel Connors."

"Pleased to meet you," he said. "Moses Fogg." At this point, he didn't have a hand free to shake, and she patted him on the arm.

"And this is Mrs. Caliban," Natalie Tunney said, gesturing in my direction.

She turned her smile on me, and I instantly forgave her her ditziness.

"You can call me Cat," I said as she folded my hand in both of hers.

"Cat." Wide blue eyes crinkled in merriment. "I like that.

"Now, don't let me interrupt you," she said, and sat down abruptly.

"Anytime you're bringing cookies, ma'am," Moses said, passing them to me, "feel free to interrupt."

She beamed at him. "I can see you're a man who appreciates good baking. But is there something wrong with your leg, Mr. Fogg?"

As Moses described his roller skating exploits, her face changed: her eyes widened in horror, then creased with concern. She sat on the edge of her chair. I was beginning to understand her popularity with the women of WCI. I glanced at Natalie Tunney, who smiled as if she were reading my mind.

When she thought they'd discussed Moses' medical condition—and his grandchildren—long enough, Mrs. Tunney spoke, and Hazel Connors transferred all of her attention to the other woman as if pulled by a magnet.

"Before you came in, they were asking how CAMAWAC became involved with WCI," Mrs. Tunney said. "We didn't have a contract with them at first, we just offered our services free of charge. We started a Saturday morning support group. That was about a year ago. Then, this summer they contracted with us to do some educational programming on women's health."

"Was that their idea?" I asked, surprised.

She laughed. "Hardly. I had to talk them into it."

"She doesn't look dangerous, now, does she?" Hazel Connors put in. "But my goodness, the woman can be persuasive when she wants to be." She had a way of tossing her head to flick the hair out of her eyes that reminded me again of a horse. And every time she did it, she jingled.

"How did you get interested in WCI in the first place?" I asked.

"We had a woman come to one of our programs on women and depression, and she had been incarcerated," Mrs. Tunney said. "She talked to me afterward about how much the women there needed programs like that one. So I thought, what the hell? It's only twenty miles up the road. That's one of the advantages of founding your own non-profit group, and declaring yourself executive director. You can do anything you damn well please." She grinned at us.

The phone rang, and she picked it up.

"Natalie's just wonderful that way," Mrs. Connors enthused in a loud whisper. "She takes an interest in everything. Anybody has a problem, they call her, and she takes care of it."

She was beginning to sound like a hit man for the mob. Moses frowned. "Doesn't she have a board?"

"Nothing she can't handle," Mrs. Connors said, and winked at me.

"And no secretarial help?"

"Volunteers, mostly," Mrs. Connors responded. "And sometimes we get a VISTA worker. But we have good volunteers."

Mrs. Tunney had put the first caller on hold and answered another line.

"How did you get involved?" I asked.

"Well, it was after my mastectomy," she said. "Mr. Fogg, have another cookie! My daughter lives here in Columbus, and she saw something in the paper about a workshop for women who were recovering from catastrophic illness. Well, I didn't think I needed a workshop, Cat, and I'm not the workshop type, if you know what I mean. But I went, just to please my daughter. You know how that is.

"Well, to make a long story short, the workshop was wonderful, and I met Natalie. And I asked her what I could do to help, you know, because I could see she had this marvelous organization. And she had been working out at

WCI for about four months. Well, I live out that way, so she invited me to come along one time, and I got hooked. It turned out well, because she can't always get out there, and then the women are so disappointed. They love her to death, you know. These days, I'm there more than she is.

"But you know, Mr. Fogg, how important it is for the women to have a black woman to talk to," she said, turning to him. "So there are things that Natalie can do for them that I can't. I mean, I can learn about black women's issues, and listen to what they say, but it's all secondhand, isn't it? And she's such a strong role model. Sometimes, the way the women treat us, you'd think she was the Lord and I was one of the seraphim."

"I heard that," Mrs. Tunney said, returning to the conversation. "It just goes to show how warped their perception is sometimes."

"It goes to show how grateful they are when anybody pays them the least bit of attention," Mrs. Connors asserted.

"Was Rocky Zacharias like that?" Moses asked doubtfully. "Grateful?"

"Oh, Rocky." Mrs. Connors's eyes twinkled, and she exchanged an amused look with Mrs. Tunney. "Yes, well, she became quite a convert."

"A convert," Mrs. Tunney repeated. "Not an angel."

"Oh, heavens, no! Not Rocky! We wouldn't want her to be an angel—that would take all the fun out of her! Remember, Natalie, that first time she came to the group, and she spent the whole time tying Prissy's arm to the chair? And here Prissy was pouring out her soul, telling us all her troubles, and everybody felt so bad for her, and then she went and tried to get up when Dorrie went to hug her, and she couldn't move her arm! And she started screaming that she was paralyzed! I didn't know whether to laugh or cry!"

"That was very disrespectful," Mrs. Tunney agreed, but the edges of her mouth were twitching. "And very disruptive of the group. I told Rocky that if she couldn't behave, she couldn't come back. She straightened up after that, and we didn't have any more trouble from her."

"Well, except for the time—" Mrs. Connors began.

"I don't count that." Mrs. Tunney cut her off. "Rocky was provoked. But she never did anything so mean-spirited after that time with Prissy. She clowned around, but she tried not to hurt anybody's feelings. And when she did, she apologized."

"This is Rocky Zacharias we're talking about?" Moses said.

"The very same," Mrs. Tunney said. "But she was attending AA and NA as well, and I think it got through to her this time."

"Well, it might not have, if it hadn't been for the Saturday morning group," Mrs. Connors observed. "The women in that group become very close, Mr. Fogg. They help each other survive."

"Was Talia Hickson in that group, Mrs. Connors?" I asked.

"Oh, yes, those two did everything together," she said. "I don't think one of them sneezed unless the other was standing by with a handkerchief."

"What about Arletta Sandifer?"

"Yes, she and Rocky were very close," she said.

"Did you know about their 'family'?"

She nodded. "That's very common at WCI. I gather it's common in women's prisons everywhere." She looked to Mrs. Tunney for confirmation.

"Much more common than what you see in Hollywood movies about women behind bars," Mrs. Tunney agreed. "The women form families to make up for the families they've lost. It's logical, not pathological. Sad to say, a lot of these prison families function a lot better and give them a lot more support than the families they have on the outside."

"Let me ask this," Moses said. "Do either of you know of

any trouble Rocky was in, or was about to be in, when she got out?"

"What do you mean by 'trouble'?" Mrs. Tunney asked, a little sharply.

"Every woman is in trouble when she gets out," Mrs. Connor explained patiently. "She's facing a hostile world with very little money, no job, probably no education to speak of, and no support group to keep her straight. She's got a record, and often the only thing on her mind is how to get custody of her kids, if she doesn't have it, and then how to support them when she does. Mostly she's walking right back into the same situation that landed her in prison to begin with, only now she's got a record."

"And she's got to put up with the same shit from the same people," Mrs. Tunney added.

"I would agree that that's a pretty accurate description of Rocky's situation," Moses said carefully. "But I'm talking about something more than the usual problems—something that would make her violate parole and go into hiding. Something that might make her consult an attorney, and call me up to ask for help."

"You realize, Mr. Fogg, that we have to respect Rocky's privacy?" Mrs. Tunney replied. "There might be things told us in confidence that we couldn't share with you. Having said that, I think I can tell you that she didn't like her stepfather very much, and she seemed worried that he might try to get custody of her children."

Moses regarded her for a minute in silence. "Have you met Gordon Nash, Mrs. Tunney?" he asked.

"No, I haven't."

"That's too bad," he said. "Because I would have been interested in your opinion about whether you thought he was capable of running a man down in the street."

She didn't say anything.

"I haven't met the man either," Mrs. Connors said. "But I can confirm that Rocky was afraid of him and wasn't at all happy that she was being paroled to him."

I tried to help Moses out. "Did she give either of you the impression that Gordon Nash was a violent man?"

"Yes," Mrs. Connors responded, "I think he could be."

"Would he have any reason that you know to go after Talia Hickson?" I asked. I remembered that Talia had been released more than a month before Rocky had, and added, "Do you know whether Rocky thought he had?"

"Poor Talia," Mrs. Tunney said softly.

"Yes, poor thing," Mrs. Connors said. She sighed, eyes gazing down at her hands. "Rocky didn't know what to think about that. It could have been that boyfriend of Talia's, it could have been a customer or a pusher, it could have been anybody."

"Including Gordon Nash," I prompted.

"I don't see why," Mrs. Tunney said. "What would he gain by killing Talia? He knew her mother had Rocky's kids, and he probably knew that Rocky would be paroled to him. So the man got violent when he was drunk. But beating her to death on the street? It doesn't make sense."

"So I gather Rocky didn't consider him a suspect in her cousin's death?" I said.

"If she did, she never mentioned it to me," Mrs. Tunney replied. "Hazel?"

"No, not to me either."

"That business about consulting an attorney," Mrs. Tunney pursued. "Of course, the women are always talking to lawyers about something. Maybe she wanted to see if she could change the conditions of her parole—get out from under Nash's thumb. Or maybe she just wanted to see if there was any way he could get legal custody of the kids."

"Possible," I conceded.

"What can you tell us about Arletta Sandifer's death?" Moses asked.

The two women exchanged a look, and Mrs. Connors sniffed.

"You don't want to get me started on that one, Mr. Fogg."

"Why not?"

"The way they handle that medication up there, it was an accident waiting to happen," she said, tossing her head angrily and setting her bells to jingling. "Arletta knew it herself. 'Miz Connors,' she used to say to me, 'I'm afraid I'm going to die in here.' And she was right!"

"Have you been to WCI, Mr. Fogg?" Mrs. Tunney asked.

"I visited an inmate there once," he reported, "but that was about fifteen years ago."

"It probably hasn't changed much," she said. "They've probably replaced the barbed wire with concertina wire, but that's about it. The whole institution is very badly run. And bad management is more than an inconvenience when the management has that much power over your life. Arletta had to go to the dispensary every day for her insulin. She should have gone on a regular schedule. But nothing at WCI follows a regular schedule. Your escort might be late, or not show up at all. Then you have to convince someone that you need an escort, that you've been waiting thirty minutes or an hour or an hour and a half, and your escort hasn't shown up yet, or your escort told you to sit on this bench in this hallway and she never came back to get you. I say 'convince' somebody, because you might get a CO who is stupid, or lazy, or vindictive, or just on a power trip, and you'll be told that you're lying, because you've already been to the dispensary. Meanwhile, your blood sugar is falling, and you are quickly losing the ability to explain anything to anybody. The symptoms of hypoglycemia can include confusion, which allows a CO to dismiss you as crazy, and personality change, which can land you in the hole for cussing out a CO."

"Nights are the most dangerous times," Mrs. Connors picked up the thread. "Diabetics dread lockdown, because it's harder and takes longer to get help in an emergency. Outside, a diabetic will usually have access to fruit or fruit juice if she feels her blood sugar falling. Inside, if they find fruit in your room, you're written up for breaking the rules."

"You're kidding!" I was shocked.

"Arletta died in the middle of the night," Mrs. Tunney said soberly. "She'd been written up five times for having food in her room."

"She had four kids in foster care, and she wanted parole very badly," Mrs. Connors added. She fished a wad of tissues out of a pocket and dabbed at her eyes. Then she blew her nose. Her bells jingled.

"So," Moses said after a pause, "you're satisfied that Arletta's death was accidental — that it was due to negligence? There's no question that she might have been killed?"

"Oh, she was killed, all right," Mrs. Tunney said. "But if you wanted to convict the people who were responsible, you'd have to hold the trial in a football stadium."

"I wonder," I said slowly. "Would that be a possibility? I mean, could Rocky have gone to Peter to find out whether the prison could be sued for wrongful death on behalf of Arletta's children?"

"It's possible," Mrs. Connors said thoughtfully.

"Let me check something." Mrs. Tunney stood and went into the other room. The phone rang almost immediately, and we heard her answer it.

I turned to Mrs. Connors. "The women in Rocky's family — is there any way we could get in to talk to them, to see if they know any more than you do about what was going on with Rocky?"

"Well, you'd have to go through channels, Cat," she said, frowning, then brightened. "But I tell you what. Maybe you'd like to come with me on Saturday, as a visitor to the Saturday group."

"You could get me in?"

"Sure. I'm not going to tell the administration, of course, that you're looking for information. But if I take you in with me, it'll be easier." She smiled regretfully at Moses. "I'm sorry I can't invite you along, Mr. Fogg. But I'm afraid that a male stranger would make the women feel uncomfortable."

"And I won't?" I asked.

"Maybe a little," she said. "But I think you'll find they're very generous in some respects, and they'll appreciate any interest you show in their problems. Anyway, I'm sure Mr. Fogg will welcome the opportunity to rest that bum leg of his."

I raised a hand to my face to hide my grin. Welcome Wagon lady, indeed!

"Sorry!" Mrs. Tunney apologized, returning with a folder open in her hands. "Arletta died very early on Monday morning, the eighteenth. That would have been six days after Rocky was released. When did you say she visited the attorney?"

"We don't know exactly," Moses said. "Sometime that week, Monday, Tuesday, or Wednesday. He was killed on Thanksgiving Day."

Mrs. Connor clucked her tongue sympathetically. "His poor family!"

"So it's possible that Rocky could have heard of Arletta's death," Mrs. Tunney speculated. "One of the women would have tried to call her, I'm sure." She laid the folder down on her desk and tapped it with her fingers. "I'm going to say something, and I hope you'll understand me. These women are not, generally speaking, very altruistic. They are not motivated by the interests of others. In certain very limited contexts—within their prison families, say, or maybe in the Saturday support group—they are capable of being loyal and supportive. But their strongest loyalties are typically reserved for their children. You can't blame them; their lives have been hard, and they don't have anyone but themselves to look after their interests. There are many reasons why we'll never see a prison riot at a women's prison that even approaches the mildest riot at a men's prison, but the insider's joke is that you'd never get the women to cooperate enough to organize an uprising."

"What you're saying," Moses said, "is that you don't

think Rocky would have gone out of her way to do anything about Arletta's death?"

"I'm saying that it would be very unusual," she responded, "especially if going out of her way would have involved her with the law. But Rocky's a funny mix of feistiness and submissiveness. It's hard to predict what she'd do."

"Let me ask you this. Have there been any other drug-related deaths since June?" I asked. "What I mean is, deaths that could be blamed on the wrong dosages, or the wrong medications, or even missed medication. Anything like that?"

Mrs. Tunney hesitated. "No," she said slowly. "Not that I know of."

Mrs. Connors spoke up. "There was Maida Neeley's miscarriage two weeks ago. She was sure it had something to do with the medicine they gave her for her urinary infection. She wrote down the name of it—Nor-something, with an *x* in it. I went to the library and looked it up. And don't you know she was right? The book said not to take it if you were pregnant."

"But as far as deaths among the women themselves—" Mrs. Tunney began.

"You always hear rumors, of course," Mrs. Connors said. "Peg Holliday had a heart attack, and the women all say that she missed her medication or they gave her the wrong medication, but who knows if it's true? I don't think much of the health care they get, but poor women on the outside get the same kind of care or worse, so maybe they're better off. Well, like the AIDS women. Up until recently, if you were HIV-positive, you were quarantined. Those women complained bitterly, and I sympathize with them, but they still got better health care than they would've gotten outside. Now, of course, they're in general population. But the point is, they can see the doctor for free—no cab fare, no paperwork. So they're more likely to get small things treated before major infections develop."

Mrs. Tunney shifted impatiently in her chair. "The difference is—how do I put it? In the outside world, the chaos is general, and the abuse of power is relatively impersonal. But inside, health care represents one more arena for the exercise of a power that can be highly personal. If you make an enemy inside, that's just one more way for your enemy to get back at you."

"By an enemy, you mean a guard," I said. "Or rather, a CO."

"A CO, or a trustee, or an administrator—anyone in a position of power."

"Do the women make a lot of enemies?" I asked.

Mrs. Tunney pressed a hand to her forehead and began rubbing it as if she had a headache.

"Let me put it this way," she said. "A lot of people who work in a prison are small people who want to be big. They take everything personally, so they're easily offended. Enemies are easy to come by, and hard to get rid of. And—they can be very, very dangerous."

Twenty-three

"Mother, Mother, I am sick,
Send for the doctor, quick, quick, quick.
Mother, Mother, will I die?
Yes, Miss Retty, and so will I.
How many coaches will I have?
One, two, three, four . . ."

Sneakers squeaked on the pavement. Mel had one end of the rope, and I had the other. Retty was bobbing up and down in the middle, her body perfectly coordinated with the turning rope. Patsy stood by, hugging a squirmy Sidney to her chest. The sun was low in the sky, and already long shadows were reaching for us with chilly fingers. I shivered inside my jacket and glanced around to see Leon headed up the walk from the front of the apartment building.

Leon was mildly retarded, or so I'm told, but that didn't stop him from becoming one of the most diversified junior business entrepreneurs in Northside. He also knew more people than the whole city council combined, and would be a shoo-in for any elective office he cared to hold once he was old enough to run. In fact, he had a whole range of talents that I hoped he wouldn't waste on the electorate. He was frequently useful to me in my line of work.

Today, he was toting a box the size of Brooklyn, which he set down carefully on the pavement when he reached the back parking lot where we were.

"Hey, M-miz Cat," he said. "Hey, M-m-mel. I got y'all Christmas cards and wrapping p-p-paper y'all ordered."

One of Leon's many enterprises was selling dopey greeting cards and hideous wrapping paper. He probably earned as much on these sales as my stockbroker daughter. I'd tell you I ordered some in a weak moment, but all moments were weak around Leon. He had a gift for selling, no doubt about it.

We introduced him to the girls, and I handed my end of the rope to Retty so Patsy could jump. Leon consulted a notebook, pencil stuck behind his ear like a misplaced antenna.

"Let's see," he said, very businesslike. "Mel, you g-got the ones with the h-h-horses, s-say, 'Mar-ey Christmas.'"

You see what I mean? Mel doesn't even celebrate Christmas. But Leon doesn't stock solstice cards, which was probably just as well.

"M-m-moses have the ones where S-s-santa looking for the elf, say, 'No-elf,'" he continued. "That's a c-cute one." He nodded with satisfaction, a salesman pleased with his wares. "I like that one." He turned the page, then bent down and studied the contents of his carton.

"K-kevin have the ones with B-b-baby Jesus in the m-m-manger. That one p-pretty." He held the box up for us to admire.

"M-miz Cat, you g-got the ones with the b-b-bird and the b-berries, say, 'Have a b-berry m-merry Christmas.'"

I could feel Mel's eyes on me. But I figured I could use these cards up on my family. They never understood me, anyway, so I didn't see the point in wasting my good cards on them. They wouldn't know from tacky if it bit 'em on the leg.

Speaking of tacky, Leon had moved on to our wrapping paper orders. He was rummaging in his box again.

"I g-got three roll d-d-dancing reindeers," he reported. "I g-got two roll M-m-miz Claus with elfs. I g-got one with a chicken and a t-tree—that yours, M-miz Cat."

"It's a partridge, Leon," I said. "A partridge in a pear tree."

"Uh-huh, well, I g-got that. And I g-got one with f-funny writing and that forky c-candlestick for Al." He turned to Mel. "What you call that, M-mel?"

"A menorah."

"Right. And I g-got that D-d-day-Glo tissue p-paper Kevin want. That's it," he summarized.

"Do we owe you, or did we already pay for it?"

"No, m-m'am. Ain't you k-kep' your receipt?" His forehead creased with concern.

"Oh, sure." I lied smoothly after long years of practice. "I've got it in there somewhere." I gestured vaguely toward the house.

He frowned at me. "You ought to k-keep them receipts, M-m-miz Cat," he said sternly. Then he spoiled his image by losing his balance somehow and falling, butt down, into the card box. I swear, Leon could trip over air.

"Don't w-worry," he reassured us, as I helped him up. "The cards is all in b-boxes."

Me, I didn't think he could make them any worse than they already were.

The sun was moving fast now, rushing to get home, I guess, like everybody else. Moses pulled into the parking lot. Retty was trying to persuade Leon that he could jump rope, which I saw as a disaster in the making.

Brother bounced across the parking lot, eyes shining, dragging his Smurf jacket and something made of red and green construction paper. Behind him, Moses unfolded himself carefully from the front seat of the car and limped toward us.

"Let me, Patsy! Let me!" Brother shouted.

To my surprise, Patsy gave way gracefully and took the rope from Mel.

"Watch this," she said to me. "He's really good."

And then he was in. He had a style all his own, his torso bobbing rhythmically as if all his energy and will were concentrated there, and his arms and legs were just along for the ride. He reminded me of a marionette, limbs attached by elastic and dancing frenetically as if they might fly off at any moment and begin their own dance. The whole was crowned by that beatific smile, a little milky around the edges but dazzling all the same.

He sang:

"Patsy is my sister, Retty is my sis,
When they jump, they go like this."

His body contorted, his eyes crossed, and his limbs shot out in all directions. He executed a bump and grind, then segued into something that looked like what used to be called the Funky Chicken. Then he hopped on one foot, waving the other leg around as if he were doing a ragged Charleston. But the rope kept turning, and one sneaker always hit the pavement just in front of the rope.

We all laughed. Sidney gazed at him, mesmerized.

"Rocky Zacharias could do the splits.
Rocky Zacharias could kick like this.
Rocky Zacharias could turn around.
Rocky Zacharias didn't never fall down.
Rocky Zacharias always set the table,
Just as fast as she was able,
With salt, ketchup, and RED HOT PEPPER!"

The rope whirred in the air and cracked on the pavement; Brother seemed suspended in midair, but his arms continued to flail. He kept it up for several minutes. Then, as if an invisible signal had been given, the rope slowed.

"Late last night and the night before,
Twenty-four robbers come a-knocking at my door.
They come in to steal my loot,
How many robbers did I shoot?"

Now he crouched in various firing postures and picked off imaginary robbers in the dusk. This rhyme sounded familiar to me, but it didn't used to go quite like this. I raised my eyebrows at Moses, who gave me a wry smile.

"Come on, y'all," he said. "It's time for dinner."

"What're we having?" Patsy wanted to know.

"Spaghetti-Os, peanut butter sandwiches, and Jell-O."

This information was greeted by cheers, and three kids raced for the back door. I hadn't seen so much mealtime

enthusiasm at my house since I opened a can of people tuna
by mistake.

"Oh, yeah, I forgot," Leon said, as Mel hoisted the box
of Christmas cards. "What that s-steak thing you d-do
s-sometime, M-miz Cat?"

"A stakeout, Leon."

"Oh, yeah. A s-stakeout." He repeated it over several
times to himself as if fixing it in his memory, but I knew
he'd ask me again. I didn't mind; menopausal women don't
go around criticizing other people's memories. We would,
but we don't remember.

He turned to go, and waved at us. Over his shoulder he
said, "I'm g-gonna g-g-go ax that m-man if that what he
d-doin'—a stakeout. If he s-still there."

I paused, one hand on the back door handle. Mel bumped
into me, and Moses bumped into her.

"If who's still there?"

"That man. He jus' s-sittin' in his c-car, don't look like he
d-d-doin' nothin'. Jus' watching' the s-street."

We all turned around and stared at him.

"Where is he, Leon?" Moses asked.

"'Cross the s-street." Leon pointed in that direction.

"Show me."

Moses, Mel, and I followed Leon to the front of the house.

"There he is," Leon said, and pointed.

In the dim light, we could make out a dark sedan parked
across the street, and a figure behind the wheel. I couldn't
make out his features.

Before we could react, the car started up, pulled out, and
sped down the street. At the corner, its lights came on, but
I still couldn't make out the license plate. As the sedan
disappeared around the corner, one taillight winked at us.

Twenty-four

"His mind kinda cloudy, Cat, but his information good," Curtis said.

Let me say up front that I had serious doubts about this informant. He looked like he'd already used up his last brain cell. His head hung forward, giving me an excellent view of his bald spot, which was surrounded by long, dirty black hair. I couldn't tell whether he was actually trying to look up at me from this position through the hair in his bleary mud-colored eyes, or if some principle of physics simply floated his eyeballs to the tops of their sockets and fixed them there. He was wearing a gray suit that had seen better days, and it smelled like he'd gotten lost on the way to the dry cleaners and taken it to the distillery instead. But I trusted Curtis's judgment. He might be homeless, but he wasn't stupid.

So when Curtis had called up on Tuesday and asked me to meet him at a bar in Over-the-Rhine, I'd gone.

But now that I was sitting across from the object of my visit, I had my doubts.

The establishment was as disreputable and decrepit in appearance as the man, whom Curtis and Steel called "Slats." The bar itself looked one termite away from collapse, and I could tell this even though there wasn't a bulb in the place above forty watts. My elbows stuck to the table, my legs stuck to the bench, and my feet stuck to the floor. I could smell well-aged sweat, strong spirits, cigarette smoke, and marijuana. As a matter of fact, I think the bartender was the one smoking a joint, and I'd ordered beer because it didn't involve any high order mental dexterity. A faint crescent of lipstick smudged the rim of my glass.

"Come on, Slats," Curtis encouraged him, edging his glass closer to his hand. "Tell Cat about the men who're looking for Rocky."

"Rocky," he repeated fuzzily. "Rocky's gone."

I leaned forward, anxious in spite of my resolve to consider the source.

"Damn, I loved that little guy," he mumbled. "And the moose, too. What was his name? Bullwinkle."

I leaned back and exchanged a look with Curtis.

"Not that Rocky, asshole," Steel said, ever the diplomat. "The other Rocky. Rocky Zacharias."

"Oh. Rocky Zacharias. The jump rope queen." His hand jerked spasmodically and encountered the glass. He looked surprised at his good fortune, straightened up a little, and took a drink. "D'jyou know Rocky holds the unofficial record for jumping longer'n anybody else? 'Sa fact." His eyes focused on me. "It would be in that book they put out. You know the one I mean? Only Rocky cussed the man out when he came to write it up, so he just—" Slats gestured with his other hand, and found a cigarette in it, so he took a puff.

"I used to live next door to Rocky in the old days," he continued, and his eyes rolled up to the top of their sockets again. Then he closed them. "I'm talkin' about the real old days. Girl had a mouth on her, that's for sure. This one time, I 'member, she got pissed at Darnell Jones, socked 'im in the kisser, knocked him out. Then she tied 'im to the tree with her jump rope. Darnell'd still be sittin' there, 'f she didn't need that jump rope for jumpin'." He opened his eyes, and they drifted down like deflated balloons. "Lot of girls woulda been scared after that, but Darnell knew better than to tangle with Rocky. Everybody did, except—" He drifted off, and the cigarette dropped from his lips, scattering ash. The wood tabletop was already heavily pitted and peppered with burn marks, so I didn't figure one more made any difference.

"Rocky hidin' out now, Slats," Curtis prompted. "And Cat want to know who she's hiding from. You say it's some men been lookin' for her."

Slats registered the dropped cigarette in a delayed reaction and swiped ineffectually at the ashes, which were by now glued to the tabletop. "Well," he said, "Orlando Walker was lookin' for her, but somebody told me he's dead."

"That's right," Curtis said patiently. "Who else?"

His eyeballs reversed themselves and floated up to visit his eyebrows. "A cop. Maybe two cops."

"Tell us about them," I said.

"Not much to tell. Cops just do their cop thing, don't they? Ask questions, throw their weight around."

"Did one of them identify himself as a police officer?"

He gave an expression of disgust. "Nah. But they were cops, all right. Or maybe private dicks. Coulda been private."

"Were they together?"

He shook his head, then thought better of that and stopped abruptly. "One was in Lucky's when I was there, and another one came in here after that."

"When was this?" I asked. Curtis and Stool gave me a look.

"What's today?"

"Tuesday."

"Well, then, maybe it was Saturday. Or Friday maybe. I don't recall exactly." He frowned at Curtis. "When they have that parade— with Santa Claus and shit?"

"That was Thanksgiving, you asshole," Steel replied caustically. "That was two weeks ago."

"He ain't so good on time," Curtis explained to me.

"Do you remember what these guys looked like?" I asked.

"The first one—he had on these real dark sunglasses. Walked like a cop."

Wyszanski, I thought. I wished I could get a fix on the date.

"Other guy— I don't know. Looked like the first guy, except for the sunglasses."

"Then how the fuck do you know they weren't the same guy?" Steel pressed him belligerently. "If anybody wore sunglasses in this dump, they'd be blind, you idiot!"

Slats seemed unperturbed. "Coulda been the same guy, I

guess. Light-colored hair, kinda stocky. Coulda been the same. They were both askin' 'bout Rocky."

He found his glass, and it was empty. Curtis called for another round. The bartender glanced at me, and I nodded. So the bartender wasn't so far gone he had forgotten who was paying the tab.

Slats scratched his shoulder meditatively. "Then there was that other guy. He was talkin' to the ladies in the laundromat. Sometimes I go in there to get warm, and I saw him leave. Juanita Jenkins said he was askin' about Rocky."

"What did he look like?" I asked.

He studied the circles of condensation on the table. "No sunglasses. I didn't notice him much when I saw him. Blond hair, I guess. Wore a suit."

"You dipshit!" Steel exclaimed in disgust. "He coulda been the same fuckin' guy as the other two!"

"Coulda been, I guess," Slats again admitted placidly. "I don't think he was, though."

"Was his build stocky, like the others?"

"Yeah, I guess," he said. "He was big in the shoulders. And he had big hands. I 'member I saw his hand on the door as I was comin' in and he was goin' out."

"And what about the other guys' hands, Einstein?" Steel said. "What did they look like?"

"I di'n't notice. Look, I gotta go take a piss." He half-rose unsteadily. "Pardon me." He slid to the end of the bench and sank like a stone to the floor.

"You better take him, Steel," Curtis said, "or we never get him out of there."

"I'll take him," Steel said grudgingly, "but if he falls in, it's no fucking loss, if you ask me."

As Steel steered him toward the restrooms, I heard Slats mumble, "Who'sa ol' lady?"

"I know he ain't no star witness, Cat," Curtis began apologetically.

"That's okay, Curtis," I assured him. "I'm inclined to trust his instincts, I just don't know if I can trust his vision."

Slats could have seen two cops, I thought. One of them—or both of them—might have been Wyszanski of the dark sunglasses. Or Wyszanski's "partner," whose crumpled card I was carrying in my jeans pocket. Moses had checked with Walter Bunke in the Investigations Bureau, and had confirmed that Wyszanski was working on the Abrams investigation, but I still thought there was something funny about him and his partner.

One of the men Slats had seen might have been Bunke himself. Or one of them might have been somebody who gave the impression of a cop—a parole officer, for example. I didn't consider Toby Grisham's build stocky, or his demeanor very coplike, but what if he'd been wearing a leather motorcycle jacket? The guy with the big hands might have been Gordon Nash; I'd certainly been impressed by the size of his mitts. But hell, there might be other players in the game that I didn't even know about yet. In the mysteries I read, somebody always had a snake tattoo or some other distinguishing mark. Damn, I'd pay a lot of money right now for a snake tattoo.

Steel and Slats returned. Steel wore the look of a martyr as he stuffed Slats into the booth.

"He remembered why the two cops couldn't have been the same guy," Steel reported.

"That's not what I said, man! You di'n't listen to me. It was another cop I was talkin' about."

"A third cop?" I asked.

"Tha's right. He was in Dewey Mayberry's place—when was it? Shit, what you say today was?"

"Never mind," Curtis told him. "What this cop look like?"

Slats's eyes descended long enough to focus on his drink. "Black guy, with a mustache. Had kind of a game leg."

Twenty-five

The cop in question was nowhere in sight when I reached home. His car was gone from the parking lot, so I deduced, with my Holmesian powers of deduction, that he had caved in and taken the kids to Chuck E. Cheese's for supper. In fact, there were no cars in the parking lot.

So imagine my surprise when I pushed open the back door, walked into the hallway, and found a man lying on the foot of the stairs. Officer Wyszanski.

He was sprawled on his back. His dark sunglasses were slightly askew, but he lay so motionless that I thought I could risk removing them. His eyes were closed. He was either asleep, or out cold. Or—but no, his chest was rising and falling.

That was a relief. I didn't like the guy much, and I didn't trust him, but however much trouble he could make for me alive, I was willing to bet he could make more dead.

I squatted on my haunches and studied him. That was when I saw the jumprope coiled around his ankle and pulled taut. I followed it up to where one of the wooden handles was wedged between the balusters.

My insurance company was going to love this.

How long had he been lying here? Did he wear his mirror sunglasses after the sun went down? We were now approaching the shortest day of the year, so that would mean he'd been lying here for more than an hour.

I felt a surge of panic. Maybe he was brain-dead. Maybe his heart would continue to beat and his lungs continue to fill with air and he'd be hospitalized for years—decades, even! The hallway suddenly felt hot and close. The walls began to bow and dip crazily, the ceiling rushed toward me. I pitched forward onto Wyszanski's inert form.

That woke him up.

"What? What? What are you doing?" he asked thickly.

I jerked myself upright.

"Just a panic attack," I mumbled. "Are you all right?"

He stared up at me, as if trying to remember who I was.

"You're—you're—" He shook a limp finger at me as if it would help him to place me.

Oh, shit! I thought. Amnesia! The room took another turn around my head.

"Caliban," he said finally, "the broad with the—"

I didn't get to find out how he had me pegged, however. He seemed to catch himself, planted his fists on the floor, and tried to sit up.

"What happened?" he asked.

I shook my head. "I just got home. You tell me."

"Oh, man!" He felt the back of his head. "I got a knot back there the size of a bowling ball!" Then he noticed the jump rope.

Damn! I thought. If my hormones hadn't taken over, I could've removed the evidence.

"It was the jump rope!" he said slowly. "It was the fucking jump rope! I was goin' up the stairs—"

"Can I ask how you got in the building?" I inquired coldly. Now that I could see he wasn't badly hurt, it was time to go on the offensive.

He stared at me. "The door was open," he said after a minute.

I stood up slowly, walked to the door, and pulled.

"No, it wasn't. It was closed and locked. I just came in the back way. That was also closed and locked."

He shrugged. "It was open when I came in, lady, what can I tell you? Maybe whoever closed it didn't close it all the way. I pushed it closed behind me."

This, unfortunately, was a plausible explanation. I had

noticed before that Brother's door closing skills left something to be desired. And he lived in the eternal present, so anything that didn't get done right the first time around was history, as far as he was concerned. The idea of going back to do it again was alien to his consciousness.

Wyszanski glanced at his watch, then did a double take. "I been out that long? I'd better call the wife."

I didn't let on that he'd just confirmed my general impression of him by alluding to his marital partner as "the wife." I helped him up, and let him use the phone in my apartment.

"You know when Moses will be back?" he asked.

"No. Like I said, I just got home myself."

I doubted that Moses' tolerance for Chuck E. Cheese's would run to more than an hour. That meant that even if the traffic was heavy on Colerain Avenue, he could be home any minute. But I wasn't about to share my suppositions with Wyszanski.

"You know, you two weren't exactly straight with me the other day, Mrs. Caliban," he said, tucking his sunglasses into his breast pocket. "You never told me that the kids belonged to Rocky Zacharias. You said they were second cousins or something. You knew we were looking for her."

"So were we. We still are."

He studied my face. "You want me to believe that you have the woman's kids, and you don't know where she is?"

"That's right."

"You trying to tell me she hasn't contacted you?"

"Not yet."

He gave me one of those cop stares they give when they're trying to intimidate you. Forget it, cookie, I thought. I been stared at by a teenager who just learned she isn't going with her friends to a Grateful Dead concert. You ain't even in her league.

"When she does, I want to hear about it," he said at last. "Good night, Mrs. Caliban."

"Have a nice night," I rejoined.

Cops can be so thickheaded sometimes, I thought. They

get so used to using their badge and their muscle and their firepower to intimidate people, they never even consider other strategies for getting their way. Take this cop. He'd never thought to say the one word I was most afraid of: lawsuit.

Twenty-six

The cop I lived with had more imagination. He'd played up his game leg, or legs, to be accurate, when declining my invitation to join the pilgrimage to Santa Claus on Wednesday night.

"Y'all go on, Cat," he said with feigned regret. "I'd just slow y'all down."

Slowing us down was just what I'd been hoping for. I must be out of my mind, I thought, as the hour of my doom approached. But I'd been conned by an expert, who'd presented me with a torn and wrinkled collage of green and red construction paper liberally sprinkled with *x*'s and *o*'s and smelling of Elmer's Glue-All.

"I's a Christmas card," he'd told me when I'd gone to say good night to him the night before. "I made it for you."

He laid his cheek, which had been slashed with red marker and dusted with green glitter, across my knee, looked up at me, and smiled.

"Will you take me to see Santy Claus, Cat?"

I'd have felt like the grinch who stole Christmas if I'd said no.

So Kevin was at work, Al was going to dinner with her support group for women in the law, Mel was baby-sitting a kiln, and I was on the road to Florence Mall with three kids, at least one of whom was hyperactive. It was raining, which did nothing to improve my night vision. And we were driving I-75 toward downtown at rush hour. The only good thing about the numbers was that everybody got a window seat.

The bad thing was that in one of my menopausal memory lapses I'd put Patsy and Brother in the backseat. Brother bounced up and down, singing "Rudolph the Red-Nosed Reindeer" at the top of his lungs, making it up as he went along. Patsy kept telling him to shut up, emphasizing her position by taking swipes at him.

If I hadn't been glancing so often at the rearview mirror to monitor the progress of the battle in the backseat, I wouldn't have noticed we were being followed.

It's just your hormones, I told myself, as I felt adrenaline flooding my system. Sweat popped out of my scalp, which bristled with electricity.

The world is full of dark sedans, I said. There are at least three in your rearview mirror at this very moment. They can't all be after you.

No, but only one had something familiar about the grillwork in the front.

Even so, said my reason. The car Leon spotted in front of your house wasn't the only car of that make and model in the city. You're getting paranoid, Cat.

"What kind of food they got at this place?" Retty was asking. "Brother won't eat nothing but a hot dog, but I like Chinese. They got Chinese food at this place?"

The lights brightened as we reached downtown Cincinnati, but the sedan was too far behind me for me to make out the driver's face, especially through the wet glass. Besides, the traffic was moving fast—too fast for the weather conditions, in my opinion.

"Quit it, Patsy!" Brother broke off his singing. "Santy gon' bring me a laser gun, and I'm gonna blast you into a zillion pieces!"

Someone cut in front of me.

"Asshole!" I shouted at him, even though he couldn't hear me. "I got kids in the car!"

"Yeah, asshole!" Retty contributed.

"Santa Claus ain't bringin' you no laser gun," Patsy snarled at Brother in the backseat. "You ain't been good all year!"

"I have so!" he exploded. "Asshole!"

At the point where the traffic merged from I-71, someone eased into my lane and then slammed on the brakes.

"Christ!" I swore. "What the fuck is the matter with you people?"

"Yeah!" Retty said. "Fuck you!"

A part of me was aware that I ought to be more careful with my language around the kids. But right now, that part was overruled by the part that was panicked by the headlights in the rearview mirror, and the demolition derby that surrounded me.

I have to get behind him, I thought to myself as we crossed the Brent Spence Bridge into northern Kentucky.

"Cat, I have to go to the bafroom," Brother wailed in my ear.

He diverted my attention just long enough for me to miss my chance to exit at Fifth Street into Covington, Kentucky. A streak of lightning lit up the sky, closely followed by a peal of thunder that made the car vibrate. Brother screamed in my ear.

We were headed toward Death Hill.

Death Hill was a winding stretch of three-lane highway climbing up from the river through Covington. It followed the contour of the hills left by the glacier that had carved out the Ohio River Valley, and therein lay the problem. Semis slowed to a crawl, clogging the right lane of traffic. Frustrated right-laners pulled out abruptly in front of center lane speeders. Center lane drivers rounded the curve and slammed into frustrated and overly optimistic semi drivers who could push their rigs up to thirty or forty on the incline, and were determined to pass their pokier counterparts. Left lane drivers ignored the speed limits and warning signs, and, crowded by the lane-jockeying going on to their right, lost control of their cars on the curve and bounced off the guardrail. Rain made everything worse.

I monitored the sedan in the rearview mirror while I formulated a strategy. I was cruising along in second gear in the right lane, confident that he couldn't see me around the trucks.

"Everybody still got their seat belts fastened?" I asked brightly.

I glanced in the mirror again. To my relief, the panic was receding and leaving behind it an anger that swelled my chest and narrowed my eyes. Goddamn it! I thought. I can't even take the kids to see fucking Santa Claus without some bastard on my tail! Didn't these guys have any respect? This must be how Barbara Hickson felt all the time. No wonder she stayed pissed off.

I felt Retty's eyes on me, but Brother and Patsy were still squabbling in the backseat. I watched for an opening large enough to give me a comfortable margin. I smiled at Retty, winked, moved left and pressed the accelerator.

The sedan was two trucks back in the right lane. He swung out now, barely missing another pair of headlights. But I couldn't give him my attention. I pushed the speedometer up to fifty, the legal speed limit. Cars flew past me on my left.

Then, just as I rounded the curve, I saw my opening and moved back into the right-hand lane. I felt the seat belt tighten against my chest as I applied the brakes to slow down, but I managed it smoothly. The voices in the backseat never diminished. Retty's knuckles, however, were pale on the armrest.

I'd lost sight of him when we'd rounded the curve. But now he popped out in my side view mirror, and he didn't have time to react. He turned his head so that all I saw was a partial profile as he sailed past in the center lane. He could have been anybody. But one of his taillights winked at me as he passed.

I took the next exit and doubled back in the direction of Cincinnati. I stopped at a gas station on Main Street in Covington.

"He don't have to go no more," Patsy giggled. "He peed his pants when he heard the thunder. Bad as he been, I guess he don't have to see no Santy Claus neither."

Brother thrust his bottom lip out far enough to build a campfire on.

"No, goddamn it!" I said. "We started out to see Santa Claus and we're damn well going to see Santa Claus, come hell or high water!"

Twenty-seven

So Brother had a long heart-to-heart with Santa, and came away clutching a commemorative snapshot and looking smug. Despite my efforts with the hand dryer in the women's room, he left a small damp spot on Santa's lap. I had planned to leave Retty and Patsy in the girls' department at Lazarus, since they seemed to be at the age when trying on clothes was still considered entertainment and not cruel and unusual punishment. But the incident en route made me wary of letting any of them out of my sight. So before we went to Lazarus, we stopped at a toy store and I bought Brother one of those handheld plastic pinball machines. He lobbied hard for a GameBoy, but when I threatened to go back and have a word with Santa, he gave in. I considered that this threat was only good for twenty more days, and hoped that by then Brother would no longer be my problem. But I still made a mental note to make sure he got what he wanted for Christmas.

Patsy and Retty went through the girls' department like locusts, snatching up everything in their path and disappearing into the dressing room with it. They had very different tastes, but between the two of them, they covered the full range of preadolescent haute couture. Brother and I camped out in a couple of chairs by the mirrors. He proved a surprisingly astute, if not particularly diplomatic, critic. I found myself grateful for his willingness to voice opinions I was reluctant to offer.

"That one so ugly I wouldn't give it to a dog," he ventured, when Patsy pranced out in a hideous plaid.

"That one look like they already wash it, and all the

colors run together," he told Retty, frowning at her image in
the mirror.

"What you want that one for?" he asked when Patsy
appeared in a faded denim jumper. "Look like somebody
already die in it, and you got it from the Goodwill."

He opened his mouth to complain about Retty's latest
selection, when she said softly, "Momma used to have one
like this."

A silence descended like a final curtain. Damn, I thought,
my eyes tearing. Rocky would probably give anything to be
here right now. To me, shopping was a pain in the butt, and
shopping with three kids, though it had its moments, ranked
somewhere below waxing the linoleum on my list of
preferred activities. But it would mean a lot to Rocky. It's
the little things we take for granted.

"Momma's don't have them buttons on the front," Brother
said finally. But for a change it wasn't an objection, merely an
observation.

"And hers have pockets," Patsy said sadly. "That one
don't have pockets."

"I don't think she have that dress no more, anyway,"
Retty said, studying herself critically in the mirror.

I wondered if Rocky herself knew what she had in her
wardrobe, or where that wardrobe was. In prison, she would
have had no choices. The color she wore would be chosen
for her, not according to her tastes but according to her
success at conforming to prison life. Good girls wore one
color, bad girls another. All the clothes were hand-me-
downs, and she would be lucky if they fit. If they made her
look sickly, or dumpy, or frumpy, that was too bad. Prison
was not about building self-esteem.

I stood abruptly. "I'm hungry," I announced. "Let's eat."

The mall food court was crowded, and everybody wanted
something different, but I was reluctant to let them split up.
We got Brother's first, and then let him eat it while we stood
in line at the other stands. By the time we arrived at the last
one, he refused to eat any more of his hot dog and insisted

that he wanted a hamburger now instead. Then we finally sat down at a table.

"They got better pizza than this at Pizza Hut," Patsy observed, her mouth full.

"I like the kind Aunt Barbara make, out the box," Brother said.

"Your elbow's in the ketchup, Brother," I said.

He raised it, and then pushed it up with his other hand for a closer inspection, which resulted in a matching stain on the other sleeve of his sweatshirt.

"When I grow up, I'm gonna go shopping every Saturday," Retty said dreamily.

"Me, too," Patsy enthused. "I'm gonna have a kazillion pairs of shoes."

"Your taco is leaking out of the other side, Retty," I said.

Rocky hung around in my imagination like a ghostly dinner guest. I found myself wondering if she'd had the same dreams her daughters did when she was their age. In my judgment, television has made it harder than ever to be poor, especially for kids, because you can't avoid seeing all the things you don't have, and you can't avoid the kind of sophisticated advertising that makes you want them. At the moment, Retty and Patsy were in ecstasy because they'd been given money to spend, and they'd spent it. I'd given them twenty-five dollars apiece, reckoning that a munificent sum until I'd seen the prices in the girls' department. Luckily, Moses had matched my twenty-five. So they were happy. But how long would it last?

They were now on the subject of marriage and motherhood.

"I'm gonna have lots of kids," Patsy declared. "Maybe five."

"I'm gonna have two sets of twins," Retty said. "One girls, and one boys. Aunt Barbara say you gonna have twins, too, Patsy."

"We always have twins in our family," Patsy explained to me. "Aunt Barbara and Grandma Zacharias was twins."

"Momma have a twin," Brother said into his straw.

I looked at him, startled.

The two girls turned on him.

"You ain't supposed to talk about that!" Patsy exclaimed furiously.

"Well, she did!" Brother countered sullenly.

"Momma have a twin, but she die," Retty said to me. "We ain't s'posed to talk about it."

"What she die of, Retty?" Brother asked.

"None of your business," Retty replied. "Finish your hamburger."

I didn't push them, but I made a mental note to ask Moses later about Rocky's twin.

Brother burped loudly, and laughed. Patsy refused to sit at the table with him any longer, so she moved to an adjoining table to eat her ice cream with her back to him.

The squabbling intensified as time wore on, and the volume increased. By the time we were headed back to Cincinnati, I would have sent them all into Time Out if I could have found a place to pull over. Better yet, I thought, I could just lock Brother in the trunk.

By now, his pinball game was broken. Between Moses and me, he'd been given a modest six dollars to spend. I'd vetoed the Uzi squirt gun he'd wanted to buy, setting off the kind of tantrum that made me willing to hand him over to the first stranger to show an interest. Nobody did. He'd eaten half the candy he'd bought, giving him a stomach-ache; the rest he'd left rolling around on the floor of the women's restroom. That same restroom sported a new notice low on the door of the third stall on the right: ELVIS WAS HEER! Retty had not been fast enough to deter this criminal activity, but she'd confiscated his orange crayon. He'd retaliated by hiding inside a rack of clothing at Sears. Then he'd sampled every perfume on the counter at Pogue's before he was returned to me by a security guard who was limping. He'd been dragged screaming to the car, insisting that he still had money in his pocket to spend. We'd had to roll the window down because of the smell, although I had to admit that the perfume cut the scent of urine from his earlier mishap.

A gusty wind blew rain in through my window. My shoulder and arm were soaked. Brother was kicking the back of my seat, and my back was sore. Patsy was crying because Brother had sat on her new hat. Retty was quiet because she was missing her mother. I had a headache of monumental proportions.

And parked in front of my house was a dark sedan with a dark figure inside.

I drove past slowly, turned the corner, and pulled into our parking lot. In my rearview mirror, I saw a man get out of the car and start toward us.

"Stay in the car," I barked at the kids.

"Lock the doors," Retty said, reaching for Brother's door. "It's Granddaddy Nash."

If only I had a gun in the glove compartment, I thought. But if I'd had a gun in the glove compartment, I would already have taken Brother out.

Should I drive to the police station? Should I turn the kids loose on him? He didn't appear to be armed, but who knew what he had under his jacket? Maybe he'd just stopped by to show me some more carpet samples.

He was calling me. I kept the window cracked.

"Hello, kids," he said when he reached the car. He bent over to look at them. "Retty. Patsy. Elvis. How you doin', boy? I know you kids remember me. Doesn't anybody have a hug for old Granddaddy Nash?"

The silence in the car was deafening. Retty stared straight ahead.

He placed one meaty paw on the open window, and I wondered if he could rip it out of the door. He sniffed, then sneezed. The perfume had apparently reached his nostrils, and I guess his senses weren't as dulled by carpet glue as I thought. Maybe the smell would knock him out.

"I brought y'all some presents," he said. "They're in the car."

Nobody moved.

He cleared his throat. "Listen, why don't you kids go on in the house so I can talk to Mrs. Caliban?"

"Why don't we all go in the house?" I said.

In the house I had a gun, a telephone, three attack cats and a beagle with an annoying bark. I ought to have had a fucking police officer, I thought, glancing up at Moses' windows, but I didn't put it past Moses to have taken his gimpy self bowling after he'd gotten out of a trip to the mall.

Retty reluctantly unlocked the door. We gathered up the packages and headed inside. I sent the kids to Kevin's to watch television.

"But just for a little while," I warned them. I was about to add that it was bedtime, but caught myself. I didn't want to confirm that they were actually staying with us, even though one look at Gordon Nash told me he probably already knew.

"Sit down, Mr. Nash," I said, figuring I'd probably just lost my first-name privileges. "What can I do for you?"

"You can tell me what in the hell you think you're doing with my grandchildren," he said belligerently. "What right do you have to interfere in my family business?"

"I took the kids to see Santa Claus," I snapped. "I didn't think I needed a goddamn federal license to do that."

"And in whose custody would you say they are at this moment?"

"Probably Walt Disney's."

"This is not a joking matter, Mrs. Caliban!" he warned me. "I thought we could work together to find my daughter. I thought we had an understanding. Come to find out, my daughter's children are living at your house!"

"They are here on a visit to Mr. Fogg," I said, restraining my temper. I didn't even correct his use of the term "daughter" to describe Rocky.

"And what right does Mr. Fogg have to keep my grandchildren from me?" he demanded.

"Goddamn it, kids are not a trophy you pass around like the America's Cup!" I exploded. "They should be with the people or person who can take the best care of them, and love them in the bargain! You want my honest opinion, you're not up to the job. You think somebody's doing a number on you, and you're all indignant about it. You don't own those kids! They're not in your custody! But if we really wanted to get to you, hell, we'd let *you* take 'em to see Santa Claus! I don't know when was the last time you spent time in a closed car with Brother, but it's not an experience I'd recommend.

"Now, if you don't mind, I want to get the kids to bed so that I can treat my bruises and swallow a little painkiller. To say that I've had a bad night is like saying the *Hindenburg* developed a leak. And you have just jumped on my last nerve!"

"I want to speak to Mr. Fogg," he said icily.

"Believe me, so do I."

"He doesn't answer his door. Where is he?"

"I don't know. When he returns, I'll give him the message."

"You haven't heard the last of this, Mrs. Caliban!" he warned.

But he spoiled his exit by stepping on a miniature race car, which was instantly transformed into a roller skate. He caught himself on the doorjamb, but he whanged his elbow on the doorknob, and probably wrenched his shoulder to boot.

I didn't lift a finger to help him.

"Watch your step," I said.

He glared at me, and stalked out.

From the front window, I watched him get into his car and drive up the street. There was nothing wrong with his taillights, as far as I could tell, and the grillwork on the front of his car didn't look familiar. But did that mean that he hadn't been the one following us on Death Hill, or only that he'd switched cars?

"I don't feel so good, Cat," Brother announced when I tucked him in later. He had his favorite stuffed animal, a worn sock monkey named George, in a headlock when I pulled the covers up.

"It's probably just the excitement of seeing Santa Claus," I told him.

Patsy piped up from a sleeping bag on the floor.

"It's probably all that candy he ate. He'll probably throw up in a little while, and then we can all get some sleep," she predicted.

Something to look forward to in a day that seemed destined never to end.

Twenty-eight

"What do measles look like?"

It seemed as if I had barely closed my eyes when Moses started pounding on my door the next morning.

Let me point out, in case you've missed it, that morning is not my best time. Even before menopause came along to liven up my nights, my brain had worked like one of those vintage generators that require a lot of cranking to get them going. And as my joints had gotten creakier, it took more persuasion to convince them that they wanted to be up and moving rather than lying in bed.

I stared at Moses stupidly.

"What do you mean, what do they look like? Haven't you ever had them?"

"Nineteen twenty-eight," he said. "Mem'ry's a little hazy."

"Didn't your kids have them?"

"Yeah, Cat, but I wasn't exactly on duty at the time, if you know what I mean."

So I pulled on my blue chenille bathrobe—the one that the cats had been attempting to unravel loop by loop—and trudged upstairs.

The patient turned fever-brightened eyes on me and swallowed with a visible effort. George the monkey was sharing his pillow.

Sure enough, as I bent forward, I could see the eruption of red spots on his cheeks and neck. I reached behind his ears and felt his glands. They felt like golf balls.

"Looks like measles to me." I sighed. "But I don't know what kind." I looked at the girls gloomily. "I don't suppose you two have had them."

"Me and Patsy had measles when we was in first grade," Retty reported.

"Do you know which kind?" I asked.

They didn't, of course, but they argued about it, all the same.

"You'd better keep Brother home and take him to the doctor, Moses," I said. "We won't keep the girls home until we hear what the doctor has to say. We'll have to talk to Barbara Hickson, too. If it's German measles, and the girls haven't had it—well, then we'll have to decide what to do."

Every parent dreads German measles. It's one of those ordeals you have to get through, like your son's first haircut or explaining menstruation to your daughters. Kids need to have German measles when they're young so that they'll be immune when they're older and more susceptible. And that's especially true for girls: a case of measles during pregnancy can cause serious birth defects in the baby. I tried to convince myself that Brother had just developed a rash from all that perfume.

"We was gonna make clay handprints in school today!" Brother protested, bottom lip protruding to better punctuate his lament. "We was gonna use gold spray paint, and I was gonna give mine to Momma for Christmas!"

"Momma got a trunkful of them handprints already," the hard-hearted Patsy observed, unmoved. "You make a new one every time we change schools."

"Not with gold paint!" he pouted. "I ain't never made one with gold paint."

The way our luck was running, of course it turned out to be German measles. And of course the girls had had the other kind. So after extensive discussion with Aunt Barbara, we all agreed it was best to go ahead and expose them. But Barbara had sounded desperate at the prospect of coping with six measles cases in the next month, and who could blame her? In the end, Moses had expressed the opinion that Rocky's children would be better off staying put for a while.

I was all for sending them over to Grandpa Nash, on the

off chance that he'd never been infected. But I held my tongue.

It was now December 6. The incubation period for rubella was two to three weeks. Need I say how much I was looking forward to Christmas?

"Al never had measles," Mel announced later that afternoon. Now that he knew he was in for the long haul, Moses was trying to make more room in his apartment. Mel was helping him carry his stationary bike and his NordicTrac down to the basement. He never used them, anyway. The stationary bike was the result of a brief period of resolution he'd passed through after last year's army reunion. The NordicTrac had been a birthday present from his younger son, and you should have seen his face when he opened the box.

"She hasn't?" I said. I was trailing them in a vaguely supervisory fashion. "Hold on, Mel. You've got one of the doojiggers caught on the railing."

"If she hasn't had it," Moses wheezed, moving gingerly on his bad leg, "she ought to get it."

"Well, it's not like I'm ever going to get pregnant," Al said that night, when we broached the subject. "Unless Mel's keeping something from me."

"Way I hear it, lesbians have biological clocks, same as everybody else," Moses observed.

"That's right, Al," I said. "For someone who moves in the circles you do, you sure have a lot of pregnant friends."

"They're right, sweetie," Mel agreed, putting an arm around her shoulder. "You want to keep your options open."

Al looked at her in surprise. "I thought you supported adoption!"

"I do, to the extent that I support parenthood at all—at least as far as we're concerned. But Moses is right about this biological clock stuff. Stranger things have happened. Look at Mary Ann: she never wanted kids, and now she moons around in her maternity jeans, crocheting booties and driving Libby crazy with pronouncements about breast milk."

"But—but—measles! At my age!" she sputtered. "It's so undignified!"

We sent her into the quarantine zone with a deck of animal rummy cards and a Chutes and Ladders game.

"Look on the bright side," Mel told her. "Maybe we can go spread it around your family on Christmas Eve. Spoil your brother's annual Super Bowl party."

Moses' lady friend Charisse, who put me in mind more of Big Nurse than Nurse Adams, had not been overjoyed to hear that Moses had turned his apartment into a pediatrics ward. In fact, she had taken a dim view of his abrupt relapse into fatherhood, but she had really pitched a fit when she heard that he'd signed on as head nurse. Not that I'd heard her, you understand. But I could read between the lines, especially with Kevin around to help me fill in the story. With a bad grace, she had brought the kids some kind of gourmet ice cream they'd never touch, and departed in a huff.

Moses' daughter Chrystal had taken a more practical view. She had sent her three kids over to get infected. This meant that around three-thirty in the afternoon on Thursday, the Catatonia Arms had turned into Sesame Street. The date had still been December 6, and by the end of the day our house had looked like the beaches at Normandy after the invasion.

"Let's play the glad game," Kevin had observed at around four o'clock. "We don't have to keep them home until the spots show up, so at least the girls can still go to school."

"Are you sure this is such a good idea, Moses?" I asked finally. "I mean, we seem to be surrounded by dark sedans driven by bad guys. I don't mind about the measles, but there's other things I don't necessarily want to expose the kids to."

"Long's we don't leave them alone in the house, Cat," he said, "I think they'll be safe. I feel better having Rocky's kids here with all of us around than over at Barbara's.

"Anyway," he continued, "Gordon Nash may be a pain in the ass, but so far he's been up front about it."

"As far as we know," I said. "And isn't it true that men who kidnap kids in custody cases usually threaten to do it beforehand? I mean, when the kids disappear, don't the police usually have an obvious suspect?"

"Yes, that's true," he conceded.

Moses had had his own shouting match with Nash on the telephone that afternoon. Moses doesn't usually shout, but his nerves had been frayed by the Walker shooting, and the outbreak of measles had done nothing to soothe them.

"But, Cat, the kind of guy that usually kidnaps kids in a custody case is somebody who doesn't have much to lose by moving around," he said. "I mean, the women who do it are usually desperate to protect the kids, and they'll leave a good job and a support system and all. The men, in my experience, tend to be either unemployed or marginally employed. They don't have many ties to the community they're living in. Gordon Nash seems to have a good job—probably a better one than he ever had before. Plus, he's got Amy. It ain't easy to move around with a teenager in tow. No, I think he's going through the courts. And to tell you the truth, if it's between him and Barbara Hickson—if Rocky doesn't come back and claim the kids and start making a home for them—he might just win."

"There's a depressing thought," I said.

"Now, Cat, you don't know that," he cautioned me. "Like I said before, just 'cause we don't like him don't mean he wouldn't be good for the kids. I know he pissed you off when he came here, and my conversation with the man wasn't exactly cordial, but if I was in his shoes, I'd probably be just as angry as he is. Rocky wasn't an easy kid to live with, and he inherited a lot of problems when he married her mother. By the looks of things, Amy ain't no cakewalk either. So we probably ought to give him credit for wanting anything to do with Rocky's kids."

"And I say it's damned suspicious that he does," I said. "I

still think it has more to do with getting at Rocky than it does any aspirations he might have to take another crack at fatherhood."

But something Moses had said reminded me of another question I'd wanted to ask him.

"Say, Moses, whatever happened to Rocky's twin?" I asked.

"Who?"

"Rocky's twin. The kids say their mother had a twin sister who died."

"I don't know anything about it, Cat," he said. "Must've happened before I knew her."

"Didn't she ever mention a sister?"

"No, not to me."

"That seem odd to you? I mean, she told you her troubles, right? Don't you think she would've mentioned a sister who'd died?"

He shrugged. "I wouldn't say she told me *all* her troubles, Cat. In fact, I'd say she was highly selective. And I didn't meet her till she was nine or ten. Sister could've died when they were babies, could be ancient history as far as she was concerned."

"Maybe so," I said. "I'd still like to ask her."

But when Rocky called that night, nobody was thinking about dead sisters.

Twenty-nine

Brother claimed the privilege of illness: he got to talk to Rocky first. While he was counting his spots for her, Moses came down to tell me she was on the phone, no doubt assuming I'd never forgive him if he didn't.

Retty and Patsy each got a turn. Their shopping trip figured prominently in their reports, but they also discussed their new school, what they were studying, who they'd made friends with, and, as a recurring theme, how eager they were to see her again. The conversation with his mother had made Brother so hyper that he bounced around Moses' living room like a pinball. He kept trying to interrupt his sisters with things he'd forgotten to say.

Finally, Retty handed the phone to Moses with tears in her eyes.

"She want to talk to you again, Moses."

"I'll take it in the bedroom, honey," he said.

I followed him and flopped down on the bed, listening.

From Moses' side of the conversation, I could tell that he wasn't having much success getting out of Rocky the information we needed: where she was, why she was in trouble, and what we could do about it.

"Rocky, do you know who killed Peter Abrams?" he asked at one point.

"What about Talia, and Arletta Sandifer? Were they mixed up in whatever trouble you're in?" he asked a few minutes later.

I looked around for a pen and paper, and settled for a stubby pencil and a bookmark he had stuck in the pages of a Western on the nightstand. I wrote him a note: *medication logs*.

"Can you tell me this?" he said at last. "Can you tell me if any of this has to do with the photocopied pages from the medication logs that you gave to Mrs. Weldon to keep?"

He hung up with a sigh.

"She says she doesn't know anything for sure," he said. "Says she doesn't have any evidence about any of the deaths, can't say if they're related. Said she didn't know what I was talking about when I asked about the medication logs. Maybe she did, maybe she didn't, Cat, I don't know. Girl always was a good liar."

He paused and rubbed his forehead the way you do when you're getting a headache.

"That's all she'd tell me. She says she has to work things out on her own. Wouldn't tell me where she is, or what she's doing for money. She sounded all right, but damn, I hope she's not dealin' or stealin'."

He sighed again. "To tell you the truth, Cat, I think she might let me help her if I didn't have her kids. She says the best thing I can do for her right now is protect the kids. She asked me to keep Nash away from them, but I pointed out that while we might be able to do that right now, in the long run she'd have to fight for them in court. She thanked me for looking after her kids, and asked me to thank my friends, too. She especially wanted me to thank you for taking the girls shopping and Brother to see Santa Claus."

The phone rang again and startled us. Moses answered it.

Brother yelped in the other room, and I went to see what was up. Patsy had socked him for trying to feed Winnie chocolate ice cream. Brother appealed to me, but I told him I probably would have socked him myself.

Retty, ever the diplomat, said, "I know it seems mean not to let Winnie have any, Brother, but it ain't that way. Winnie could get sick and die from eating chocolate. We explained that to you."

Back in the bedroom, Moses seemed to be winding up his

conversation. I flopped down on the bed again and propped up my head on my elbows.

"No, I appreciate your concern," Moses was saying. "If I find out anything, I'll let you know. Thanks for calling."

"Liar, liar, pants on fire," I said. "You never tell anybody anything."

"That was Grisham," he said. "Wanted to know if we'd found Rocky. He'd talked to Nash, knew about the kids."

"I hope you didn't tell him Rocky had called here."

He gave me an exasperated look. "I told him the truth: we don't know where she is."

"Is it unusual for a parole officer to go looking for somebody?" I asked. "I mean, I guess she's violated parole if she's not living with Nash, but is he the one who's supposed to go after her? I thought bail bondsman and cops did that sort of thing. I never thought about parole officers doing it."

"They don't usually," he said. "I get the impression, though, that beneath his hard-boiled exterior, Grisham is really a soft touch. I think he's really worried about her, Cat."

"Either that, or a good actor," I observed. "Where's it going to end, Moses?"

"I don't know, Cat," he admitted. "I don't know. Maybe you'll find out something tomorrow."

Tomorrow I was going to prison.

Thirty

Welcome to Marysburg—where the grass is greener!

I had awakened at the ungodly hour of seven, and watched the sun rise over I-71. It was competing with some dark clouds that had gathered in the west. In Columbus, I found my way to Hazel Connors's house, and she was driving us to Marysburg, a small town about twenty miles northwest, home of the Women's Correctional Institution. I wondered which Mary the town was named for—the penitent prostitute or the virginal intercessor. The town motto was derived from one of its resident industries, a major lawn care corporation. Its implications for the women living inside WCI chilled me to the bone.

We turned up a street in what looked to be a mixed residential and commercial neighborhood. Then the view opened up on our left, and we were looking across an open field at an imposing set of buildings set back from the road like a medieval castle. We turned into a long drive.

"That's it?" I asked in surprise.

"That's it," Hazel Connors said.

"It doesn't look like I expected," I said. "If it weren't for the razor wire at the top of the fence—"

"I know. It would look almost like a college campus."

The buildings looked old but venerable. They were surrounded by walkways and open space, and because our weather had been relatively mild so far, the grass was still green. From a distance, the scattered spots of color moving about could have been college coeds on their way to class.

"I met a criminologist once who said that the architecture of women's prisons reflects society's patronizing attitude toward women," Hazel observed. "Men's prisons look like they house dangerous criminals—psychopaths and sociopaths. Women's prisons look like they house bad little girls. Here, they live in cell blocks called 'cottages.' It sounds really rustic and charming, but believe me, you wouldn't want to live there."

I realized then why she seemed different to me today. She wasn't wearing any jingle bells. That made her quieter, but the quiet ran deeper than that.

The atmosphere changed as soon as we walked into the reception area. The contents of my purse and Hazel's briefcase were examined, and we passed through a metal detector. On the other side, we stood around for ten minutes, waiting for an escort. Nobody, I soon realized, seemed to be in a hurry to do anything around here. Time was different on the inside.

We passed several pairs of prisoners and guards, or COs. Hazel spoke to everyone, sometimes calling them by name. The prisoners wore solid colored shirts in a limited range of colors and dark slacks. The COs wore gray.

"The color an inmate wears reflects her security level, and her status," Hazel explained. "Ohio only has one women's prison, so they have all security levels here. That makes it harder on the women, because the prison is forced to apply the standards it would apply to maximum security prisoners, even though most of the women aren't maximum security. So things are pretty strict."

We entered a building built around a large rectangular courtyard. The hallway looked institutionally dingy, but the courtyard seemed pleasant enough. I wondered if anyone was allowed to sit in it without an escort. Perhaps they were only allowed to sit on one of the hall benches and contemplate it through the window.

We ended up in a large room that reminded me of my kids' grade school. It could have been a choir room or a band room, with its motley collection of folding metal chairs, dilapidated window shades, and curtains crusted with dust. Some of the chairs had been formed into a big circle, and several of these were already occupied. Three women sat talking together on one side of the circle, another woman sat alone on the other side, bent over, head in her hands.

The session was supposed to start at ten, but it was ten now, and women continued to trickle in for fifteen minutes. Most appeared to be in their twenties, but a significant majority were probably teenagers. Most were black. Apart from the uniforms, they didn't look at first glance very different from any collection of young women on the outside, except that they moved with a curious lack of purpose, as if they had happened onto this room at this particular moment and might as well stay until something moved them elsewhere.

Hazel was deep in conversation with two women who were speaking in low voices. She was frowning and nodding.

"You come with Miz Connors?" somebody asked me. It was a friendly inquiry.

"Yeah, that's right," I answered. "I'd like to sit in today, if it's okay."

She shrugged. "Okay with me."

Another women came and propped her arms on the first woman's shoulders.

"Miz Tunney ain't comin' today?"

"Not today," I said.

"You know Miz Tunney?" the first one asked.

"I just met her," I said.

"She's a good lady," the second one told me. "We love her to death. Miz Connors, too."

I didn't know what to expect when the meeting started. I knew this was some kind of support group—normally something I avoid like the plague. I soon discovered that it wouldn't have done me any good to expect anything.

"Where's Tracy?" Hazel asked. "Does anybody know?"

"She in the hole again for fightin'," somebody said.

"What about Dessa?"

"She didn't get a pass," somebody said. "She asked me to ask you to be sure she's on your list."

I was introduced as a guest who "might want to talk to some of you later."

"C.J.?"

"She in the infirmary again." A look passed around the circle. "She startin' to get them spots on her face, Miz Connors, like they do when they get sick. I think we better pray for her."

Hazel nodded gravely.

"Let's talk about your week," Hazel began. "Anybody have a particular crisis this week they want to talk about?"

There was a moment of silence. Then a woman spoke up.

"Jane have her one-year anniversary," she said, and seized the hand of the tall thin woman sitting next to her.

"Want to talk about it, Jane?" Hazel asked kindly.

"It was Thursday," Jane said softly. "December the sixth. I been here one year and one day. I felt so bad. I thought, how I'm gonna get through this day? I got four years to go—five years for bustin' checks, second offense."

Her eyes were dry, but her voice was thick with despair. "First time I come here, I say, never again. But my boyfriend, he lost his job. Got car payments. Plus he owe his pusher. He say, 'Come on, baby! It's a piece of cake! You ain't gonna get caught again, you too smart for that.'" Her laugh was brittle. "Smart. Yeah, I'm so smart I caught five to fifteen. And he ain't never even come to see me."

"I'm sorry to hear that," Hazel said.

"I didn't want to come today, Miz Connors," Jane confessed. "Seem like I don't want to do nothin', jus' lie in the bed. But the Lord guided my steps here today."

"The Lord gon' help you, girl, you know He will," said another young woman. Heads nodded agreement around the circle. "And Jesus will visit you any time you want, 'f you jus' open your heart and let Him in."

"Aw, can that Jesus crap, Selena." A white woman with stringy blond hair spoke up. "If what she wants is her boyfriend, Jesus ain't gonna do the trick."

Selena started to say something, but the new speaker turned to Jane and stepped on Selena's line.

"I know just how you feel, girl," she said. "I got fucked over by a sweet-talking bastard—you know the kind I mean?"

Now there was an audible murmur of assent.

"His place was too hot, he said. He had a nosy landlady, he said. My place was real close, he said. And all the time he's sayin' it, he's slidin' his hand up my thigh, you know? I didn't want that crap in my house! What did I want that shit for? I got two kids, I didn't want that shit around them! But one minute he's sweet-talkin' me in bed, and the next minute I'm busted, and my kids is in foster care! And don't you know that bastard had another bitch in his bed by the time I got sentenced?" Her voice dropped. "Sometimes, I think it's just as well I'm in here, 'cause if I was out there, I'd shoot the bastard, sure as I'm alive!"

"You shouldn't say that," someone corrected her gently, but it sounded a little perfunctory. Most of the women looked like they'd help her load the gun.

"My little brother had surgery this week," someone said, "so I'd appreciate it if everybody could pray for him." She glanced at the last speaker. "Or—whatever. I just about raised him, on account of my momma died when he was four years old." She sighed. "I miss him so bad sometimes. And now he's got something wrong with his heart. I wanted a release, but they said he wasn't dying—I could only go home if he died." She swallowed. "I guess he's doing okay, but sometimes I think I shouldn't ever have requested that pass. I mean, what if I—you know—jinxed him or something?"

"Oh, I don't think you did, Trina," Hazel said. "I'm sure he'll be fine. But I think we can all send him our thoughts."

"Dorrie didn't come today, Miz Connors," someone else said. "She too depressed. Her kids been put up for adoption."

"Maybe she ought to be thankful," another said. "Maybe they'll go someplace nice, get them some good parents. My kids—" Here her voice started to tremble, but I couldn't tell at first that the emotion in it wasn't suppressed sadness, but suppressed rage. "My kids is with the same bastard who used to play games with me in the bedroom while my aunt and my momma was workin' night shift at the GE plant."

"Didn't you talk to your lawyer about challenging the custody?" Hazel asked. "I thought we discussed that."

"I talked to him," she said bitterly. "He say, one thing at a time. What I can't get him to see is that there ain't no time. In two months, my daughter will be seven years old. That's when my uncle started in with me." She pushed back her hair with both hands. "Maybe he already started on her. How will I know? He won't bring the kids to see me."

Hazel was writing on a small pad of paper. "I'll call Hamilton County Children's Services again," she said. "Maybe they can at least put him on notice by visiting the house."

"I ain't never told y'all this," another woman said, her Southern accent thick as syrup, "but my kids was with me when I was arrested. I'd been shootin' some Ts and Blues, and then I went to the store to boost me some cigarettes and some aspirin for the baby, 'cause he was sick. And then — I seen this book of paper dolls. It was ladies from different times in history, and all the costumes was so beautiful. And I thought, 'Annie would just love them paper dolls!' I know it was the paper dolls that gave me away. I jus' stood and stared at 'em so long, you know? And then the Security come after me, and the cops come, and I tried to tell 'em about the kids in the car, but they didn't never go lookin' for 'em. It wasn't till I finally got hold of my sister three hours later, and then she went down there and found 'em scared to death. I ain't never been so ashamed!" She swiped at her eyes with one arm, dragging her sleeve across her face. "I'll never make it up to them. My oldest boy still won't speak to me."

"Sometimes," a woman said in a voice barely above a whisper, "when you wake up in the morning, you can't hardly believe you made it through another day. Every-body's makin' noise, they's fightin' in the showers, the guards is in your face about some new rule they just thought up or about to think up, it's cold as a witch's tit 'cept where the steam is turned up so high you burnin' like a sinner in hell. Your boyfriend don't write, your girlfriend in the hole, and you just been turned down for parole again. If you lucky and your lawyer show up, you can go talk to him, long's you willin' to have Becker or Saint Rheba stick they hand up your ass when you come out. And he ain't got no good news for you anyway, so he probably ain't comin'. And they got your medication screwed up so you seein' double and pukin' your guts out, only thing you ain't doin' is gettin' better."

She paused to take a breath. "And then you get a letter from your kids askin' when you comin' home." Tears began to slip down her cheeks, and she rolled her bottom lip under her top one.

"You'll get through this, Opal, with the Lord's help," someone said.

"I know He's helpin' me," Opal said. "I know He is. But some days—some days, it's pretty hard to see."

The door opened, and a stocky man in a gray uniform sauntered in, wearing a bored expression.

"I need McKinney, Smith, and Lingenfelter," he said.

Three women, including the last speaker, got up.

"I'll see you next week, ladies," Hazel said.

They nodded dispiritedly. Next week was a long way off.

"Yeah," one said. "Thanks for coming, Miz Connors. You, too, Miz Caliban."

They followed the guard out. None of them appeared to be annoyed by the interruption. None of them appeared upset. They appeared resigned.

I glanced at Hazel Connors, but she had moved on. Was I right about what had just happened? From Rocky's letters, I'd identified two of the three women who had just left as members of Rocky's prison "family." Had somebody just deliberately taken them out of my reach?

Thirty-one

"Mrs. Caliban would like to talk to you about Rocky Zacharias, whom most of you know," Hazel Connors said at last. "She believes that Rocky is in trouble, and she's trying to find Rocky in order to help her. Several people who were close to Rocky have died." Her intense gaze slowly swept the circle of faces. "Now, I'm not asking you to violate any confidences that you don't feel you can violate. Nor am I asking you to put yourself in danger. I just want you to listen to what Mrs. Caliban has to say, and if you feel you can help her, let her know."

I told them the story of Rocky's phone call to Moses. I didn't want to misrepresent myself: I was working with an ex-cop. I told them as much of the rest as I thought they needed to hear, including my concerns about Talia's and Arletta's deaths. I told them that Rocky's kids were staying with us now, and that she probably didn't want us to draw any heat.

"Does anybody here know what kind of trouble Rocky is in?" I began.

"Rocky always in some kind of trouble," someone said at last. "That the way she is."

"Yeah," another woman agreed. "Trouble follow Rocky like her shadow."

"This would be something bigger than usual," I prompted them.

Some women stared at their laps, or their shoes. Some just stared at me, brows furrowed.

"What can you tell me about Arletta's death?" In for a penny, in for a pound, I thought. If Arletta hadn't died entirely on her own, then I was asking them to rat either on a fellow inmate, or on the guards and administration. Both paths were dangerous.

"Arletta have the sugar diabetes," a woman explained to me. She was sitting on her hands, as if to restrain them. "When you got the sugar diabetes, your medication have to be just right, 'cause you changin' all the time, see? I know 'cause my aunt have it."

"Arletta used to have these attacks all the time," another woman contributed. "She'd get dizzy and have to eat something. But she always worried about the nighttime— about what would happen if she got an attack in the middle of the night. They wouldn't let her keep food in her room."

"Kep' writin' her up for it," another woman said. "You think if someone was sick like that, needin' food to keep from passin' out, maybe dyin', they let her have a damn apple to take to her room at night!"

This observation was greeted with a chorus of appreciative grunts, uh-huhs, and shakes of the head.

"She always know how it was gonna end," the first woman said. "She use to say, 'Lord Jesus, jus' let me out of here before I die.' But she didn't make it."

"That's the way it goes in here, Miz Caliban," someone summarized.

I nodded.

"Talia Hickson was killed shortly after her release," I said. "Anybody know anything about that?"

Somebody grunted. "Prob'ly that crazy motherfucker she run with. Walker. I use to know that motherfucker, see? And he was always crazy! Even before he was on the needle, he was out his mind! You ask your friend the cop to lock that motherfucker up and throw away the key, you hear what I'm sayin'?"

I cleared my throat and shifted uncomfortably on the hard metal chair. "Actually, Walker's dead," I said. "My friend the cop shot him when he was about to throw one of Rocky's kids out of a third-story window."

"No shit?" Her small thin face split in a grin that exposed a gleaming gold tooth. "Well, you give your friend a big ol' kiss from me! Tell him Cassie sent it!"

Since nobody was offering any alternative theories about Talia's death, I moved on.

"I'm interested in two dates," I said slowly. I had given a lot of thought about how to frame this next question, and I'd decided that I'd been focusing too narrowly on medication. "The first is June eighth, and the second is June twenty-first."

"June twenty-first is my baby's birthday," a heavy woman said in a high-pitched, breathy voice.

"Girl, she don't care about that!" someone scolded her in exasperation. "She ain't axin' 'bout your baby, she axin' 'bout what happen here!"

"It was hot in June, I 'member," someone else put in. "Real hot. Didn't seem like it was no air in here, like they put a lid on the whole place and stuck it in an oven."

"That's right. It was like that for weeks," another woman confirmed.

"And everything was worse 'cause of what happened with Frankie and Joan," Cassie said. "When that happen? Anybody remember?"

"It was the eighth," a soft voice spoke of. "The ninth is my birthday. That's how come I remember."

"What happened between Frankie and Joan?" My little Cat whiskers were standing on end.

"They had a fight," the woman named Trina responded. "Frankie threw Joan down the stairs, and killed her."

In the silence that followed, I felt as if I'd just closed a circuit. A subtle current was running through the circle of women.

"That's what they say," Cassie said finally.

"And you don't believe it," I said.

Cassie shrugged.

"They was only one witness," the Southern accent reported. "She don't b'lieve the witness."

"Who was the witness?"

"A CO we call Wiseass," Trina said. "W-i-ise-a-a-ss." She drew it out and finished in a hiss. I felt my eyebrows hop. "I don't know his real name."

"Don't nobody ever use it," Cassie said. "Can't pronounce it. One of them Polack names, got a zee in it."

"That's okay," I said. "I think I know what it is."

I hadn't been thinking straight. I'd thought maybe I was looking for an ex-con who'd been inside with Rocky and Talia, and then got out. But what I was really looking for was someone who could operate both inside and out. I'd just found him.

Thirty-two

Here's what had happened, according to Hazel Connors. A male guard, the one the women called "Wiseass," had been bringing a woman named Frankie Williams back from a trip to the clinic for medication. He had taken her to her building, climbed the stairs to the third floor, and stepped into the hallway. Joan Small had been standing in the doorway to the bathroom when they passed, and had made a remark under her breath to Frankie. The guard claimed not to have heard what was said—some sexual innuendo, he thought. Frankie wheeled around and punched Joan in the stomach. Joan slumped over. Before he could react, Frankie picked Joan up and slammed her against the fire door leading to the stairwell so hard that she knocked it open and lay sprawled on the landing. Frankie sprang at her, picked her up again, and pitched her down the stairs. Joan Small died instantly of a broken neck.

Nobody saw what had happened except Wiseass.

"Technically, he shouldn't have been on the third floor in the living area," Hazel remarked.

She and I were sitting in a McDonald's on the outskirts of Marysburg, drinking coffee. I had lost my appetite inside the high fence and razor wire. I had just spent more than an hour listening to anguished women pour out their souls. The experience was more grueling than anything prime-time television had to offer. I realized that it took these women more courage to get through the day than I was ever likely to have to muster in my lifetime. And at the end, they thanked me for listening, and promised to pray for me.

"The cottages are supposed to be off limits to male guards.

I guess they used to be allowed to go anywhere, but a few years ago, the rules changed. If he thought Frankie really needed an escort all the way back to her room, he should have called a female guard. But sometimes the rules get bent." Hazel tossed her head in that habitual way she had.

"When exactly did this happen?"

"It was June eighth, like they said. It was a Saturday morning."

"Did you know Frankie Williams?" I asked. "Do you think she could have done it?"

"I didn't know her well," Hazel confessed. "She had asked to join the Saturday morning support group, so I'd put her name on the list. That was maybe two weeks before all this happened. But she hadn't shown up yet. I didn't know Joan Small either. But Frankie was notoriously volatile. She had these incredible mood swings, apparently, and the medication didn't really keep them under control. She'd been in the mental health ward at some point, but then she was moved to general population. Nobody knows why. But then, nobody seems to know why anything is done the way it is there at the farm."

"The farm?"

"Oh, that's what the women call the prison. Anyway, if the CO was lying, we'll probably never know what really happened."

"You don't think Frankie will testify?"

"She can't." Hazel looked down at her coffee cup. "She killed herself in solitary not too long after it happened."

I pushed my own cup away, propped my chin on my fists, and thought.

"What do you know about the CO?" I asked.

"Only what the women call him—Wiseass," she replied. "I know they don't like him much. I gather that he's one of the ones who relishes his authority. I suspect that he has sexual relations with some of the inmates—mostly from comments made in passing, you know. Natalie might know more. Sometimes the women tell her things they won't tell me."

"By sexual relations, do you mean rape?"

"No," she said, frowning. "I really don't think there's much of that at WCI, if any. Technically, you'd have to call them consensual relations, but there's usually a payback— phone privileges or cigarettes or something. In my book, the women are still being victimized by someone in a position of power. They don't have anything to bargain with except their bodies."

I nodded. "How did Frankie kill herself?" I asked.

"She had a piece of broken glass. I don't know where she found it. She used it to cut her wrists, and then—this is really awful, Cat." She swallowed and looked away. The McDonald's Playland was empty in the cold, bright light. "She immersed her wrists in the toilet bowl to make the blood flow."

We didn't speak for a minute. Then, I decided to change the subject.

"Why did the CO call those women out of the meeting? What was that all about?"

"Oh, who knows?" she said in exasperation. She flicked her hair out of her eyes. She was digging around in her purse. "Maybe they had a phone call, or maybe they had to go for medication, or maybe they were in trouble."

"But the group seems pretty important to the women," I observed. "And if they attend every Saturday morning, why can't that hour be reserved for the group meeting? I mean, it doesn't seem like a logical time to schedule them for medication, does it?"

"Of course not!" she said, dabbing at her eyes with a handkerchief. "That's probably why they do it! But no, that's unfair. It gives them too much credit for being able to think things through. Cat, the fundamental principle of life on the inside is chaos. Don't be fooled by all the uniforms and passes and escorts and checkpoints. Or even the rules. The rules change so fast that you can be written up for breaking a rule before you even know the rule exists! Not all the crazy people inside are behind bars." She blew her nose.

"But, Hazel, I think two of the women who left, Opal Smith and Precious McKinney, were members of Rocky's family. Isn't that so?"

"I don't know, Cat," she confessed. "I don't know who's in whose family."

"But if they were, isn't it possible that somebody got them out of there before I had a chance to talk to them?"

She dropped her handkerchief into her purse, snapped it shut, and pondered my question. "It's possible, I suppose," she said slowly. "But really, Cat, I do think that implies too much planning and organization on somebody's part. And, like I say, it's unusual for someone to be pulled out of a group session. It's damned aggravating, especially given the emotional content of the sessions. But it's not unusual."

"How can I get in to talk to those women?" I asked. "Do I have to wait until next Saturday?"

She sighed. "Even then, they might not show up. Let me see what I can do. The problem is that the phones aren't really secure, you know. Not secure enough for what we want to discuss. It almost has to be face-to-face. You may have to wait, though. They could request a special visiting pass for you, but they only get one of those every three months. Would you be willing to go back next Saturday?"

"Sure," I said. "I guess. It'll probably take me all week to recover from what I heard today."

She nodded. "It's pretty intense. They have so many problems, and their problems aren't easy ones to solve." She smiled, and added, half apologetically, "I don't usually cry, Cat. The thing is, if you really thought about it all, and started crying, you might never stop."

"I couldn't believe the woman's story about how her kids were in the custody of the uncle who used to molest her when she was a kid."

"That's more common than you might think, Cat," she said, sounding tired. "After all, these women don't have a lot of options. They don't trust the foster care system, and some of them have good reason. Besides, if their kids stay in foster care too long, they run the risk of losing them to adoption."

"But handing the kid over to a sexual molester!"

"A lot of these women have been sexually abused, Cat," she said quietly. "A lot of them have been physically abused, too, but a lot of them have been sexually abused as kids." She paused.

"When I started working at WCI, I was pretty naive. The first time a woman told me a story about how her father used to take her to work with him so that he could play games with her in a storage room, I was shocked. Then came the second story, about the older cousin who used to baby-sit. Then the one about the neighbor who offered free piano lessons. And on and on." She gazed at me intently. "And I haven't heard all their stories. Not all of them will talk about it. The figures you see on official surveys of incarcerated women are bad enough, but the reality is much worse."

"Are you suggesting that the sexual abuse has something to do with the incarceration?" I asked.

"I'm not a psychologist or a psychiatrist," she said. "What I see is women who have lost control of their lives. I don't mean that they've had a bad day or a bad week or a bad year. I mean that they feel fundamentally out of control. I think someone took it away from them somewhere along the line. That's why boyfriends and husbands and male family members figure so prominently in stories about how they got into trouble. They spend their lives waiting for a man to come along and tell them what to do."

"But Rocky's not like that, from what I've heard," I said. "Everybody describes her as tough, defiant. And her cousin Talia was the same way, wasn't she?"

"But remember, Cat, both Rocky and Talia got mixed up with this guy Walker," she said. "Talia may have been killed by him. Sometimes women like Rocky and Talia develop a tough, hard persona to cover up their vulnerability. They're the kind of women—well, let me put it this way. On the one hand, you can't imagine a man being attracted to them, because they're so 'unfeminine.' On the other hand, you can't imagine how they could be attracted to the men they choose—domineering, even brutal, types like Walker."

I mulled this over. It made a certain kind of sense.

"But if these women are all looking for someone to tell them what to do, then they ought to be comfortable in prison," I ventured. "They ought to love the place."

"Some women do feel more comfortable in prison than out," she responded. "But most of them hate it. Just because they're used to being bullied, doesn't mean they enjoy it. They're not full-blown masochists. See, Cat, just because you feel incapable of making any decisions for yourself doesn't mean you like the decisions other people are making for you."

"In that case," I concluded, "prison is the worst place for them, because nobody is forcing them to make their own decisions."

"Bingo!" She flashed me a dazzling smile. "What most of them need is drug treatment and psychological counseling—counseling that can help them deal with their past experiences, and with a whole range of dependency issues. Counseling that can build their sense of self-worth and their self-confidence. Without that, the world is a minefield, and they're going to keep stumbling into the same mines, over and over. And most of them have kids, so every time they stumble, they get separated from their kids, and everybody suffers." She wadded up her coffee cup. "But that kind of large-scale counseling is a lot harder—though not necessarily more expensive—than warehousing them."

"Let me make sure I understand you. You're suggesting that women prisoners are fundamentally different from men prisoners."

"I don't have any experience with incarcerated men, Cat," she protested, "so I can only speculate. But statistically, women are more likely to be incarcerated for a first offense, far less likely to be violent or have a record of violent crime, and are more likely to be on drugs when they're arrested. What does that tell you?"

"That maybe we're taking the wrong approach to women criminals."

I glanced around the room. Micky D's has never been my favorite restaurant. But I was sitting here, in a place I chose to be, with a purse full of money and what, under some circumstances, would be considered "personal items," wearing the clothes I'd chosen to wear, having a conversation with a person I wanted to talk to. If I wanted, I could even lean across the table and kiss her without anyone objecting. I felt overwhelmed by my privileges.

Thirty-three

I had planned to drive back to Cincinnati in the afternoon, but instead I asked Hazel if I could use her phone to make a few calls.

First, I called the prison. I wanted to check my theory about a Polish name with a z in it, nickname "Wiseass."

"Is Officer Wyszanski working today?"

"Wyszanski? Not today," said the woman's voice on the other end of the line.

So Officer Wyszanski of the Cincinnati PD had a relative who was a prison guard. Curiouser and curiouser.

"Hmm. Well, I have some catalogs he wanted to see. Maybe I should run them by his house. Do you know his address?"

"We're not allowed to give out home addresses, ma'am," the voice replied in a monotone, as if accustomed to answering the question. "Phone numbers either."

"I see," I said. "Well, I only met him the one time, there at the prison. Can you tell me his first name? Maybe I can get his number from information."

"Len." To my surprise, the voice responded promptly.

I thanked her and hung up. Did she have it in for Wyszanski? I wondered. Did she secretly hope that I was planning to deliver a letter bomb to his house?

But I soon learned why she had been willing to give me his first name. His number, according to the 513 operator, was unlisted. I supposed, in retrospect, that this practice might be common among prison guards.

I called Moses.

"How's tricks?" I asked.

"Ask me a serious question," he mumbled.

"Okay," I said. "I want a home address for a Len or Leonard Wyszanski, who is a corrections officer at the Women's Correctional Institution. Can you get it for me?"

"Wyszanski? That's the cop's name."

"Right," I said. "I think this guy must be related. You told me once that law enforcement runs in families. And don't some cops start out as corrections officers before they go to the police academy? So how about it, Moses? Maybe you can check his vehicle registration or something. It would be nice to know his tag numbers, so I can check the car."

"Cat," he said grumpily, "if you mean what I think you mean, as in can I run this check right now, the answer is no. I just got the girls out of the house, and Brother is downstairs seein' the dog movie again, and my plan is to sit back in my recliner with a six-pack and watch Ohio State cream Michigan. Now, that is my plan."

"Moses," I said sweetly. "Right now happens to be the time when I am probably a twenty-minute drive away from Wyszanski's house. Which makes it the perfect time to find out where he lives. Come on! You've got friends who can dial it up on a computer in no time."

"You don't dial a computer, Cat."

"Whatever."

"Anyway, what you goin' to do at this guy's house? Try to sell him Avon?"

"Maybe I'll be the Welcome Wagon lady."

"Cat, if this the dude been watchin' the house, he already knows what you look like," Moses pointed out irritably.

"Okay, then I'm going to find out what *he* looks like, to level the playing field."

He sighed. "You think this guard's a killer?"

"I think he might be. There was a suspicious death at WCI back in June, and Wyszanski was the only witness— supposedly. I think he might be eliminating other people who know something about what happened."

"All right," he grumbled. "But you got to promise me that

all you're goin' to do is look, and you're not goin' to get close. Give me the number where you're at."

I gave it to him.

"Where are the girls?" I asked.

"*Nutcracker,*" he mumbled.

"Oh, that's right. Did Charisse take them?"

"You know Kevin took 'em and don't start in on Charisse, or I'll hang up and unplug the phone!"

"Moses, have you got something in your mouth?"

"Yes, Cat, I got a thumb in my mouth, on account of that's where I put it after Brother slammed it in the kitchen drawer, and it started bleedin'. He said he was sorry, though, and he kissed it."

"Oh, goody! Now we can find out if you've really had German measles."

It took him about twenty minutes to call back, and I could hear the game in the background. He gave me an address in Ostrander.

The ranch style house had pale green aluminum siding, and a satellite dish in the backyard that loomed over it like King Kong. The landscaping was strictly low maintenance—a stolid line of unclipped yew bushes along the front under the picture window, and some forsythia along the side. There was a bicycle leaning against a wrought-iron support on the front porch. The front curtains were closed, and I wondered if Wyszanski, like the rest of the population of central Ohio, was planted in front of the tube, watching the Scarlet and Gray.

I trained a pair of binoculars on the front of the house where I was parked, two houses down, but they didn't reveal anything more exciting than a pile of shoes, a bag of salt, and a snow shovel near the front door. Either the Wyszanskis were the kind of well-organized people who liked to plan ahead, or they were the careless kind who left the shovel there all summer because they couldn't be bothered putting it away. I wished Moses were there to discuss the matter.

Now, you can scoff at this kind of psychological profiling, and you can dismiss it as frivolous. But maybe you've never been stuck sitting on your butt in a car on a cold day in December, with nothing to do except twiddle your thumbs. The most I could hope for was probably a beer run at halftime. So I passed the time pretending I was Sherlock Holmes and studying the house for clues to the people inside it. A yard sign would have made my day.

At 2:18, the front door opened. A woman dressed in gray sweatpants and a red sweatshirt, stepped out on the porch and removed the mail from the mailbox. I didn't get a good look at her sweatshirt, but the colors were encouraging.

The afternoon wore on. There were no houses on the other side of the street, just an open field and what looked like a warehouse off in the distance. The street was narrow, a blacktopped lane marred by potholes. There were a few other cars parked along the street, but not many. If Ohio State hadn't been on TV, I would've stuck out like a stripper at a revival meeting.

At 3:28, the garage door went up. A dark blue Buick pulled out of the driveway, with the woman behind the wheel. I felt a shock of recognition as it swung around to face me: the last time I'd seen that grillwork, it had been framed in my rearview mirror. I slumped down as she passed—a nondescript woman with permed and frosted hair, and seemingly nothing on her mind.

There was no point in following her; she wasn't the one I was after. But I'd just learned that Wyszanski was the kind of guy who'd send his wife for beer at halftime while he stayed home to watch the halftime show. Big surprise. She was back in ten minutes, but she left the car out. I took that as a hopeful sign.

In the late afternoon, I watched a line of clouds advancing from the west. The sun disappeared, and I shivered inside my jacket. I was glad I hadn't drunk much of my coffee at McDonald's, but my appetite was returning. I wondered if it was kosher on a stakeout to borrow a neighbor's phone and

order a pizza delivered to your car. A rangy brown dog came
trotting down the street, sniffed at my front tire, and marked
it.

My muscles ached. My daughter Franny was into meditation, and it occurred to me that this might be a useful skill to
have in my repertoire, especially for these grueling stakeouts
when an out-of-body experience would be welcome.

At 6:30, the door opened again, and the woman appeared.
Behind her was a stocky man with blond hair cut close as
grass on a putting green. As he fumbled with the car keys,
I trained my binoculars on him. Close-set eyes, thin lips, a
cleft chin. Hands not as beefy as Gordon Nash's, but big
enough to give him trouble with small objects like car keys.

I slumped down under the wheel just before his headlights raked my car. When I heard him pass, I straightened
up.

One taillight winked at me in the rearview mirror.

Thirty-four

The clouds I had watched all afternoon unloaded on me just south of Columbus. The temperature had also plummeted in the last hour, and the wind had picked up. I had to stop for gas at Washington Courthouse, and my hand nearly froze to the nozzle. There's never a hot flash around when you need one.

At home, I walked in on an argument between Retty and Patsy over which rock station to listen to on the radio, and I'd heard both sides before the snow melted off my jacket. I left tracks on the linoleum like the Wicked Witch of the West on her deathbed.

Moses put the kids to bed finally, and then stood outside the bathroom door, lobbying me to come out and tell him what had happened at WCI and afterward. I added more hot water to the tub, drained my second gin and tonic, and set the glass carefully on the floor, between numbers one and three. I sank down into the bubbles. It would do him good to wait.

Shortly thereafter, a small black paw appeared under the door. Moses had sent Sidney to lobby in his behalf.

"You snooze, you lose, Sid," I told him, stirring my third G&T with my index finger. "I'm not coming out till I'm good and ready."

An hour later, I sat in Moses' living room with my notes in my hand and the photocopied logs spread out on the coffee table.

"I think I was looking at these the wrong way around before, Moses," I told him. "I was looking to see whose name appeared on this list. I think I should've been looking to see whose name didn't."

"And who would that be?" he asked.

"Frankie Williams," I said. "I think she's supposed to be on permanent medication of some kind. Wyszanski was supposed to have been bringing her back from the clinic on June eighth when she killed Joan Small. I think this page"—I tapped the sheet on the left—"shows that she wasn't at the clinic just before the murder took place."

"What time did it happen?" He picked the sheet up, raised his bifocals with his other hand, and squinted at the record up close.

"I don't know exactly," I confessed. "I just know it was morning. Frankie had signed up to attend the Saturday morning support group, but she hadn't attended yet. Maybe that plays some part in this; I don't know."

He shook his head. "It doesn't seem like the kind of lie you could pass off that easily, Cat. There are too many witnesses involved—the nurse that hands out the medication, the other women standing in line, the guards."

"I know, Moses, it sounds pretty far-fetched," I said. "But Hazel says things are pretty chaotic there. And Frankie probably went every day, maybe even several times a day. People might not remember if they missed seeing her once. As disorganized as things are, she probably doesn't even stand in line with the same people every time. And a CO's story carries a lot of weight—a lot more weight than the word of an incarcerated woman who's standing in line for tranquilizers or antidepressants or methadone."

"What about these other pages?"

"I'd have to confirm the date of Frankie's suicide; Hazel didn't know. But I think Frankie didn't get her medication the night she killed herself. That's criminal negligence at least, but it might be something more calculated."

"Cat, I don't think I'm ready to follow you out on that limb," he said. "You sayin' Wyszanski withheld her medication in the hope that she'd commit suicide? Like, he didn't show up to escort her when he was supposed to, and nobody noticed?"

"It's just a theory," I said defensively. "He might have done it more than once, just to unbalance her."

He pressed his lips together, and kept on shaking his head. "So he's on escort duty one Saturday morning in June, and two weeks later, he's on the night shift?"

"Well, he doesn't work Saturdays now," I pointed out. "Maybe he changes shifts."

"Even so." He laid the page down. "You got a motive for the killing of Joan Small?"

"No," I admitted. "But how important is that? It could have been an accident. Maybe she slipped on the stairs and fell when he was with her, and he was afraid of losing his job."

"So he didn't murder Small, but he goin' around murderin' everybody else?"

"Okay, okay, maybe not. So maybe she mouthed off, and he just lost his temper and lost control."

"Doubtful, Cat," he said, inspecting his bandaged thumb. "I guess we could find out how long he'd worked there, and whether there's any other 'incidents' in his file, but guards who can't take the heat usually wash out pretty fast. You got to be able to put up with a lot of bullshit to be a CO."

"The point is that he was the only witness," I said patiently. "So if Frankie didn't kill Small, then he becomes the prime suspect."

"Prime, maybe," Moses conceded. "But he could also be covering for somebody."

"Well, could you at least talk to this Officer Bunke? The guy who's supposed to be investigating Peter Abrams's murder? They could probably run lab tests on Wyszanski's car, couldn't they? I mean, I guess you'll have to be careful, if this other Wyszanski—what's his first name, do you know?"

"George."

"If George Wyszanski really does work with Bunke, then

I guess you have to be careful about fingering Leonard Wyszanski, who's probably his brother or cousin or uncle or something."

Moses sighed.

"I could *talk* to Bunke, Cat—"

"But what?"

"I don't see that we've got anything to give him that he'll take seriously." Moses leaned back, propped his feet on the coffee table, and gestured at the papers I'd laid out. "I mean, you got to have a lot of imagination to move from a name that doesn't appear on a couple of pages of a medication log to—what are we talking about here? Quadruple, quintuple homicide? Committed by a relative, possibly a near relative, of another homicide cop? Where's the evidence for probable cause? You can't just go around confiscating folks' cars. You need a search warrant. And no judge is going to issue a search warrant based on what we got. Ain't like you can have a lineup of cars, have 'em all drive around in the dark so the eyewitnesses can take a look at their taillights. Even if you could, you'd have to run a lineup of cars with faulty taillights to make the lineup legitimate, and even then I guarantee you that the eyewitnesses wouldn't agree."

"But I saw the car, too," I protested. "It tailed me. You saw it parked up the street."

"You saw a car with a bad taillight, on a rainy night, with three squabbling kids in the car," he said. "You thought it was tailing you. I saw a car parked up the street, and I saw it drive past. It also had a bad taillight. But, Cat, I hate to break it to you, baby, but the world is full of cars with bad taillights. It takes more imagination to assume that the cars we saw were the same, and that the driver was lurking with malicious intent than it does to assume that we got bad taillights on the brain, and so we happened to spot two of them in our general vicinity."

"But you don't believe it was a coincidence?"

"My beliefs don't constitute probable cause," he pointed out. "Look, if it's any consolation to you, the killer's car could be clean. The lab might not find anything. It was November. If Abrams was wearing a topcoat, there might not even be any blood on the car. You might see some evidence of the impact, but I doubt you could prove what the car hit."

I felt sick at heart.

"Well, when you put it that way, what kind of evidence could we find that Wyszanski committed any of these murders? If we showed his photograph to people who live in the neighborhoods where Talia Hickson and Peter Abrams died—"

"You'd get more circumstantial evidence, but not enough to arrest or convict him."

"And if the autopsy results on Frankie Williams and Arletta Sandifer showed that they hadn't taken the medication they'd been prescribed to control their life-threatening conditions—"

"You'd have evidence of negligence, maybe, and maybe the families could sue."

I planted my chin on my fist.

"Gee, Moses, you're a real ray of sunshine. Thanks for sharing."

"The only real chance we've got for any kind of forensic evidence against Wyszanski would be Talia's murder," he said speculatively, "and that's assuming Walker didn't kill her, like everybody thinks. In all the other cases, he either didn't get close enough to the victims—if they were victims—or any evidence he left could be explained by his position as CO. Maybe I can arrange to take a look at the Hickson file, but it's a long shot. The only thing right now that could make Wyszanski an official suspect would be eyewitnesses."

"Then," I said grimly, "we'd better find the ones that are left before Wyszanski does."

Thirty-five

But I knew where some of the witnesses were, and they weren't going anywhere. Or at least, I hoped they weren't. The only way they could leave was feet first—the way Frankie Williams and Arletta Sandifer had left. I was worried about them, wished I could protect them. It occurred to me that Rocky was safer outside the prison than they were inside. I began to develop a superstitious belief that as long as I didn't find Rocky, nobody else would find her either.

The cold front that had blown in on Saturday proved to be an unseasonable blast of arctic air that settled over the Ohio River Valley like unwelcome in-laws. When Moses stepped out the door to go to church on Sunday, he sank in snow up to his pant cuffs. He shoveled his way to the car, but then the car wouldn't start. Retty and Patsy, who were wearing new outfits, ignored his suggestion that they change into something warmer, and they finally drove off in my Rabbit, which behaved in cold weather more like a snow bunny. So far, they didn't have a measle between them, but there had been an outbreak of general scratching at the Catatonia Arms which we put down to sympathetic itching.

When the cold front first arrived, people talked cheerfully about the prospects for a white Christmas. But as the week wore on, the mood soured. The emergency rooms were jammed with folks who had slipped on ice. Secondary roads remained slick. Cars died, and the tow trucks worked overtime. A hapless duck froze in the pond in Burnet Woods, and the SPCA had to chip him out. Grocery stores ran out of salt. Homeless shelters were filled to capacity, and the city had to open some emergency shelters. The thermometer hovered near zero.

You can probably guess the mood inside the Catatonia Arms, where nerves had already been frayed before the temperature dropped. The girls rebelled against the layers of sweaters, heavy socks, long underwear, coats, hats, mittens, earmuffs, and boots we made them wear to school. Brother went into an extended pout because he couldn't go to school, and he couldn't go outside to play in the snow. We kept the girls in, too, when they weren't in school, and since none of the animals cared to venture outside, we had our own two-story, three-ring circus. Moses' car finally went into the shop on Tuesday, with no release date in sight.

With Brother still in quarantine, and the girls cooped up inside when they weren't at school, the kids squabbled night and day. On Wednesday, Brother choked on a Monopoly game piece, giving Mel an opportunity to practice her Heimlich maneuver; apparently, Brother had snatched Retty's marker in a snit when he landed on a hotel-laden Park Place and discovered how much he owed her. Retty refused to play afterward because her marker now had cooties on it. Patsy threw the *101 Dalmations* tape against the wall and smashed it. Brother pitched her Barbie doll out the window in retaliation, and it seemed unlikely that we would find all of Barbie's accessories before the spring thaw. Patsy did something to Al's computer that put a murderous glint in Al's eye. Sidney unraveled Retty's knit scarf, which she'd left hanging on the newel post at the bottom of the stairs. Winnie ate a mitten, and threw it back up on my living room carpet. Maybe she and Gordon Nash were in cahoots.

Somewhere in there, the hot water pipe broke, and we were without hot water for twenty-seven hours and forty-three minutes.

The only good thing that happened was that Kevin went into a baking frenzy, and baked enough fattening edibles to get Washington's army through the winter at Valley Forge.

Unfortunately, however, the sugar content made our troops more hyperactive.

Oh, and Charisse slipped on the ice and sprained her wrist.

"You know, Moses, maybe she shouldn't wear that heavy gold bracelet," Kevin said, his face screwed up with concern. "It probably throws her off balance."

"Those spike heels don't help either," Mel observed.

"I hope she didn't fall on that nice Gucci bag she carries!" Al put in. "Those bags don't hold up well at all."

I kept mum. I had to work with Moses.

He glared at them, and stomped off.

Kevin raised his arms in an elaborate gesture of bewilderment.

"I thought we were all sympathy," he said.

Moses and I made the rounds of the homeless shelters, just to have something to do. But nobody we talked to admitted to having seen Rocky, and we didn't find her.

Barbara Hickson came to visit several times, but if she knew where Rocky was, she wouldn't tell us. On the other hand, close confinement with the adult residents of the Catatonia Arms, who were all on their worst behavior these days, was beginning to have a salutary effect on the kids. Aunt Barbara was greeted like a long-lost friend. Santa Claus himself couldn't have anticipated a warmer reception. All of her cruelties seemed forgiven if not forgotten. This boded well for our return to a childless state in the not-too-distant future.

In fact, she proposed that the kids spend Christmas day with her, if Retty and Patsy remained measleless till then, and they eagerly agreed. She clearly missed them, and they missed their cousins. I was reminded that normally they had someone besides their own siblings to harass, torment, and beat up on.

On her first visit, I took her aside.

"Tell me about Rocky's twin," I said.

"Jamie?" She frowned. "Where did you hear about her?"

"The kids mentioned it in passing," I said, reluctant to get them into trouble. "They didn't mean to."

"There's not much to tell," Barbara said, a crease like the Grand Canyon appearing between her eyebrows. "Jamie died when the girls were seven."

"How did she die?"

"Just one of those freak accidents. She was running in the house, tripped, and fell. Her head hit the radiator, and she was killed. They said it was unusual, but not unheard-of."

I wasn't satisfied. Call me suspicious, but that night I was on the phone to Miss Iva Weldon.

"Jamie?" she ehoed in some surprise. "Oh, yes, Rocky told me about her. I gather that those two were real close when they was little. Sometime I used to wonder if maybe losing her sister like that didn't make Rocky into that sad little girl I knew. Maybe she was different before, I don't know. I didn't like to mention Jamie to you before when you asked, because the family didn't ever talk about it."

"Was Rocky's mother married to Nash at the time?"

"No, now, I don't believe she was," Miss Iva said.

"And as far as you know, the death was accidental?"

There was a silence on the other end. Then she said, "You know, Cat, I don't know if I should say this. I guess the police and Children's Services was satisfied at the time. Jeannie never went to jail, anyway. But one night when Rocky had a bad dream, and I was holdin' her, you know, like you do, she said, 'I'm always afraid Momma will get mad at me, like she did with Jamie.' I didn't ask her no more about it at the time—she was already in foster care, after all. And I don't guess I cared to hear the details, I surely didn't.

"Rocky's mother was a sad woman, Cat." Miss Iva continued softly. "I felt sorry for her. She loved that child, and Rocky loved her. They just couldn't live together. Jeannie's drinking made it too dangerous, and then—well, they just couldn't get along. Then Nash moved in, and, Lord have mercy, they was fireworks all the time after that!

"I never raised a hand to that child, Cat," she concluded.

"Not like my own kids. Them kids knew they could count on a swat on they behinds if they was misbehavin'. But I couldn't never bring myself to hit Rocky. She come from a house where a little girl maybe got hit so hard she cracked her head open against a radiator and died. I didn't want Rocky to be havin' no nightmares about me."

"Do you think Barbara Hickson knows what happened?" I asked.

"Oh, yes," she said. "She know everything what went on in that house. But she ain't never wanted to face the truth about her sister. And I don't reckon she ever will."

So I didn't speak to Barbara Hickson again about it. What was the point?

But on Friday, December 14, Aunt Barbara brought news that filled me with dismay, even though I'd expected it: Gordon Nash had filed for custody of the children.

I pored over Rocky's letters, looking for any evidence of her current whereabouts, or anything that could lead to anything we could use against Wyszanski. Nothing.

"She'll call again, Cat," Moses said. "You know she will."

"And what if she doesn't?" I asked. "What then? We won't even know where to look for the body."

Thirty-six

"Don't get your hopes up, Cat."

That was the last thing Moses had said to me as I'd gotten out of the car on Saturday morning in the parking lot at the Women's Correctional Institution. It was good advice, I knew. We were on Wyszanski's turf now, and the chances that he'd let me get close to anyone who could tell me what I wanted to know were slim.

Moses had insisted on accompanying me because he was willing at least to entertain the possibility that Wyszanski was a dangerous man.

I met Hazel Connors and Natalie Tunney in the reception area, and we passed through the metal detectors to wait for an escort. The sun was deceptively bright. The grass, however, had turned a muddy yellow where the snow had melted under an exhaust pipe which vented billows of steam into the yard.

We saw no one until we reached the building where the support group sessions were held.

Several of the women greeted me like old friends. They greeted Natalie even more enthusiastically. A group of them crowded around the two women, exchanging news, making special requests, asking for advice. As the room filled, I saw many familiar faces and some unfamiliar ones. Some of the people I remembered from last time weren't here. Opal Smith was one of these. But Precious McKinney sat quietly as if isolated by her own thoughts.

"Opal's in the hole again," Natalie said in a low voice behind me.

"What for?" I asked suspiciously.

"Sexual misconduct," she said, sighing. "She was caught making out with her girlfriend."

I stared at her, dumbfounded.

"She can get put in solitary for *that*?"

Natalie let out an exasperated puff of air. "It's a Class II offense. The state of Ohio considers it a threat to security—along with masturbation."

"What?!"

"Anyway, Precious McKinney is here. I'll see if she's willing to talk to you."

We'd decided that if I was going to talk to anyone in private, it had better be early in the meeting, before we were interrupted.

I watched Natalie perch on a metal chair next to Precious and engage her in conversation. It quickly became apparent to me that the negotiations were not going well. I saw Precious glance across at me and shake her head. She raised her palms, and continued talking. But after a few minutes, Natalie brought her over to where I was standing, leaning against one of those long folding conference tables outside the circle of chairs. She was still shaking her head as I gestured to the table and invited her to sit.

Up close, Precious McKinney was a sweet-faced, light-skinned black woman who probably once had the looks and air of a movie star from the forties. You could imagine her hair, which now hung stiff behind her ears, waved into one of those curvy forties dos I'd once aspired to, a Lana Turner style, maybe. Her face was puffy from the prison diet, and a body that might have been voluptuous once had gone skinny on her. But her light brown eyes were the most unsettling things about her: they looked unfocused, dead.

"I told Mrs. Tunney, I don't know why you want to talk to me, Mrs. Caliban," she said in a voice with a curious cadence, as if she'd returned from a long stay in a non-English speaking country, and had forgotten the rhythm of English speech—had forgotten where the emphasis belonged. "I ain't seen Rocky since she left here. Ain't had a letter from her either. I can't tell you where she's at."

"Why don't you call me Cat?" I said.

It didn't appear to register. Maybe she didn't want to be on familiar terms with me.

"Rocky been gone almost a month now, Mrs. Caliban," she said.

"But I think she's in trouble on the outside because of something that happened on the inside," I said. "I thought you might know what that would be."

"I wouldn't know," she said.

"Look," I said carefully, "a lot of people who were close to Rocky or who had contact with Rocky recently have died. Can you explain that?"

"No," she said. Her glance seemed to drift over my right shoulder. "A lot of people die. A lot of people I knew have died, and there's some others—" She left the statement unfinished.

"I want to figure out what's happening before anyone else dies," I said.

She didn't answer.

"I'm worried about Rocky, Ms. McKinney." If she chose to be formal with me, I ought to respect her choice and be formal with her, I thought. "About Rocky, and Opal—and you."

"Ain't nothing going to happen to Opal," she said finally. "Opal don't know nothing. I can't help Rocky. I can't even help myself. I just do the best I can to get by."

"Can't I help you?"

For the first time her eyes came to rest on my face. "I don't think you understand, Mrs. Caliban. I'm on death row. Didn't nobody tell you that?"

I stared at her, in shock.

"No," I croaked.

"I killed my husband," she said without emotion. "I was sorry after I did it, but that wasn't the first thing I felt. The first thing I felt was relief, because I knew he wouldn't never hit me again. I still dream about him sometimes, though, and wake up in a sweat. Sometimes I think the bastard will kill me yet. And maybe he will."

She passed her fingers through her hair.

"We got one more appeal," she said. "Then, the only chance I got is clemency. If it wasn't for my kids, I wouldn't go through with this shit. If it wasn't for my kids—" She gazed out the window.

"You can't afford to help me," I said, nodding. "If you help me, you rock the boat. You might ruin your chances of getting out of here." I leaned closer to her, breathing in the odor of fear. "But, Ms. McKinney, will he let you get out of here alive?"

She didn't react at first, and I thought maybe she hadn't heard me. She was still staring out the window.

"I guess I'll have to take that chance," she said softly at last.

"You were in Rocky's prison family," I observed.

"I'm the mommy," she said, and turned her eyes on me again.

"Can't you give me anything?" I thought about Moses' questions. "Even a motive for Joan Small's murder would help."

She frowned down at her hands folded in her lap.

"I'll tell you something about Joan," she said slowly. "Joan had three kids in foster care. She thought she'd get her parole and get them back. Then she got written up. I don't remember what for—some petty bullshit thing. She blew up at the CO, and ended up in the hole. It fucked up her parole. Next thing, a letter come, saying her kids were being put up for adoption. She'd left them in foster care too long." She paused and glanced at me to see if I was following this.

"Joan went crazy," she said. "Them kids meant the world to her. She said she'd get that bastard if it was the last thing she did."

"Who wrote her up, Ms. McKinney?"

Her eyes met mine again.

"I don't think I have to tell you that, Mrs. Caliban."

Thirty-seven

"So, you saying that this Joan Small blamed Wyszanski for losing her children, and she was so angry that she took him on, tried to throw him down the stairs, and ended up getting thrown herself?"

That wasn't what I was saying exactly, but I could see how it had potential from Moses' perspective—probably more potential than my own theory, which he'd consider half-baked.

"It could've happened that way, couldn't it?" I asked.

"Yeah, Cat, it could've happened all kinds of ways," he said testily, "but we don't know 'cause we got no evidence."

"Well, I can't blame Precious McKinney for not wanting to get involved," I said.

"No, I don't blame her either. But it doesn't help us any."

"It all comes back to Rocky," I conceded. "We need to know what Rocky knows."

That night, she called. Again, she talked to the kids, and then to Moses.

"I want to see my kids," she said.

"I want to talk to you," Moses said.

They agreed to meet the next day, Sunday, at one o'clock on the riverfront, near the public landing by Yeatman's Cove.

"*Outside?*" I objected. "Are you crazy? Do you know what the temperature is out there? Moses, I am not freezing my ass off to hang around and wait for Rocky! Brother's just getting over the measles, for crissake!"

"If his appetite and his energy level are any indication,

he's over 'em," Moses observed wryly. "I ain't seen a spot since Thursday night."

"He's still infectious, though," I protested. "Read the book. And the girls are probably just getting sick."

"We'll bundle 'em up good," Moses said. "Look, Cat, Rocky's got no transportation. She must be staying somewhere near there. She wanted a nice empty open space, where she could see everything. She didn't want any places around where somebody could hide and sneak up on her—that's what I figure."

"Hell, why not the pitcher's mound at Riverfront? Or why don't we just pretend to go ice fishing in the middle of the fucking river?"

"Those good suggestions, Cat," Moses rejoined mildly. "If Rocky calls back, I'll pass 'em on. Meanwhile, we got a date to meet her at one in the parking area near the *Showboat Majestic*."

Along the riverfront below Second Street was a cobblestoned incline used for parking. The *Showboat Majestic*, which featured live theatre in the summertime, was moored there, and at the east end was a boat launching ramp, and a sidewalk which wound through some green space, across a set of railroad tracks, to a large fountain. It was, as Moses had described it, an open space, empty now that the river was frozen along both banks and nobody was trying to get anywhere in a boat. The emptiness was apparent as soon as we passed under the underpass below Second Street. Kevin was behind us with a friend of his named Earl somethingor-other; he'd insisted on following us for "backup," but I suspected that what he really had in mind was a peek at the woman who'd given birth to Brother. Me, I knew better than to make assumptions about mothers based on their offspring. God knows I didn't want to be judged by mine.

As usual, the kids had been squabbling in the backseat. It started when the girls returned home from church with some folded paper flowers they'd made in Sunday school. Brother, whose sense of the injustice of having been kept home again was piqued by this evidence of how much fun they'd had without him, shredded all the flowers, provoking Patsy to call him a "toad turd." That was how it started, and to tell you the truth, I hadn't really been tuned in.

"I told Santa Claus about you," Brother had taunted Retty somewhere in there. "I told him you been bad, and he told me he wasn't going to bring you *nothin'*!"

"That wasn't Santa Claus, you dodobrain!" Patsy scoffed. "That was some guy dressed up in a Santa Claus suit! Them malls hires guys to play Santa to fool little dodobrains like you!"

By then, we were approaching downtown on Central Parkway. We had taken my Rabbit, but Moses was driving, since I figured he might be better at taking evasive action if it was warranted; he'd pointed out that juvenile officers didn't get a lot of practice at shaking tails, but even so. As it turned out, the day was warmer than I'd feared. The thermometer had finally broken twenty, and it felt like a goddamn heat wave, especially to someone with my unbalanced hormones. The kids had already shed their hats and gloves.

"You the dodobrain!" Brother was shouting. "I don't mean that Santa Claus! I mean the *real* Santa Claus!"

"There ain't no real Santa Claus!" Patsy countered.

"You ain't never met the real Santa Claus, Brother," Retty put in. "He live at the North Pole—only come to Cincinnati on Christmas Eve."

"You don't know what you talkin' about! He come to Cincinnati to see *me*!"

I caught a certain smugness in his voice, but I was busy checking the rearview mirrors for tails other than the one that was supposed to be there.

"You lie!"

"You the one lyin', girl! I seen him with my own two eyes!"

"That fever got to your head, boy!" Retty said. "Now you seein' things that ain't there."

"Nuh-uh!" he shouted. "I seen him in our parkin' lot this mornin', while you and Patsy was at church! And I told him about you, Patsy, and he said—"

We turned off Second and passed under the underpass into the deserted parking area.

"—had a white beard and a red suit and everything!"

Moses parked in the middle of the lot, and yanked on the parking brake. The place was deserted.

Suddenly, I experienced a kind of reverse hot flash—an icy finger touched the bottom of my spine and traveled up between my shoulder blades. It was a delayed reaction to what I'd been hearing. I turned around in my seat.

"When did you say you saw Santa Claus in our parking lot?" I asked Brother slowly.

His face was flushed with anger, but now I watched as his expression changed and the blood slowly drained from his cheeks.

"I was just kiddin', Cat," he mumbled.

"Did Santa Claus tell you not to tell us you'd seen him?" I asked.

He hunched his shoulders. His face contorted in a full-blown pout.

"Did Santa ask about your mother?"

"I ain't s'posed to tell," he said, a tear forming in the corner of one eye. "It's a secret."

By now Moses had turned around, too, and was staring at Brother.

"How come nobody else saw Santa but you?" I asked. "It's important for you to tell us, Brother."

"You got to tell, Brother," Retty said gently, taking his hand.

"He call me first on the telephone," Brother said. "Say he Santa Claus. But Aunt Barbara say don't never talk to strangers on the telephone; don't never tell 'em your business. He sound like Santa, but—"

"When did he call?" I asked.

"This mornin', after Moses an' them went to church," he

said. "So I ax him what I want for Christmas, 'cause if he Santa, he gonna remember what I told him."

Score one for Brother, I thought.

"But he say he don't remember, 'cause he talk to so many children. Got to keep notes, he say, and the notes is in his other suit. So I say, maybe he should call back when Retty and Patsy is here. He say, he is so Santa Claus, and I ax him what his reindeers is name—"

Moses glanced anxiously at his watch.

I interrupted Brother's saga. "Cut to the chase," I said. "When did he show up in the parking lot?"

"After while," Brother answered. "He say, 'Look for me out behind the buildin', but don't tell nobody I'm there. It's a secret, jus' between you and me.'"

"Did he ask about your mother?"

"Uh-huh, after I opened the car door and tried to sit on his lap." He frowned. "I think maybe I hurt his knee when I did that. Seem kind of grumpy for Santa Claus, but he wearin' the suit, and he have white hair and a beard."

"Did you tell him you were coming to see your mother?"

"Uh-huh. He say—"

"Did you tell him where?"

He nodded, and his face crumpled. Between disobeying Santa Claus and disobeying us, he knew he was in trouble.

He had no idea how much.

Moses rolled down his window to speak to Kevin, who'd pulled up next to us.

"Brother tipped him off," he said. "We'd better—"

"Moses!" I gripped his elbow and nodded up to where Second Street crossed over the underpass. A man in dark clothes stood watching, the sun glinting off something he held by his side.

Then everything happened at once.

"Momma!" Brother screamed, and scrambled over Retty and out the door before anybody could stop him.

From the sidewalk at the other end of the parking area, past the boat ramp, a diminutive figure emerged, striding toward the car. She bent down suddenly and opened her arms just as a loud report cracked in our ears and bounced off the opposite riverbank.

"Get down!" Moses shouted, already out the door, gun in hand. Doors slammed and feet pounded behind me as I ran toward Brother, who was oblivious to everything except closing the distance that separated him from his mother.

I saw her lift her head and spot something over my shoulder, as another shot rang out.

"Brother, get down!" she shouted.

But his momentum carried him forward. I heard another explosion, and then he was down, flailing to regain his balance. His small body skittered on the ice, and then slid down the boat ramp toward the frozen river.

I was still running. And Rocky was on her feet again, running, too. Little puffs of ice exploded around her. The sounds of shouts seemed to come from everywhere, as if we'd been caught in a cross fire.

She slipped on the ramp and slid into Brother at the bottom. She scooped him up and held him close to her chest. Bending low, she pulled herself up awkwardly, and headed out across the river without a glance behind her. She was moving away from the danger she knew.

My mouth dropped open. I stopped and sank to my knees. Icy fingers of terror clawed at my lungs. I heard nothing except the pop of exploding ice, and the creaks and cracks that followed it. But now it seemed they were falling short. Rocky had moved out of their range.

In the distance, somewhere outside the bubble of fear in which I was enclosed, I heard the roar of a gunned engine.

Then I heard another crack.

The ice was breaking up under Rocky's weight. I saw an island of it break off and tilt crazily into the water a split second after Rocky's foot lifted. For just a moment, she paused, rigid with terror.

"Keep moving!" Moses shouted, running past me. "Keep to the shore! Don't go so far out!"

She turned toward the voice. Perhaps she realized, as I did then, that the fusillade had stopped.

She almost lost her balance as a fissure opened up between her feet.

"You can make it, Rocky," I said under my breath. Then louder: "You can make it, Rocky! Come on, girl! What are you waiting for? Get those feet in gear!"

She stepped lightly, then leaped—short, nimble one-footed hops until she was skipping along the surface of the ice, her feet just ahead of the cracks springing up on its surface.

"You got it, baby!" Moses shouted. "That's-a-way! You almost got it beat, girl! One more step!"

He reached out to take Brother from her arms. Standing next to him now, I extended an arm, grabbed a fistful of her jacket, and hauled her onto solid ground. We collapsed into a heap and held each other, crying.

I was shaking with relief.

After a few minutes, Rocky's sobs subsided. She pulled her thin, hard body away from me, swiped at her face, and looked into my eyes.

"You must be Rocky Zacharias," I said.

"You must be Cat Caliban," she said. "Thanks for takin' care of my kids for me."

Thirty-eight

Rocky Zacharias had a gaunt face, prematurely wrinkled and shadowed by worry. Her wispy red hair had been pulled back into a low ponytail, but half of it had escaped and hung across her forehead and cheeks. She brushed it back as her gray eyes scanned the parking area and came to rest on the cluster of figures gathered at the far edge.

Then it shifted to the middle ground, where Retty and Patsy had climbed out of the car, clutching each other in tears.

"Got a bump on his head," Moses was saying, setting Brother back on his Smurfs. "I guess he wasn't hit—just slipped on the ice."

"Come on, Brother," Rocky said, holding her hand out to him. "Let's go talk to your sisters."

Moses and I joined Kevin and Earl, who were standing over the sprawled form of a man I'd never seen up close: Leonard "Wiseass" Wyszanski. Kevin was pressing a towel to his shoulder. The towel was rapidly darkening with blood. To my amazement, Earl was holding a shotgun on him.

"He got a license for that thing?" I muttered to Kevin in an aside when he straightened up.

Kevin looked at me. "Sure, he does, Mrs. C.," he said. "Earl's a deputy sheriff."

"Nobody ever tells me anything," I groused, as Kevin turned back to the others.

"Anybody gonna call the police?" I asked brightly. "Or are we gonna kick the shit out of him first?"

"Toby already went to call," Earl reported.

"You know Toby Grisham?" I cocked an eyebrow at him.

"Do now," he commented laconically. "Rides that Harley like a son of a bitch."

"See, Earl clipped him on the shoulder," Kevin said. "But he started to run. And then this Harley comes out of nowhere. Ran him right over the edge."

I followed his gaze up to the guardrail along Second Street. It was maybe a two-story drop.

"My back is broken," the man on the ground wheezed. And then he mumbled something that sounded like "sue the shit out of you," and coughed.

"Save it for the coroner," I said, unmoved. The man's eyes jumped to mine. "Sorry, did I say 'coroner'? I meant 'prosecutor.' "

Moses had scouted the vicinity and picked up a high-powered rifle with an impressive-looking scope on it.

I bent over Wyszanski and felt both knees. On the left knee—apparently the one Brother had kicked—I was rewarded by a yelp. I tightened my grip.

"And that's for dishonoring Santa Claus and tricking little kids," I said.

I leaned closer.

"You want we should ask the hospital to run a blood test?"

The look of fury that came over his face made me wonder if I'd gone too far.

"Bitch! Bitch! Bitch!" he rasped. At first I thought he meant me. Then I caught, "That bitch!"

I hardened my heart and my eyes.

"We're sending you up, Wyszanski," I said in a low voice. "Only this time, you're going to be on the other side of the bars, and in a place less hospitable than the women's prison, especially to former guards."

Sometime later, I was sitting in the back of the patrol car with Rocky and the kids, heat blasting from the vents. Brother and Patsy seemed to be enjoying the experience, though Retty's sober mood matched her mother's. I was thinking that it was a good thing the front seat was separated from the back by a steel grill; otherwise, Brother would have broken the radio for sure. Then I thought to ask him something.

"Brother, did you kiss Santa Claus this morning?"

He nodded.

"Where?"

"In the car."

"No, I mean—"

"She want to know did you kiss him on the mouth, dodobrain," Patsy interpreted.

"Uh-huh."

I started to laugh. Once I started, I couldn't stop. Tears rolled down my cheeks. Then Retty caught it, then Patsy, and finally Rocky broke down.

"Lord," she said, "I hope that bastard ain't never had the German measles!"

Thirty-nine

That was the last moment of happiness I was able to share with Rocky Zacharias. She was taken off, handcuffed, in the back of a patrol car. We sent the kids home with Kevin, and the rest of us drove over to District One to make our statements—Moses, Earl, and I. Toby Grisham brought up the rear on his Harley.

"Damn!" I said. "Every time I look in the rearview mirror, I'm practically blinded by the reflections off all that chrome! What was he doing there, anyway?"

"Just one of those coincidences, Cat," Moses shrugged. "He was in our neighborhood visiting another parolee, and he decided to stop by and see Rocky's kids. He spotted Santa Claus having a heart-to-heart with a kid out behind our building, and he decided to stick around and see what happened next."

"He staked us out? In our neighborhood? In twenty degrees on a *Harley*?"

"I don't think it was exactly a stakeout, Cat," Moses said. "He tailed Santa back to Stagecraft, where Santa was returning the costume."

Stagecraft was a costume rental store at our end of the viaduct that marked the boundary between the neighborhoods of Clifton and Northside.

"After the guy came out, he went into the store and found out that Santa's real name was Wyszanski. But he'd met a Wyszanski, only one in his life—a cop working the Abrams case who was looking for Rocky. This wasn't the same guy. This guy could be related, but what was a cop's relative doing talking to one of Rocky's kids? So he figured maybe this guy was impersonating Wyszanski. Says he was pretty confused, so he went over to the Blue Jay for breakfast to think things over. He decided to have another talk with us, but he got back just in time to join our convoy. When he saw where we were headed, he figured we were taking the kids to see Rocky. He stayed up on Second Street to watch, and then the shooting started."

"Wyszanski was a hell of a bad shot," Earl commented.

"Rocky was moving pretty fast," I said.

"And he was drawing fire from you," Moses pointed out. "If you hadn't brought a shotgun, man, we would have been out of luck."

"When Kevin described the setup, it seemed like a good idea," Earl said modestly. "But I wish I'd been close enough to see his face when he saw that Harley bearing down on him."

We spent three hours on hard metal chairs down at the station. I called Al, who called somebody she knew at the Public Defender's office, who showed up to sit in on Rocky's interview. When we got home, the kids were making Christmas cookies at Kevin's. Christmas carols blared from Kevin's quadraphonic speakers. Retty and Patsy appeared subdued. Brother was dancing with Winnie, making up his own lyrics, as usual.

I didn't get the whole story from Moses until the next day. He had a long interview with Rocky, and returned looking exhausted. For the first time in a week, all three kids were back in school. The house was eerily quiet.

"You were right, Cat. About why Wyszanski killed Joan Small," Moses said, removing his glasses to rub his eyes. Then he paused abruptly, and went to the sink to wash his hands and face. He smelled faintly of institutional disinfectant.

"I kept thinking about what Hazel said—about how the women didn't have anything to bargain with except their bodies," I said. I handed him a towel. "Then I thought, what if I were in that position? What if I thought I had nothing left to lose, and no power, and I wanted revenge? I knew there were some AIDS cases among the prisoners, and there are probably some more prisoners who are HIV positive—probably more than the prison knows or admits. Especially if so many of the women have been involved in prostitution at one time or another. I thought, hell, if I didn't care anymore, I'd go have sex with someone who had AIDS, then turn around and seduce my enemy. It's a power trip for the COs anyway; they'd probably just as soon think you hated their guts but felt forced to have sex with them in spite of it."

I pulled two beers out of the fridge and popped the tops. I handed one to Moses. "Then I remembered what Mel and Al said about lesbians being the goddess's chosen people and all, because you don't get much AIDS transmission through lesbian sex, and I figured there were better ways to make sure I got infected, if that's what I wanted. I realized that the beauty of this scheme was that I wouldn't even have to get infected by an AIDS carrier; I'd only have to say I did. That would be enough to ensure years and years of fear and anxiety."

"Joan Small did get infected by an AIDS carrier, though," Moses confirmed, rubbing his eyes and then settling his glasses back on his nose. "They cut their wrists or hands or something, then rubbed 'em together. Woman was happy to do what she could to bring Wyszanski down. She's dead now. Anyway, Rocky says it wasn't enough for Joan to make him worry about AIDS. She wanted to do everything she could to make sure he'd get the disease. She had sex with him several times before she sprang her trap."

"On June eighth," I supplied.

"Apparently," he said. He wiped foam off his mustache. "Rocky was the only one who knew about Small's plot, but she didn't know when Joan was going to tell Wyszanski. She says that as soon as she heard Small was dead, she knew who'd done it. That was even before she'd figured out that Frankie Williams couldn't have killed Joan."

"Did that have to do with the medication logs?"

"Right again," he said. "Cat, let's sit in the living room. I need to sit on something soft."

He settled on the couch, and I flopped sideways into an upholstered chair, my legs hanging over the side—the way I always told my kids not to sit.

"Frankie started out to go to the support group that day. But when she got there, a CO showed up to tell her she had to go for Special Meds, and to sit on the bench in the hall and wait while the CO escorted somebody else back to their cottage. Talia saw her sitting there when she got to the room where the group meets. Talia was called out of the meeting because of some kind of disciplinary hearing, and didn't notice whether Frankie was sitting there or not. But Arletta and Rocky saw her sitting there when the meeting was over, and she complained to the CO who was escorting them that she'd been stuck on the bench for more than an hour."

"Then the other CO has been colluding in the cover-up," I said.

"She could be, Cat," he said cautiously. "Or maybe she just never bothered to put everything together. She may not realize the significance of what she saw."

"And what about the one who abandoned Frankie in the first place? She'd be a witness."

"Again, if anybody stopped to wonder whether a witness was needed," he said. "After all, they had a perfectly reliable eyewitness to the murder itself."

"CO Len Wyszanski."

"That's right. And nobody believed Frankie—probably didn't even listen to her story—because everybody knew she was crazy. The women figured it out—Rocky, Talia, and Arletta—but they didn't think anyone would listen to them either. And while they were still talking about what to do, Frankie died in solitary."

"It really stinks, Moses."

"Yeah, baby, it really does."

"But how did Wyszanski find out what they knew?"

He sighed and slumped further down on the couch.

"That was Talia's fault," he said. "Wyszanski pissed her off one day, and—" He gestured vaguely with his beer can.

"It was the only way she could think of to get back at him," I guessed. "So she said something like, 'You can push me around now, but you just wait! We know who killed Joan, and we can prove it!' She must have realized right away what a mistake that was, but you can see how it happened. Did she tell him who the witnesses were?"

"I'm afraid so. In the heat of the moment, she probably wanted him to feel ganged up on."

"Did Rocky tell Precious McKinney what she knew? And Opal Smith?"

"She told Precious, but even if Wyszanski suspected, I guess he figured a woman on death row didn't pose any threat to him. Opal didn't know anything."

"And I suppose Wyszanski enlisted help from his relative to keep him out of jail. How *were* those two bastards related, anyhow?"

"Cousins," Moses said. "Just like Talia and Rocky. George Wyszanski has been suspended from the force while they try to figure out whether he actually did anything that violates regulations. But there's a good chance he'll just get a slap on the wrist for sharing information with his cousin."

"So how many people did he kill, Moses?" I asked. "CO Len Wyszanski, I mean. What do you think?"

"I'm skeptical about the drug-related deaths," Moses said. "He could have been involved in those, but they're kind of messy. I'd probably put them down to institutional incompetence. You'll probably never get a conviction on those. I think he killed Peter Abrams, because Rocky went to talk to Abrams about legal protections." He paused, then said in a low voice, "She didn't exactly put it this way, Cat, but I think she went to Abrams when she couldn't reach me."

"It's not your fault, Moses," I reassured him gently. "Just like Orlando Walker wasn't your fault."

But he didn't say anything at first.

"I'm still not sure about Talia," he said finally. "That could've been Wyszanski, or it could have been Walker. Or somebody else."

"Too coincidental for my money," I said. "But let me rephrase the question. Which murders is he being charged for?"

"He's not being charged with any of them, Cat," he reported gloomily. "Not yet, anyway. The crime lab has the car, and the best we can hope for is something there—fibers from Peter's coat or something. Otherwise, he's down for assault with a deadly weapon."

"You're kidding!"

"Ain't somethin' I'd kid about, Cat. He's already made bail."

"He's *out*?"

"Well, I don't think the hospital's going to let him out any time soon," Moses observed. "But they took the ankle bracelet off."

"Goddamn it, Moses! He hasn't even spent a night in jail!"

"Man's flat on his back in traction, Cat. I don't think he's a happy camper."

"Will he plea-bargain?"

"He'll try, sure. And he might get it down to aggravated assault. But he'll do time, unless the prosecutor screws up. And wherever he gets sent, it's going to be hard time. The boys inside would love to get their hands on an ex-CO."

At this point, Winnie chased Sidney into the room. Sidney skidded to a halt, turned, arched his back and hissed at her. I suspected this entertainment was put on for our benefit, to cheer us up.

"Y'all better rest up and save your strength," Moses advised them. "Kids be home in a little while."

"Sounds like a good excuse for another beer," I said, and retrieved two from the refrigerator.

"So Wyszanski is free, and Rocky is back in jail," I

observed. "Where was she all that time we were looking for her?"

"She was staying with a friend down at Anna Louise Inn. You know where that is?"

I nodded. "Down by Lytle Park."

The Anna Louise Inn is a five-story transitional housing facility for young women. Built in the early 1900s and named after one of the Taft girls, it is a Cincinnati institution. It would have been an easy walk from there to the riverfront parking area.

"Wouldn't say what she did for money," he said. "I imagine Barbara gave her some, and Amy probably stole some from Nash to give to her."

"How long will she get for parole violation? Won't they take into account extenuating circumstances—like she was running for her life?"

Moses didn't answer at first. He took the beer from me and set it down absentmindedly on the end table. Winnie was lobbying for his attention, so he scooped her up and set her on the couch beside him.

"It ain't that simple, Cat," he said slowly. "After Rocky talked to her lawyer last night, she had another session with Bunke this morning. Then the cops went out to Westwood. They found Gordon Nash lying on the floor in the living room with a jump rope wrapped around his neck."

I gaped at him.

"I don't guess he's going to get custody of Rocky's kids after all," he said.

Forty

"Ladybug, ladybug, fly away home.
Your house is on fire, and your children will burn."

Patsy and Retty had learned some new hand games in school. They were seated cross-legged on the living room floor, knee to knee, chanting, fingers flashing. It had been so long since I'd had kids around, I had forgotten all about this particular form of amusement. I was pleased to discover that there were still some recreational activities that technology couldn't replace. They'd started with "This Old Man," and worked their way through a repertoire of old favorites and newer chants unfamiliar to me.

Brother was itching to join them, but I had him down on the floor in the kitchen, scrubbing ELVIS WAS HEER! off the cabinet door.

I was, I'll admit it, indulging in a little sentimentality, now that the kids were about to leave us. Tomorrow, school would let out for the Christmas holiday, and on Saturday they would all move back to Aunt Barbara's, spots or no spots. Nobody could stand the separation any longer. They would come back for dinner, accompanied by their aunt and cousins, on Christmas Eve, but they would sleep in their own beds at Aunt Barbara's that night, so Santa Claus would know where to find them.

Patsy rolled her eyes when we said this, but Retty pinched her, so she held her tongue. Brother was confused enough about Santa Claus; he'd asked me that morning if the real Santa drove a Buick when the reindeers were taking a nap.

The fake Santa was still on his back in a hospital bed, and I'd heard he was wearing a shoulder cast and back and neck braces. I was counting the days and keeping my fingers crossed.

"If there's a just God in heaven," Kevin had declared, "that man will get measles under his cast."

Meanwhile, the forensics lab had come up with some promising fibers from the grill and hood ornament of Wyszanski's car. But the case against him in the Abrams homicide could literally hang by a thread.

"I'd settle for the death penalty," I told Moses wistfully, "but I'd rather see him do life up in Marion, where the tough guys hang out."

Rocky's lawyer was hopeful that he could successfully argue extenuating circumstances in both of the cases against her. Toby Grisham was willing to go to bat for her on the parole violation. The murder defense would be harder to argue. Yes, Rocky had been sexually abused by her stepfather as a teenager. Yes, her half sister was carrying a baby alleged to be Nash's. And yes, this record of sexual abuse indicated a clear danger to Rocky's own daughters if Nash had won custody of them. But had she killed him in cold blood, or in the heat of an argument? Had he threatened her physically? The only one who knew for certain was Rocky and she wasn't talking.

Amy had run away from home the night before to move in with an older girlfriend, so she hadn't been there to witness the confrontation. Had the timing been coincidental as Amy insisted, or had Rocky made a point of getting her out of the way? It made the difference between excusable homicide, and murder one.

Me, I considered it excusable, either way. But I doubted that Wyszanski's lawyer was going to allow me on the jury.

I stood in the doorway and watched the girls.

"Ladybug, ladybug," they sang.

Retty looked up at me.

"Momma taught us that one," she said softly.

None of us would be getting what we wanted for Christmas.